He stared at the ceiling, refusing to meet her gaze. "When you build a stone wall," he said, "you've got to pick each stone and put it in exactly the right place. If you want the wall to be stable, you have to do it right. The size of the stones. The shape."

She wasn't sure what he was getting at, but at least he was talking. She waited for him to continue.

"We didn't lay the foundation right," he murmured. "We're standing on that wall and it's shaking beneath our feet. It's going to collapse. And we're going to fall."

"We'll get through this, Bobby. I know we will."

He shook his head. "We're falling, Jo. And it's a long way down."

Lying in a bed now cold, with her husband right beside her yet a thousand miles away, and that awful silence once again settling into the space between them, Joelle wondered how long the fall was and how broken they would be when they landed.

Dear Reader,

When my editor, Beverley Sotolov, asked me if I'd be interested in writing a book for Harlequin Everlasting Love, my immediate reaction was no. My books focus on the joys and challenges lovers face at the start of a new relationship, not the complexities and struggles they confront in a relationship that has endured years of wind and rain and burning sun. Also, I write mostly romantic comedies, and Everlasting Love novels were billed as deeply emotional stories.

Yet within a day of Beverley's phone call, Bobby DiFranco and Joelle Webber presented themselves and told me their story—the story of a relationship between two proud, defiant, working-class kids who face some staggering obstacles but are determined to build a good life for themselves, only to have that life threatened when the lie on which it's based is exposed. Can a marriage built on a falsehood survive the glaring light of truth? Can a love that's deeply felt but never acknowledged hold a marriage together?

I was enthralled by the poignancy and power of Bobby and Joelle's attachment to each other, their stubbornness and grit, and the bond that holds them together even as reality tries, again and again, to tear them apart. As soon as they were finished telling me their story, I phoned Beverley and told her that, yes, I'd be writing a book for Everlasting Love.

I hope you come to care as much about Bobby and Joelle as I do.

Judith Arnold

The Marriage Bed

Judith Arnold

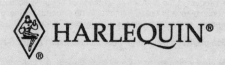

HARLEQUIN®

TORONTO • NEW YORK • LONDON
AMSTERDAM • PARIS • SYDNEY • HAMBURG
STOCKHOLM • ATHENS • TOKYO • MILAN • MADRID
PRAGUE • WARSAW • BUDAPEST • AUCKLAND

ISBN-13: 978-0-373-65409-3
ISBN-10:   0-373-65409-X

THE MARRIAGE BED

ABOUT THE AUTHOR

The Marriage Bed is Judith Arnold's eighty-fifth published novel. During those rare moments when she isn't writing, she loves to travel, read, jog, listen to music (classical, rock and everything in between), daydream and read some more. She prefers eating to cooking, but is willing to do the latter because it enables her to do the former.

She is happily married and the mother of two wonderful sons, who tower above her in height but—she hopes—still look up to her. She lives with her family near Boston, Massachusetts.

She loves to hear from readers. You can reach her through her Web site, www.juditharnold.com.

To the XromX gang
With gratitude and love

Chapter 1

What the hell was he doing here?

Joelle stared at the man standing on her front porch and stifled the urge to scream, slam the door in his face...or pretend she didn't know who he was.

She did know, of course. Thirty-seven years might have passed since she'd last seen Drew Foster—she was aware of exactly how long it had been, considering how drastically her life had changed that night—but she recognized him immediately. His hair was a little sparser and grayer, his laugh lines deeper, his jaw softer. His well-cut pinstripe suit didn't hide the slight paunch that had sprouted above his belt, but despite carrying a few excess pounds, he appeared generally fit for a man only a few years away from his sixtieth birthday.

How had he found her? Why hadn't he called to give her some warning before he appeared on her doorstep? How could she get him to leave? He'd come close to destroying her life once, but she'd painstakingly rebuilt it—and now here he was, perfectly capable of destroying it all over again. Fear gathered in her gut and squeezed.

"Joelle," he murmured, his gaze deep and intense. "God, you look great."

She clenched her dust rag so tightly her fingers began to go numb. She'd been cleaning the house, as she did every Saturday morning, and she hadn't bothered to put the rag down before answering the door. If only he'd arrived a few minutes later, the roar of the vacuum cleaner would have drowned out the doorbell and she'd never have realized he was there.

At her continuing silence, his smile faded. "You don't re-member me, do you?"

"Of course I do." She shook her head, then forced a smile. "I'm just…surprised. How did you—I mean, what are you…" She pressed her lips together to stop from stammering.

"It's a long story. May I come in?"

Back then, his voice had been as smooth and sweet as warm honey. It still was. Just like his warm, honey-sweet grin.

She didn't want him inside her house, but she couldn't think of a way to keep him out without leading him to assume she had something to hide. If he suspected her of hiding something, he'd be right. What had happened thirty-seven years ago, the decisions she'd made, the turn her life had taken—he mustn't find out. She couldn't let him.

But if she barred the door, he'd grow suspicious. Re-luctantly she stepped back and allowed him to enter. If luck was with her, he'd tell her he just happened to be in Gray Hill, and someone at the gas station had mentioned her name and he'd thought he would stop by and say hello. They'd chat for a few minutes about old times and then he'd be on his way.

"You have a lovely place," he said, surveying the foyer before he peered through the arched doorway into the living room. "Beautiful landscaping, too."

"Yes. Bobby—" She cut herself off. If she talked about Bobby, she might start talking about their children, and she couldn't do that.

"Bobby D. Who would've thought you two would get married?" Drew smiled wistfully. "He's a damn lucky guy. Is he around?"

"No, he's—" Again she cut herself off. Bobby often spent Saturdays meeting with clients who weren't available during the week. But if she said he was working, Drew might assume he did some kind of labor that demanded weekend shifts. She wanted to assure Drew that Bobby's business was a success, that he had clients as far away as Hartford and Bridgeport and even across the state line in New York, that his sons were now working with him, that he and Joelle were no longer kids from the poor side of town. She wanted to shout that Bobby was more of a man than Drew could ever hope to be.

All she said was, "I'm afraid he's out right now."

Drew shrugged. "Well, at least you're home."

"Cleaning the house." She held up the dust rag in her hand and smiled faintly. The air smelled of lemon-scented furniture polish, and through the arched doorway into the living room the vacuum cleaner was visible, its electrical cord snaking across the rug to the socket near the bay window.

"I'm sorry for springing myself on you like this. I was afraid that if I called you, you might tell me not to come."

Good guess, she thought, then reminded herself that acting rude would rile his suspicions. If she could force herself to behave civilly, he'd be less likely to ask questions.

Everything had happened so long ago. Maybe he'd forgotten, or he no longer cared about the mistakes they'd made when they were teenagers. Maybe none of it mattered to him anymore.

"Would you like something to drink?" she asked. "Coffee? Tea?" He was standing too close, and she backed up another couple of steps. "Wine or beer?" she offered, even though it wasn't yet noon.

"Have you got anything stronger?" His voice was tinged with laughter, but she sensed that he was serious.

"No." Bobby preferred no hard liquor in the house, and she respected his wishes.

"Coffee's fine."

Nodding, she pivoted and headed down the hall to the kitchen, her footsteps muffled by the runner rug. She was barefoot—the house was hot, despite the air-conditioning units Bobby had installed—and she always worked herself into a sweat when she cleaned. Dressed in one of her son Danny's ratty old Colgate University T-shirts and a pair of denim cut-offs, with her hair pulled into a sloppy ponytail, she'd been warm until she'd opened her door and discovered Drew Foster on the other side. From that moment on, she'd felt chilled.

He followed her into the kitchen, where she tossed her rag onto the counter and busied herself scooping coffee beans into the grinder. She could feel him prowling around the room behind her. Was he assessing the quality of her appliances? Peeking through the window in the top of the back door, which opened onto the flagstone patio that Bobby had built? She refused to turn and watch her guest. She hated that he was here, hated that his presence made her hands tremble and her fingers fumble as she arranged a filter in the basket of the coffeemaker.

"You have grandchildren?"

His question jolted her. Flecks of brown powder spilled from the grinder's cup and scattered across the counter. *No,* she silently begged, *don't ask me about my grandchildren.*

She glanced over her shoulder and saw him standing in front of the refrigerator, admiring the crayon scribblings she'd fastened to the surface with magnets. He knew she was too old to have children drawing like toddlers. Obviously she had grandchildren. She couldn't lie about it.

"Yes," she said. "How about you?"

"No." The word was hard and blunt. He softened it by adding, "You don't look old enough to have grandchildren. I mean it, Joelle. You look fantastic. You must be drinking from the fountain of youth."

His flattery made her scowl.

"Do you work out?"

She emptied the grinder into the coffeemaker's basket and wiped away the grounds that had spilled. Drew was buttering her up for a reason, and sooner or later he'd tell her what it was. *A long story,* he'd warned. She hoped he'd tell her the abridged version and then disappear.

"The only workouts I do are dusting and vacuuming," she said, pulling the ceramic pitcher and sugar bowl from the cabinet above the sink. The sugar bowl was full, but she had to pour some milk into the pitcher. She wished he'd move away from the refrigerator so she could open it without standing too close to him. She also wished he'd stop staring at the primitive artwork Jeremy and Kristin had created. Those precious scribbles could ruin everything if the conversation drifted to questions about Jeremy and Kristin's mother.

Fortunately, Drew backed away as she approached the refrigerator. "I gather you and Bobby have never gone back to Holmdell for high-school reunions," he said as she filled the pitcher. Hands shoved in his pockets, he leaned casually against the counter while the coffeemaker chugged and wafted a rich aroma into the air.

Joelle surprised herself by laughing. "God, no."

"I've managed to avoid them, too."

"Do you still live there?"

"New York City. We've got a weekend place out in Amagansett, on Long Island, but we call Manhattan home." He flashed her a grin. "Manhattan and Connecticut—who would have thought you and I would wind up practically being neighbors?"

Joelle would hardly consider Manhattan and the hills of northwestern Connecticut the same neighborhood, although throughout the years she and Bobby had lived in Gray Hill. More and more New Yorkers had bought up the ramshackle old farmhouses and barns and turned them into weekend retreats. It was in part because of all those rich city folks that Bobby's business had flourished. They all wanted stone walls around their properties, brick patios with built-in hot tubs, elegant plantings and pools with waterfalls. They paid DiFranco Landscaping huge fees to tame the wild beauty of their surroundings.

"You said *we*," she noted. "You have a wife?"

Drew held up his left hand to display his wedding ring. "Helen. A wonderful woman. We just celebrated our thirtieth anniversary this year. You'd like her."

Joelle doubted that. Despite her history with Drew, she'd always known they were from two different worlds. His wife was undoubtedly from his world, not hers.

"So, what are you doing with yourself?" he asked, as if they were in fact trapped at a high-school reunion in the old West Side Motor Lodge down on Rockwood Turnpike, drinking stale punch and standing amid bouquets of helium balloons while a deejay played great hits of the sixties. "Career? Hobbies? Volunteer work?"

"I'm a kindergarten teacher," she told him. "Bobby owns a landscape-design business." Pride made her stand straighter. She and Bobby had done well for themselves, better than anyone in Holmdell, Ohio, would have predicted. Back then, folks had probably assumed Bobby would wind up a mean drunk like his father, tending the grounds of the town cemetery all day and drowning his sorrows at the Dog House Tavern all night. And Joelle...well, people might have believed she'd had prospects, but only because she'd been dating Drew, a rich boy who lived in a mansion overlooking the ninth hole at Green Gates Country Club.

The coffeemaker announced the end of its brewing cycle with a raucous gurgle. "We could sit in the living room," she suggested, "but I'd have to straighten things up in there—"

"This is fine," Drew said, pulling out a chair at the butcher-block kitchen table. He remained standing until she'd carried over two steaming mugs, waited for her to take her seat, then lowered himself onto the chair facing her. He dipped his head toward the cup and inhaled. "Smells great."

He was stalling. "Why are you here, Drew?" she asked.

He stalled some more, stirring milk into his coffee, then lifting it, blowing on its surface and taking a sip. After swallowing, he sighed. "Joelle." His voice had grown soft, his expression pensive. "I'm here because I'm a desperate man."

She wasn't sure if he was serious. His statement was so melodramatic. Yet he didn't seem to be joking. His words hung in the air, unsettling her.

"I would never have gone to all this trouble—hired a private investigator to find you and then intruded into your life like this—if I could have figured out another way, but…" He sighed again and set down his mug with a thud. "Helen and I have a son. Adam. He's the joy of our lives. You're a mother—I don't have to explain what it means to have a child."

Her heart began to pound, sending shards of pain through her chest. *Don't talk to me about my children. Don't.* He had no right to barge into her life and tell her, of all people, what it meant to have a child. If she could think of an excuse, any excuse, to get him out of her house—

"Adam is dying, Joelle," Drew said, his voice even more hushed. "And I'm here because the only person who can save him is your daughter." He paused, his dark eyes meeting hers. "*Our* daughter."

Bobby noticed the BMW with the New York plates parked out front and wondered who was visiting Joelle. Some new summer person, probably. The only rich New Yorkers they knew were the people buying up all the houses in the northwest hills and turning them into vacation homes. Thank God for those rich New Yorkers, too. Many of them paid him good money to landscape their property.

The guy he'd spent that morning with was a bond trader or something, one of those Wall Street professions that earned people ten times what they were worth. His wife was heavily into an English-country-manor fantasy. She'd already done up the house with floral wallpaper and frilly pillows on every damn surface, and now she wanted the backyard to look like an English garden, only with a free-form pool in the middle of it. Bobby had patiently explained that English gardens didn't generally include free-form pools and she ought to aim for a nice Connecticut garden, instead. He promised her lots of perennials and a gorgeous pool, and she'd seemed satisfied. The husband required stone walls so the place would look like fox-hunting country. Honest to God, why didn't they just go buy themselves a place outside London?

But they'd signed a whopping contract with DiFranco Landscaping. When Bobby was done with their property they'd be happy, and so would his company's bottom line.

He'd considered phoning Mike and Danny with the news that he'd landed the job, but decided that could wait until Monday. He had to remind himself that when it came to the business, they were his colleagues, not his sons. You didn't phone colleagues on a Saturday morning to talk shop, even if the news was good. Sons you could call anytime, but with business associates, Monday was soon enough.

He had to admit that having both his sons choose to join him in the company made work a thousand times more rewarding. He liked his business, liked the job's demands, liked the praise from satisfied customers, but he loved having Mike and Danny as partners.

You did well, Bobby D, he thought as he steered the truck up the winding driveway to the garage.

He'd done well with the house, too. Maybe it wasn't a palace, but it was spacious and comfortable and Joelle deserved no less. She'd had faith in him when he'd bought it, back when it was so shoddy a nasty blizzard would have knocked it flat, and one weekend at a time he'd rebuilt it. Claudia had helped, he recalled with a grin. Nothing like having a ten-year-old girl assisting. "Can I get your hammer, Daddy?" she'd ask, hovering behind him. "Should I hold the tape measure?" Once she'd hit adolescence, she couldn't be bothered anymore, but during the first couple of years of renovations, while Joelle had had her hands full with one and then another baby, Claudia had been Bobby's loyal assistant.

He eased the pickup into the bay next to Joelle's little hybrid. He wasn't convinced her Prius saved them much in fuel costs, but she'd craved one, so what the hell. As he swung out of the cab, he checked the thick, treaded soles of his work boots. He and the bond trader had traipsed all over the guy's four-acre property, and they'd hit a few mucky areas. Bobby would leave his boots in the mudroom. He wasn't going to track dirt into the house when Joelle had spent the morning cleaning.

Inside, he heard the muffled sound of voices in conversation, Joelle's and a man's. Yanking off one boot, he called out, "Hey, Jo!"

The conversation came to an abrupt halt, punctuated by the clatter of chairs scraping on the kitchen floor. "We're in here, Bobby," she said. She didn't have to tell him where *here* was.

The silence spooked him. He tugged off his other boot, then left the mudroom for the kitchen.

Seeing the man standing at his table was like walking into a fist. He lost his breath, his vision briefly blurred and his muscles contracted into knots. He inhaled slowly and met the man's gaze.

"Bobby," Drew Foster said quietly, his right hand extended.

Bobby nearly blurted out that only family got to call him that. To the rest of the world he was Bob or Robert or Mr. DiFranco. But to say that would make him sound like a psycho. Back in Holmdell, where Foster had known him, everyone had called him Bobby or Bobby D.

He swallowed again. Joelle slipped away from Drew to stand beside Bobby, an unspoken show of support that he appreciated. He wished he'd kept his boots on. It would be easier for Bobby to kick the bastard out of his house if he was wearing shoes.

The brush of Joelle's fingers on his elbow reminded him that he had to shake Foster's hand. He wasn't surprised by the softness of Foster's palm. The guy probably never lifted anything heavier than a pencil.

"Foster," he said brusquely, then gave a nod.

"Let me get you a cup of coffee." Joelle broke from him and crossed to the coffeemaker. He didn't like this—the fact that she hadn't asked how his appointment had gone, that she hadn't kissed his cheek, that no one was explaining the presence of Drew Foster in his kitchen, dressed in a thousand-dollar suit, with every freaking hair in place. Less hair than he'd had in high school, Bobby noted with grim satisfaction.

He wondered what Drew and Joelle had been doing before he'd arrived, and the possibilities made his stomach churn.

They couldn't have been doing much, he tried to assure himself. Joelle was dressed for housework, and despite the cooling hum of the air conditioners, her hair was beginning to frizz into little golden springs around her face. She had on no makeup, no perfume. If Foster had hoped to seduce her, he'd caught her at the wrong time.

Bobby fought off his reflexive jealousy. Joelle had been his wife a hell of a lot longer than she'd been Foster's girl-friend. They weren't in high school anymore. They'd all made their choices and Joelle's choice had been to marry Bobby. Still, his gaze drifted to her left hand, to the simple gold band she always wore on her ring finger, just to make sure it was there.

She handed him his favorite mug, filled with coffee. Claudia had given him that mug for Father's Day a few years ago. It said Number One Dad on it—silly, but he loved it.

Claudia.

Staring at Drew Foster over the mug's rim, Bobby felt the tension in his abdomen increase. Did Foster know about Claudia? Had Joelle told him? After all these years, did she still care enough about her old boyfriend to think he had a right to know?

His eyes never leaving Foster, Bobby moved warily toward the table. Something was bad here. Something was very bad.

"Drew has a problem," Joelle said gently, settling into her chair. "He needs our help."

"It's okay, Joelle. I'll explain," Foster said, resuming his own seat.

Bobby's tension spiked. He didn't like the intimacy between Joelle and Foster, the way they were speaking for each other. He lowered himself into a chair, his hands curling into fists. He rested them in his lap, under the table. If he had to pummel Foster, he would. But he hoped he wouldn't have to.

"I was telling Joelle, you've got a lovely house. Beautiful piece of property, too—"

"You didn't come here to talk about my house," Bobby cut him off.

"No, I didn't." Foster bit his lip, then leaned forward. "You see, Bobby…I have a son. He's twenty-five. A terrific kid, I can't tell you—" His voice cracked.

Bobby waited him out, his fingers flexing against his denim-clad thighs, his teeth clenched so tight his jaw ached.

"When Adam was sixteen, he was diagnosed with acute myelogenous leukemia," Foster said. "He was treated with chemotherapy and the disease went into remission. He finished high school, went to college—for more than six years he was disease free. We really believed he'd licked it. But then it returned. The chemo isn't working this time. His only chance is a bone marrow transplant."

Bobby forced himself to keep breathing, to remain still. He felt as if he was back in 'Nam, waiting for the next explosion. Peril vibrated in the air.

Foster hadn't come here to talk about chemotherapy any more than he'd come to talk about Bobby's lovely house and his beautiful piece of property. And if he didn't get to the point soon, Bobby would bring on the next explosion himself. He'd trip a land mine, just to end the suspense.

"I don't understand all the science," Foster continued, "but neither my wife nor I were a good match to be a donor. None of his grandparents or cousins matched. We worked with the National Marrow Donor Program, searching for a possible match." He studied his coffee for a long moment, then lifted his eyes to Bobby. "For some reason, a sibling makes the best donor."

Boom. No need for Bobby to trip an explosion. The word *sibling* had done it. He understood why Foster was here now— and anger turned his vision red, just the way the land mines in 'Nam used to.

"I always wondered—I mean, that autumn, after I'd left for college and Joelle called and told me she was, well…"

Pregnant, you piece of scum.

"I'm not sure what she told you or what you… Well, that's between you and her. The thing was, I never heard from her again. I had no idea if she'd gone through with…" He faltered.

An abortion. Say it.

"All I heard was that she left town and never came back. I asked my parents if they had any news of her, but—" he glanced at Joelle "—they'd never been crazy about us, and I think they were relieved she was gone. I tried to talk to Joelle's mother, too—this was years ago, Bobby, before I got married, before my son… Anyway, Joelle's mother seemed to dislike me as much as my parents disliked her. She wouldn't give me the time of day. So I let it go—until Adam's leukemia returned, and the doctors asked if he had a sibling."

"He doesn't." This conversation was over. Bobby pushed back his chair, ready to stand, ready to pick Foster up by his fancy silk necktie and drag him out to the street.

At Bobby's movement, Foster sat straighter and spoke faster. "I hired a detective, and he found you. He told me you had a daughter who was thirty-six-years old. I did the math, Bobby."

Bobby shook his head.

"I realize it's not fair, my coming to you like this," Foster said, including Joelle in his gaze. His voice wavered. "Back in Holmdell, when—I mean, I was young, and I was a fool and—"

"Claudia is my daughter," Bobby said, these words sharper than the last, slicing through the air.

"Of course she is. I would never—"

"You can leave now."

Foster flattened his hands against the butcher-block surface of the table, as if clinging to it to would keep Bobby from evicting him. "All I'm asking is to have her tested, to see if she's a match."

"No."

"Bobby," Joelle murmured, reaching for his hand.

His hand fisted again and he yanked his arm away. This man, this creep, was staking a claim on Claudia, and Joelle was taking his side. Explosion after explosion rumbled inside Bobby's skull. Could Foster really invade his home, win over his wife and steal his daughter? Could this actually be happening?

"You wouldn't have to tell her everything." Foster pressed him, pleading. "Just have her take a blood test. If she isn't a match, then it's done."

"No." Bobby refused to look at Joelle. If she wanted to ally herself with Foster, Bobby would fight on his own. "Claudia is my daughter. I'm her father. Now you're asking me to tell her that everything she's ever known, everything this whole family is about, is a lie. You're asking me to tell her some other guy—some son of a bitch who knocked her mother up and abandoned her—is her real father."

Foster sighed. "My son's life hangs in the balance, so yes," he conceded. "That's what I'm asking you to do."

If Bobby drank the coffee, he'd choke. If he sat in this room with Drew Foster for another minute, he'd start swinging. He shoved away from the table so hard his chair fell over when he stood and then he stormed out of the room. Behind him, he heard Joelle call his name and then Foster say, "It's all right, Joelle…"

Oh, sure. It was all right. The two of them—Claudia's *parents*—would figure this whole thing out once hotheaded Bobby D was out of the way.

He stalked through the mudroom to the garage and climbed in behind the wheel of his truck. He wasn't going to drive anywhere, not without shoes. He didn't really want to go anywhere, anyway. He just needed to get away from Foster. Foster and Joelle. Drew and JoJo, the lovebirds of Holmdell High School.

He had to breathe. Had to calm down so he could think. Had to hold himself together. Violent urges simmered inside him, but he was a better man than his father. He wasn't going to snap.

He rested his arms on the steering wheel and his forehead on his hands. Inhale, exhale. Control.

Claudia was his daughter. He was the only father she'd ever had. He'd wiped her butt, bandaged her scrapes, perched himself on tiny chairs in colorful primary-school classrooms to discuss her progress with her teachers. He'd taught her how to use a hammer and a tape measure, how to grout tile and repair dry rot and how to plant a rosebush without getting pricked by the thorns. He'd paced the floors when she'd stayed out past her curfew, and he'd paid her college tuition, and nine years ago, he'd walked her down the aisle in church and delivered her to her groom. Her children called him Grampa.

He and Joelle had a life. They had a family. They had two sons and a daughter, a home, an understanding. They'd put it together and made it work. They'd succeeded, no thanks to Drew Foster.

And now that prick was in Bobby's house, begging for his son's life. An ailing son didn't give him permission to undermine everything that made Bobby's life worth living. His family. His children. His wife.

Drew Foster had no right. Yet Bobby knew, with a sickening certainty, that it was too late. The mines had exploded, and soon everything Bobby held dear would be nothing but rubble.

Chapter 2

May 1970

"'Ooh, baby, baby, it's a wild world,'" Joelle sang along with Cat Stevens as she brushed blue shadow on her eyelids. The music spilled into her bedroom from the FM radio Drew had given her for her eighteenth birthday last month. Her mother had been annoyed by the gift—"He's been dating you since before Christmas. He should've bought you jewelry"—but Joelle loved the radio. The old hi-fi in the living room wasn't a stereo, and besides, her mother hated when she played Jimi Hendrix or Bob Dylan or the Byrds. She even bitched about Simon and Garfunkel, who had pretty voices but rubbed her wrong. And the Beatles. "They used to be so cute, but then they got all druggy," she complained.

With her own radio, though—the most generous gift anybody had ever given her—Joelle could listen to music in her bedroom. Druggy music, heartbreaking music, dance-till-you-drop music. Jewelry was nice, but you couldn't sing along with a bracelet.

Joelle also couldn't sing along with Cat Stevens while she applied her mascara. For reasons she had never figured out, she found it impossible to put on mascara without opening her mouth like a fish. She'd chosen a brown shade, because black would have looked tarty with her fair coloring. But her pale lashes were invisible without mascara on them.

She blinked a couple of times to dry the lashes, then shut her mouth and stepped back to assess her reflection in the mirror above her dresser. People were always telling her she was pretty, but she didn't see herself that way. She'd been spared the curse of acne, thank God, but her nose was too long and her cheeks too flat, and no matter how much she tweezed her eyebrows, one was higher than the other. Her hair was naturally blond—she didn't even have to use lemon juice in it to bring out the highlights—but without makeup, her eyes were practically invisible.

Tonight they were vivid, though—and not just because of the eye shadow and mascara. Her dress was the same blue as her eyes. She'd picked the fabric just because of the color.

She hoped no one would guess that she'd sewn her prom dress herself. The rich girls had all traveled to Cincinnati to buy their gowns, and the girls who couldn't afford to make that trip had bought their dresses at Beldon's, Holmdell's local department store. Joelle couldn't even afford the prom dresses at Beldon's. She'd gone into the store, read the price tags and realized that the only way she'd wind up with a formal gown was if she sewed one herself. She'd chosen a dress pattern with narrow shoulder straps, a sleek bodice and an A-line skirt that flared as it descended to her ankles. It appeared homemade to her, but maybe people wouldn't notice.

Yeah, right. And maybe they wouldn't notice how awful her hair had come out, either. She'd set it so it would hang in fat corkscrew curls. She'd globbed on the setting gel and drenched her hair in most of a can of her mother's Aqua Net. But the curls hadn't held. They sagged and drooped.

The rich girls all went to Fontaine's beauty parlor on prom day. Their hair would be perfect. She looked like a witch.

Tears stung her eyes, but she batted them away. She couldn't cry, not with all the mascara she'd just brushed on. Sighing, she turned her back to the mirror. She'd done the best she could. And the bottom line was that none of the rich girls, with their fancy big-city gowns and beautiful hair, was Drew Foster's prom date. Joelle was. Drew had chosen her.

"Remember," her mother had been coaching her ever since her first date with him "this boy is a catch. You don't want to lose him. He's your route to a better life. Don't screw up."

In the living room, her mother chain-smoked and gossiped with their landlady, Mrs. Proski. A chubby old widow, Mrs. Proski could pass for Santa's wife, although her chronically pink nose was caused not by arctic weather but by drinking too much sherry. Still, she was tolerable. When Joelle had been younger and her mother had had to work odd shifts at the Bank Street Diner, Mrs. Proski had been on call in case Joelle had an emergency. Mrs. Proski was always home because she didn't have a job. She managed to make ends meet between her late husband's pension and what she charged in rent for the first-floor flat that Joelle and her mother occupied in the duplex on Third Street.

Since Joelle and her mother didn't own a camera, Mrs. Proski had brought hers downstairs so she could take photos of Joelle and Drew before they left for the prom. Unfortunately Joelle's hair was going to look like crap in all the photos.

"'Ooh, baby, baby…'" she sang, then held her lips still so she could dab some pale pink lipstick on them. Through the closed door she heard the doorbell ring.

Her mother hollered, "Joelle! He's here!" She sounded more excited than Joelle felt. But then, her mother didn't have to impress anyone tonight. She didn't have to have magnificent hair and a stunning dress. No rich kids from the Hill were going to be checking her out and issuing her a failing grade.

She examined her reflection for one final minute, then pulled her sling-back sandals from their box and slipped her feet into them. She so rarely wore heels that she felt a bit wobbly, even though they were only two inches high. She practiced pacing the room—or as close as she could get to pacing, since her bedroom was so small she could move only two steps in each direction–but that was enough to get her balance and grow used to the flow of the dress.

"Never mind," her mother shouted through her shut door. "It's just Bobby."

Her tension escaped her in a long breath that ended in a laugh. She swung the door open to see Bobby DiFranco swaggering down the hall to her room. In a pair of torn jeans, a T-shirt with a fist stenciled across it and over that a faded, fraying army shirt, his long, dark hair splayed out from his face like a lion's mane and his scuffed boots green with grass stains, he was clearly not dressed for the prom.

"Far out, JoJo." He let out a low whistle as he swept into her room. "You look great."

"Really?" Feeling a bit more secure in her sandals, she pirouetted for him. "I look okay?"

"I'm speechless." He pressed his hands to his chest. "I'm in love."

"Don't you be slowing her down," Joelle's mother yelled from the living room. "She's got to get ready for Drew."

Joelle and Bobby shared a scowl, then snickered. They'd been friends since childhood. Bobby knew Joelle's mother nearly as well as Joelle did—and he knew Wanda Webber didn't put much value on her daughter's friendship with him. Wanda was placing all her bets on Drew Foster, the young man from the Hill who'd taken a liking to her daughter. Drew was Joelle's ticket out of Tubtown—the neighborhood of Holmdell where she and Bobby and all the other poor slobs lived. Everyone called it Tubtown because of the large number of bathtubs planted vertical in people's front yards, with little statues of the Virgin Mary inside them to create shrines. Mrs. Proski hadn't erected a bathtub shrine in front of the duplex where she and the Webbers lived, but she kept a rusting washtub planted with geraniums near the front porch, her idea of decorative landscaping.

Bobby was just another Tubtown boy on the fast track to nowhere. Why Joelle wasted any time on him was a mystery to her mother, one Joelle had long ago quite trying to explain to her.

"You think people will figure out I sewed the dress?" she asked him.

"If they do, they'll be throwing money at you and begging you to sew dresses for them."

Snorting in disbelief, Joelle stalked back to the mirror and frowned. "My hair looks gross."

"Are you kidding? It looks—" he sighed "—wonderful."

He touched one of the wayward curls. "Feels kinda sticky, though."

"You wouldn't believe how much hair spray I used."

He shrugged, then sprawled out on her bed. "It looks great, really. You look like a flower child."

"I don't want to look like a flower child." She located her white leatherette purse and gathered everything she needed to stuff into it: lipstick, her keys, a couple of dollars, a few neatly folded tissues. "I want to look like a princess." The kind of princess who belonged on the arm of a prince like Drew Foster.

"Don't expect me to call you Your Highness," Bobby teased. "Your heinie, maybe."

Joelle wrinkled her nose at him. If she'd hoped he would help calm her bristling nerves, she'd hoped wrong. He'd come here to give her a hard time, to tease her as if he were an irritating brother.

She decided to tease him right back. "You should be going to the prom, too," she said, turning back to her dresser and zipping the purse shut. She dabbed a little Jean Naté behind her ears. "You should have asked Margie."

Bobby snorted. "Thirty bucks for the tickets. Another thirty to rent a tux. Then I'd have to buy her a corsage. And find a car. I couldn't drive her to the prom in my truck."

"Do you think she would have cared how you drove her? She's your girlfriend. You should have asked her. I bet she would have loved to go."

"Proms aren't for Tubtown kids."

"I'm a Tubtown kid and I'm going."

"Because you're in with the Hill kids. They'll all be decked out in their fancy threads, acting stuck-up and pretending they're cool. That's not for me." He shrugged. "I'll do something with Margie tonight. Maybe we'll catch a movie. *Easy Rider* is still playing at the Bijou."

"You've seen it already," Joelle reminded him.

"So we'll see it again. Or we'll go to the lake or something."

The lake was where people went to make out. Joelle didn't know if Bobby and Margie were having sex, but she suspected they were. She sometimes believed she was the only high-school senior in Tubtown—in all of Holmdell, probably—who was still a virgin.

She imagined that everyone at school assumed she was putting out for Drew. Why else would a boy like him, who had money and good looks and was heading to an Ivy League college in September, be dating someone like her?

Because he loved her; that was why. Because he thought she was nice and fun to be with and she wasn't snobby like the other Hill girls. That was what he told her, anyway. And since she wasn't putting out for him, she figured he must be speaking the truth.

Someday she'd make love with him. But she hadn't yet. She loved him with all her heart, yet she couldn't say with absolute certainty that he loved her. She supposed most girls who put out didn't care all that much whether or not they were in love, but Joelle was old-fashioned. She wanted to be sure Drew was hers as much as she was his.

Bobby broke into her thoughts. "Listen, Jo, do me a favor."

"What?"

"Mrs. Proski is taking pictures of you and Foster, right?"

"Yeah."

"Have her snap a picture of just you alone, for me. You never looked this good before, and you'll probably never look this good again—"

Pretending to be insulted, Joelle spun around and threw her purse at him.

Bobby laughed and batted it away. "I want to remember what you looked like the night you were a princess. And I don't want Foster's ugly mug in the picture."

"Drew Foster isn't ugly." She knew that was nothing more than Bobby's teasing, but she wasn't in the mood to be teased tonight. She was anxious—about whether she was truly pretty enough to belong with Drew, whether she was even remotely classy enough to fit in at the prom. Whether after the dance he would drive her to the lake. Whether he'd expect her to go all the way with him because he'd spent so much money on the tickets and flowers and his tux. Whether he would still want her to be his girlfriend tomorrow.

Any other time, she'd welcome Bobby's taunting and give as good as she got. But not tonight.

Bobby seemed to sense that. His smile lost its sneering edge and he pushed himself off the bed. "You're gonna have a good time," he assured her. "Remember, JoJo, you're better than they are."

"No, I'm not." In front of anyone else, she would have hidden her insecurity. But not Bobby. They went back too far, knew each other too well.

She was aware that the Hill kids tolerated her only because she was Drew's girlfriend, not because they thought highly of her. She didn't wear the right brand of jeans, didn't take all the honors classes, didn't participate in glee club or cheerleaders or student government. The rich girls treated her pleasantly only out of respect for Drew—which was why, when she wasn't with him, she hung out with Bobby and the other Tubtown kids she'd grown up with. Some of them had stopped being friendly to her once she'd started going with Drew, though. They thought she was stuck-up.

She wasn't. At least Bobby recognized that.

The doorbell rang again. "Drew's here," Wanda bellowed.

Joelle didn't miss the flicker of disapproval on Bobby's face. He resented the Hill kids because they viewed him as trash. Joelle insisted that Drew wasn't like the others, but Bobby considered him just another spoiled, arrogant rich boy. If only he knew Drew the way she did, he'd realize how wrong he was.

She and Bobby emerged from her bedroom and met up with Drew in the hallway. He had asked her what color her dress was and he'd rented a tux to match—powder blue, his shirt white with blue-trimmed ruffles down the front and his cummerbund and bow tie a slightly darker, satiny blue, the same color as her dress.

Unlike her hair, his was perfect, parted on the side and slicked smooth across the crown of his head. He kept it relatively short—because it was easier, he claimed, but she suspected he just didn't want anyone to mistake him for a hippie.

"You look beautiful," he said, then glanced at Bobby. "Bobby D."

"Foster," Bobby responded curtly.

Staring at her two favorite guys in the whole world, Joelle had to stifle a laugh. One clean-cut, polished and elegant, the other scruffy and defiant. They were so different, and she loved them both. But Drew was easier on her nerves. He never seemed to struggle. He never suffered a moment's doubt. He understood what he wanted from life, and he knew how to get it. He wore his good fortune as if it were a comfortable pair of shoes.

Good fortune had never favored Bobby DiFranco. Maybe that was why he wore scuffed old boots.

"I gotta go," he said, patting Joelle on the shoulder. "Have fun. And don't forget that photo."

Joelle watched him stride through the living room, mumble a farewell to her mother and Mrs. Proski and then swing out the front door. She wished he weren't so negative about the prom and the Hill kids. He could have gone to the prom with Margie and had fun tonight, too.

If he and Margie went down to the lake, he'd probably have fun, she realized with a quiet laugh. Maybe even more fun than she and Drew would have at the prom.

She didn't go to the lake with Drew that night. Instead he and two of his buddies and their dates all drove to a nightclub three towns away. Joelle was the only one of the six without fake ID, so she'd ordered ginger ale while they'd all gotten tipsy on cocktails, and she'd felt like an idiot. But to her great relief the question of whether to go all the way with Drew never came up.

Two weeks later, they were high-school graduates. Joelle had a job running the cash register at Harley's, a convenience store where she'd worked the previous summer. She had enrolled in two classes at the community college, which would start in September. Two were all she could afford, and the light schedule would allow her to continue working at Harley's during the school year.

Drew would be heading to Dartmouth at the end of August. He spent the hot, empty days of summer playing tennis and lounging by the pool with the other Hill kids at Green Gates Country Club. He didn't bother to get a job. His parents provided him all the money he needed.

Bobby got his draft notice. He'd scored a low number in

the lottery and college had been out of the question for him, so he couldn't apply for a student deferment. "I don't want to go to Vietnam," he confessed to Joelle, "but I'm not gonna shoot my kneecap off or pretend I'm queer just to stay out. I just can't do that." With a philosophical shrug, he added, "At least Vietnam isn't Holmdell. Going there can't be as bad as staying here."

He had a job doing maintenance at the town cemetery, mowing the grass, trimming the shrubs and clearing away the wilted flowers left by visitors. He spent most of his evenings with Margie and Joelle spent most of hers with Drew. But two nights a week she had to work until 10:00 p.m. at Harley's, and Drew considered that hour too late for them to get together. On those nights, Bobby would swing by Harley's in his rattly old pickup truck and drive her down to the A&W. They'd sneak into the woods beyond the parking lot and share a joint. Once it was nothing more than a wisp of lingering smoke, they'd buy root beers and split a jumbo order of fries and they'd talk.

"You think he's gonna ask you to marry him?" Bobby inquired one evening while they were satisfying their munchies with hot, salty fries.

"I don't know. It doesn't make sense to be engaged while he's in New Hampshire and I'm here."

"But that's what you're hoping for, right?"

"Yeah," she admitted, feeling her cheeks warm. The Hill girls were all leaving town for college, and they talked about having careers and waiting until they were established before they got married. But Joelle was never going to be "established"—not unless Drew established her as his wife.

She wouldn't mind having a career, too. She wasn't afraid

of work. Before she had a career, though, she'd have to earn a college degree. Accomplishing that might take her longer than normal if she enrolled in only two courses a semester at the community college, but eventually she'd transfer to a four-year university and graduate. Drew wouldn't want to have a wife who wasn't college educated.

Sitting beneath the awning bordering the parking lot at the A&W, Bobby sent her an enigmatic smile and drawled, "You wanna get yourself a big fat diamond on your finger." He always smiled that way after he'd smoked pot, a mysterious I-know-something-you-don't-know smile. "You wanna drive a Caddy and wear a mink and have everyone call you Mrs. Drew Foster." Still smiling, he shook his head. "You should aim higher, JoJo. If you can get Foster, imagine who else you could get. The world is filled with rich guys. Why settle for him?"

"I'm not looking for a rich guy," she insisted, trying not to let Bobby rile her. "That's not why I love Drew. I don't put Margie down, Bobby. Don't you put Drew down."

She never smoked pot with Drew that summer. He preferred liquor to drugs. He seemed to believe booze was sophisticated. He preferred mixed drinks, and he liked to lecture on which brands of vodka or scotch were the best. At least he never got smashed on a regular basis, like some of his friends.

She wished he would take her to Green Gates some evenings, but he rarely did. He would complain to her that he'd already spent the whole day there and didn't want to go to the nighttime swim or sign up for the lighted tennis courts. Not that Joelle knew a tennis racquet from a snowshoe, but she would have liked to swim in the pool. She owned one swimsuit, but it was a black bikini. If Drew saw her in it, it might make him love her a little more.

They did go to the lake pretty often in his Corvette—but not to swim. Making out wasn't easy in that car, since it had no backseat. She let Drew touch her breasts and even slide his fingers inside her shorts, which seemed to excite him more than her. And she touched him, stroked him, let him come in her hand. That always struck her as incredibly intimate, his spurting all his fluid onto her palms. After she cleaned up, using tissues from the portable pack he kept stashed in his glove compartment, he'd always cuddle her and tell her he loved her.

As the summer stretched into August, he began to push for more. "We're going to be apart for months," he reminded her. "If we did this, it would make us closer. It would seal our love."

"I don't know, Drew… Maybe I'm not ready yet." Everyone was always talking about free love, but she didn't get how anything that significant could be free. If she gave in to Drew, would he love her more or less? If she gave in to him, would she love herself more or less?

"We're high-school graduates, Joelle. How much more ready to we have to be?"

"Sex isn't exactly like trigonometry," she argued. "You don't just take a course and pass."

Whenever they had these discussions, Drew always worked hard not to get impatient. Joelle could tell; she could see him wrestling with his temper, breathing deeply then holding her hand or wrapping his arm around her. He didn't yell. He didn't force. That told her he must love her.

Toward the end of August, he tried a different approach. "It would be like this gift you gave me to bring with me to

Dartmouth," he explained. "This special thing we shared that would keep us close, even when I'm away."

"If I gave you that gift, how do I know you wouldn't just leave and forget I ever existed?"

"Because I love you. You know I do."

The night before he planned to leave for college, she yielded. She still wasn't sure she was ready or if it was right, but when she imagined him traveling all the way to New Hampshire and meeting all those new, smart, sophisticated Ivy Leaguers, she couldn't bear the thought that he wouldn't have something of hers in his possession, something precious, something she would never give to anyone else. So she told him yes.

He borrowed his father's Lincoln for the occasion because it had a wide, well-upholstered backseat, which Drew carefully draped with a towel because he was aware she would bleed. He brought a condom. They drank half a bottle of Chianti, the kind with straw around the base, and Joelle told him to save the bottle when it was empty and stick a candle in it, and every time he lighted the candle it would be like a memory of her burning in his soul. He told her she was a poet.

Despite the wine and the towel and the car's wide backseat, it hurt. All she felt was pain and Drew's hot, wine-tinged breath in her face. She'd believed making love was supposed to feel good, but it didn't. It hurt, hurt, hurt.

At least it ended quickly. Drew tore into her and pounded on her for less than thirty seconds, and then he groaned and shuddered and was done. He pulled out of her so fast the condom remained behind. That was probably the worst part of it, so embarrassing, his poking around with his fingers and dragging the condom out.

"I love you, Joelle," he whispered. "I love you so much."

Hearing those words soothed the awful burning between her legs. They'd made love and now they were bound forever. Because she'd given him this, he would never stop loving her.

The next day, he was gone.

Chapter 3

Joelle stood in the open doorway, a silhouette in the light from the mudroom, and stared into the garage's gloom. Bobby watched her through the windshield. Even with her face in shadow, he could picture her features—the hollows of her cheeks, the pointed tip of her nose, the faint lines fanning out from the corners of her dazzling blue eyes. He'd fallen in love with her face when he was ten years old, sitting three rows to her left in Mrs. Schmidt's fourth-grade class, before he'd had any idea what falling in love meant. And today, forty-seven years later, he still loved her face.

He wasn't the sort who ran away from a problem, but as long as Drew Foster had been sitting in his kitchen, threatening everything Bobby cared about, everything that had ever mattered to him, he couldn't have stayed. Not because Foster scared him but because he scared himself.

His father had been a violent man, and Bobby had sworn he would be exactly the kind of man his father wasn't. But looking at Foster, listening to him calmly explain why Bobby should tell Claudia the truth about her birth, had made Bobby feel his own father's blood pulsing through his veins. He'd had to get the hell out.

Joelle was alone now. He knew she wouldn't have come looking for him unless Foster had left. She'd probably made some excuse for Bobby, explained that he had a quick temper—which, in general, he didn't—or invented some other justification for his behavior. Or maybe not. Maybe she'd just let his rage sit there in the room, simmering in the air.

He shoved open the door, swung out of the truck and walked toward Joelle. He felt the cold, hard concrete floor against the soles of his feet, right through his socks. Cold and hard suited his mood.

"He's gone," Joelle confirmed.

"I'm sorry," he said. He was sorry not for walking out on Foster but for abandoning Joelle. He should have stood by her and made clear to Foster exactly whose wife she was. Instead, he'd bolted, leaving her alone with a man she'd once loved with all her heart.

She gave him a sad smile. "It's okay."

No, it wasn't okay. Nothing was okay.

He followed her through the mudroom into the kitchen. The air smelled of coffee. He wondered if from here on in he would always associate that scent with Foster, if he would never be able to drink coffee again.

His own cup was resting in the dish rack beside the sink, already rinsed clean. The coffeemaker was turned off. Except for the aroma, he detected no sign that Foster had ever been in his house. Yet the atmosphere felt charged. The sunlight streaming through the windows seemed too bright.

In that glaring summer light, he could see Joelle's face clearly. Her mouth was tense, her eyes tired. Her ponytail hung lopsided, brushing against her left shoulder.

"He can't have Claudia," Bobby said. If that SOB wanted to reach Claudia, he'd have to get past Bobby, and Bobby intended to make that impossible.

"He doesn't want Claudia," she said wearily. She reached for Bobby's hand. Her fingers felt like icy twigs on his skin. "He wants her to take a blood test, that's all."

"That's all," Bobby echoed, then snorted. "How do we ask her to take a blood test without telling her why? And what if she's a match? What do we tell her then?"

"I don't know." Releasing his hand, Joelle sank into a chair, propped her elbows on the table and rested her chin in her palms. "It's not a simple situation."

"It's simple enough," Bobby argued, dropping onto another chair. "You and I had an understanding. We based our marriage on that understanding. Claudia is our daughter. That's the end of it."

"His son is dying," Joelle said, her eyes as overly bright as the sunshine pouring through the windows. "Can't you at least have a little sympathy for the man?"

Not as much as Joelle had, obviously. Sure, he felt sorry for Foster in an abstract way. He'd feel sorry for any man whose child was at risk. Maybe he ought to feel sorry for himself, since right now his own daughter seemed at risk.

"If she had the blood test and didn't match," Joelle argued, "she'd never have to know."

"Of course she'd have to know. What do you think—we can sneak a blood test past her?"

"We wouldn't have to tell her what it was for. We could say she's being tested to find out if she matches a distant cousin—"

"Oh, there's a plan." Sarcasm soured Bobby's voice. "You're an only child and my brother's gay. My father's family gave him up long ago. How's your mother fixed for cousins? How does Claudia wind up with a cousin?" He crossed to the sink and washed his hands, just because the whole situation made him feel dirty. "Don't you think she'd ask about this cousin she'd never heard of? Maybe she'd even want to meet this miraculous new cousin of hers."

Rather than commenting on his sarcasm, Joelle nodded in agreement. "You're right. Lying isn't going to help. It's just that we've been lying all along. What's one more lie at this point?"

Bobby dried his hands on a dish towel, buying time to consider his response. Had they been lying all along, or had they been trying to create a family? Had they been lying or simply figuring out a way to survive, a way to make life work? Had Bobby been lying from the start when he'd convinced himself he could be the father of another man's child, and the husband of a woman who hadn't loved him the way he'd loved her?

Everything—his home, his work, his family—had sprouted from a lie. Like a plant grown from a poisoned seed, that lie had broken through the ground and blossomed, but the roots were rotten. Sooner or later the plant was doomed to die.

"Nothing can change the fact that you're her father," Joelle said, twisting in her chair so she could look at him.

"If I'd conceived her at a sperm bank, it would have been the same thing."

"No, it wouldn't." He flung the towel aside and shoved his hair back from his face. The kitchen was too warm. The streaming sunlight was killing him. "A sperm bank is anonymous. This..." He waved vaguely toward the front door, through which Foster must have entered his house. "This was a guy you were in love with."

"I was a kid then."

She didn't deny that she'd loved Foster. She wouldn't. Now wasn't the time for lies. Yet acknowledging that she'd once loved that bastard—a truth Bobby had managed to avoid thinking about for years—pained him. He wished he were the only man she'd ever loved. He'd married her knowing he wasn't, but still...the truth hurt.

"All right." Her shoulders slumped and she glanced away from him. "What do you want, Bobby? What do you want to do about this?"

"I want to tell Drew Foster to go to hell." Actually, what he wanted was to turn back the clock a half hour. He wanted to drive home, excited about landing a new contract—even after years in the business, every new contract gave him a thrill—and confident that when he got home, Joelle would be waiting for him. He wanted to arrive and find her finished with her housecleaning, sweaty and heading for the shower. He wanted to pull off his clothes and slip into the shower with her and screw her silly while the water sprayed down onto them.

"What do *you* want?" he shot back, dreading her answer even though he had to hear it.

She turned back to face the table and folded her hands, as

though praying. "I keep thinking about how his son is dying," she said, her voice muted but steady.

"His daughter would have been dead if you'd done what he'd told you to do all those years ago." The words sounded brutal, but he didn't care. "If you'd done what Foster asked back then, Claudia would never even have existed."

"Here's the thing, Bobby." Her voice remained calm, her eyes dry, but she clasped her hands tighter, turning her knuckles white. "Imagine if it was Claudia who was sick today. Imagine the only thing that could save her was a bone marrow transplant from a sibling."

"She's got two brothers."

"Imagine they weren't a match." She seemed to be addressing a molecule of air directly in front of her. "Imagine her life was at stake. If there was the slightest chance that Drew might have gone on to have other children who would be her half brothers or half sisters… You know as well as I do that we'd be hiring a detective to find him. If the shoe was on the other foot, we'd do exactly what he did."

Bobby opened his mouth and then shut it. Joelle was right. He hated her for being right, but he couldn't argue. If Claudia was dying, Bobby would try anything, go anywhere, destroy any family if that was what it took to cure her.

"What happened then happened then," Joelle said. "Now we've got to deal with today. A young man is dying, and there's a chance Claudia can save his life."

Joelle's words and all they implied enraged him. He wanted to hit things, break things. He wanted to confront the doctors treating Drew's son and tell them to come up with some other treatment so he wouldn't have the burden of that boy's life pressing on his back.

He wanted to preserve his family. He wanted to protect his daughter. He wanted to keep on living the lie. It had been a good lie. It had worked for all these years.

He gazed down at Joelle. Seated, she should have looked small. But her spine was straight, her eyes clear, her chin raised. A piece of his soul shriveled inside him as he considered his choice.

If he said no, he'd lose her. If he said yes, he'd lose everything his life had been about up to this minute.

Closing his eyes, he saw red.

Claudia lived south of Gray Hill in Fairfield County. Her husband was an attorney—he made too much money to be a mere lawyer—and Claudia had been a well-paid marketing consultant until she gave birth to Jeremy four years ago. She'd contemplated returning to work when Jeremy was six months old, but she'd been so reluctant that Gary had urged her to be a full-time mother for a few years. They could live well on his income alone. And two years later, Kristin was born.

So Claudia was still a full-time mother, though she often told Joelle she intended to return to paying work someday. "Women who work outside the home can be terrific mothers," she often said. "Look at you. You're a teacher, and you were a terrific mother."

After tonight, Joelle thought, Claudia would hardly think Joelle was terrific. This was probably a huge mistake. She should tell Bobby to turn the truck around and drive home. She should forget that Drew Foster's shadow had ever darkened her front porch.

It was too late to turn around. Seated beside her in the driver's seat of his truck, Bobby appeared grim and determined as he steered south toward Claudia's house. Joelle had done too good a job of convincing him that this was the correct thing to do, that Drew's son didn't deserve to die just because Drew and Joelle had been young and stupid.

"Claudia has a right to know the truth," she said, wishing she could convince herself the way she'd convinced Bobby. "We probably should have told her years ago."

"Told her what?" He stared through the windshield at the headlight beams illuminating the road. "That I'm not her father?"

"Stop saying that, Bobby. You *are* her father. Even Drew understands that."

"If Drew understands it, then I guess it must be true."

His sarcasm implied just how bitter he was. She hadn't meant to cause him pain—not now, not ever. But she didn't see how continuing the lies would help, especially when a young man's life hung in the balance.

Claudia should have learned about her genetic heritage years ago, for her own benefit. Better for her to find out from her parents than from some doctor should a crisis arise, like the one Drew's son was facing.

But Joelle and Bobby had never told her. The secret had simply gotten buried by daily life. One year had rolled into the next until the truth had grown invisible, just one blade of grass in a thick green lawn.

"She'll never stop loving you," Joelle reassured Bobby. "You're her daddy. She's named after your mother, for God's sake."

He glanced at her. His hair was too long, but she liked it that way, a remnant of his rebellious youth. Strands of silver had infiltrated the dark waves and the outdoor work he did had weathered his face. Unlike Drew, Bobby hadn't gone soft at all. His body was still sinewy, his jaw defiant. He'd started using reading glasses a few years ago, but even when he was wearing them, he looked tough and brimming with energy, ready to take on the world.

"Are you going to explain everything?" he asked. "Or should I?"

"I will."

"What if she kicks us out of her house?"

Joelle didn't want to consider that possibility. "I'll tell her it's all my fault. Let her blame me, Bobby."

"I don't want her blaming you," he muttered. "You're her real mother."

And I'm not her real father. The words lingered unspoken in the snug cab of the truck.

Joelle had already told him countless times that he was Claudia's father. She wasn't going to say it again. She felt sick, her stomach clenching, her head thumping. *Turn around,* she thought, but she couldn't force out the words.

Just as Drew's son deserved a chance to live, Claudia deserved her parents' honesty.

Bobby pulled into Claudia's driveway, which led to a spacious colonial in a ritzy subdivision. The porch lights had been left on for them. Joelle wondered if this would be the last time Claudia ever welcomed them into her home. Even braced for the worst, she wondered if she'd survive her daughter's reaction.

Gary opened the door for them. A tall, affable man, he greeted them with a warm smile. "You're lucky you caught us home tonight," he said as he ushered them into the house. "Saturday night we're usually out carousing."

"Ha!" Claudia commented from the kitchen. "We can barely keep our eyes open after 9:00 p.m. The kids wear us out." She waltzed down the hall and hugged Joelle. Claudia resembled Joelle—the same slender build, the blond hair, the elegantly hollow cheeks—except that she had brown eyes. She'd always claimed she had her father's eyes, but now, as Joelle peered into them, she saw Drew as much as Bobby in those mocha-brown irises.

"I've got to admit, we were surprised you asked to stop by so late," Gary said. "Usually you don't even want to see us. You just come to play with the kids."

"That's not true," Joelle said, her tone more defensive than she'd intended. She knew Gary was joking. He and Claudia always kidded that their sole value to Bobby and Joelle was as the people who'd supplied them grandchildren.

Tonight, though, Joelle had told Claudia they would be stopping by after Jeremy and Kristin were in bed. This was not a visit for which the children should be awake. Lowering her tone, she said, "I'm sorry we're keeping you awake past your bedtime."

"Not a problem," Claudia insisted, wrapping Bobby in a hug. Claudia's hair was cut in a chic, angular style and her outfit, a wrinkly cotton shirt of turquoise, with slacks the same vivid fabric, probably cost more than Joelle's entire summer wardrobe. "Dad, you look terrible. Are you feeling okay?"

"It's been a rough day," he said cryptically.

"Why don't we sit down," Joelle suggested, gesturing toward the living room. "We have to talk, Claudia."

Claudia eyed Gary. "I don't like the sound of this," she said through a tight smile.

"Hey, it's Saturday night. No bad news allowed." Gary

grinned at Joelle and Bobby. "Can I get you something to drink?"

Bobby answered for both of them. "No, thanks." He sat in the wingback chair in Claudia's impeccably decorated living room.

Gary took the other wingback chair and Joelle settled on the couch with Claudia. She wanted to be close to her daughter. In fact, she wanted to gather Claudia up, hold her on her lap and hug her, the way she had when Claudia had been a little girl. She wanted to cling to her baby and assure her that nothing bad would ever happen to her. Her own mistakes had brought so much pain to Bobby, and now they would bring pain to Claudia, too—and this wasn't a pain she could kiss away, like the scrapes and bruises Claudia had suffered as a child.

Just get it over with, she ordered herself, then added a stern mental reminder that Claudia deserved the truth. "We had a visitor today," she said. "Someone Dad and I went to high school with. In fact, he was my boyfriend senior year."

"I thought Dad was your boyfriend," Claudia said.

"I adored Dad. He was my best friend." She felt Bobby's gaze on her, cool and condemning. Swallowing, she pressed on. "This old classmate of ours is married now, and he has a son. His son is sick with a kind of leukemia. He has to receive a bone marrow transplant."

Claudia's smile faded. She glanced away—at Bobby or Gary, Joelle didn't know—and then turned back to her mother. Her eyes were filled with questions. "How tragic."

"Yes. It's tragic. Claudia…that man, that old boyfriend…" Joelle drew in a deep breath. She tasted the salt of tears at the back of her throat and swallowed. "He believes you might be a match for his son as a donor."

Claudia's mouth tensed. Her eyes hardened. She didn't need Joelle to spell it out. "Oh, my God," she whispered.

"We probably should have told you years ago, but... There never seemed to be any need. We're your parents, you're our daughter and nothing else mattered. So we just never said anything. But now, with his son so sick—he begged us to discuss this with you."

Claudia spun away, seeking her husband. Gary started to rise, but before he was standing, Claudia had twisted back to her mother. "Who is this man?" she demanded. "Who is this old boyfriend of yours?"

"He was someone from our hometown, Claudia. A classmate of ours."

"What's his name?" Claudia's voice was as cold as stone.

"Drew Foster."

Claudia mouthed his name, as if testing the syllables. She closed her eyes and shook her head. "I can't believe this. I can't believe..." She glanced at Bobby. "You knew about this?"

From the corner of her eyes, Joelle saw him nod.

"But you never—you always—" Again Claudia shook her head. Her eyes glinted with moisture. "How could you?" she asked, directing her question into the air rather than toward Joelle or Bobby. "How could you keep this from me? How could you let me think..." Her voice trailed off.

"Think what, Claudia?" Joelle asked.

Gazing desperately at her, Claudia gestured toward Bobby. "Think *he's* my father."

Joelle felt her heart crack in two. She couldn't bear to look at Bobby, to witness how badly Claudia's words wounded him. "He *is* your father. He's the only father you have."

"But this other man—this Drew Foster—"

"Asked me to get an abortion. I wanted you so much, Claudia. I couldn't do that. And your dad—" she dared to peek at Bobby, whose face was frozen except for his dark, turbulent eyes "—wanted you, too, every bit as much as I did. So we raised you, and we loved you and we still love you, more than you can imagine."

"But you never told me this." Claudia's anguish carried an undertone of hysteria. "You never told me some other man was my father. My God. I don't even know who I am anymore."

The sobs in Joelle's throat threatened to choke her. She wouldn't let herself cry, though. Not in front of Claudia and Gary, not in front of Bobby. Yes, she'd made mistakes in her life. But she would never believe that giving birth to Claudia had been a mistake. Not even now, when she felt as if the pain in her heart would kill her.

Abruptly Claudia stood and stalked out of the living room. In the stillness she left behind, Joelle could hear the tread of her footsteps as she climbed the stairs, followed by the click of a door closing.

Gary shoved to his feet and glowered at them. "You can show yourselves out," he said as he stalked out of the living room. In less than a minute Joelle heard that upstairs door open and shut again, sounding miles away.

In the summer, Bobby slept nude. If Joelle's body were as sleek and youthful as his, she might sleep nude, too, but she was too self-conscious about the droop of her breasts, the way the skin of her abdomen sagged between the points of her hipbones, the damage left by fifty-six years of living. So she slept in an oversized T-shirt. Her sons had outgrown so many T-shirts over the years that she had several wardrobes' worth of castoffs from them.

Tonight she was wearing a striped cotton shirt Mike had worn constantly throughout high school, until in one of those odd adolescent spurts he'd awakened one morning to discover that he'd grown two inches and his shoulders were straining the shirt's seams. The cotton fabric felt soft against her skin, but she couldn't find a comfortable position between the sheets. When Bobby finished washing and joined her, he eased himself onto the bed, making sure not to touch her.

Usually he stretched out on his side facing her and slung one arm around her. Their bed was their refuge, their haven. In bed they were united. Husband and wife. No disagreements, no resentments, no bullshit. Just the two of them, JoJo and Bobby D, unbreakable.

Tonight he kept his distance.

She lay in the darkness until his silence began to feel like an actual presence, a stranger in their bed. Damn it, she wouldn't allow Drew to tear her and Bobby apart. No matter what had happened today, no matter how Claudia dealt with what Joelle had told her, she was not going to sacrifice her marriage.

She breached the chasm between her and Bobby—only a couple of inches, yet wide enough to contain the ugly truth they had carefully avoided until today—and stroked her hand down his chest. His skin was warm, the hair on his chest springy. When he didn't move, she shifted closer to him, snuggled up to him, skimmed her lips against the underside of his jaw.

He lay as still as a stone.

Sitting, she yanked off the T-shirt. She needed Bobby tonight. She needed him to know how much she loved him. She needed proof that they could survive this as they'd survived so much else in their lives.

She grazed his chin again, caressed the length of his torso, raised herself to kiss his cheek. He seemed to struggle against her invitation, against his own reflexes, but he was able to resist her only so long. When her hand slid downward to stroke him, she found him fully aroused.

With a curse, he pushed her fingers away—then cupped his hand around her head and pulled her down to him. His kisses were hard and angry, his tongue subduing her, his hand fisting in her hair so tightly she could feel his knuckles against her scalp. There was nothing tender or seductive in his kiss, in the way his free hand clamped onto her hip, his fingers digging into the soft flesh. After a moment, he tore his mouth from hers. Breathing heavily, he swore again.

"Bobby," she murmured. They'd gotten through bad times in the past by reaching for each other, using their bodies to communicate when they had no words. She knew that when Bobby was uneasy or afraid, he withdrew—and when he withdrew, she could bring him back this way, through touch, through sex. He wasn't much for talking. He was a physical man. He could close himself off, but she knew how to open him up again.

She brushed her fingertips against his lips, as if she could wipe away his coarse language and the emotion behind it. He jerked his head, recoiling from her gentle touch, then reared up and pushed her onto her back against the mattress. Her vision had adjusted to the darkness and she could make out the rage and sorrow in his eyes, the resentment tightening his jaw. He ran his hands down her body, his motions rough, his chest pumping as though breathing was a struggle.

Everything about him seemed to be struggling. She arched her arms around his shoulders and urged him onto her. *It's all right,* she wanted to tell him. *I need this. We both need this.* Not seduction, not tenderness—just connection. Just the knowledge that they were still together, that not even the truth could tear them apart.

He took her, his thrusts fierce and fast. When he came, his groan was tremulous, almost like a sob. She circled him with her arms, holding him on top of her, refusing to let him withdraw as her body pulsed around him. Had this been love or rage? Desperation? Fear?

He let out a long breath and with it another curse. *It's all right,* she assured herself, even though the past few minutes had failed to convince her anything was all right.

After a minute, he rolled away from her and flung an arm across his eyes, as if he didn't want to risk glimpsing her. "Sorry," he muttered.

She cupped his jaw. He recoiled from her touch, and she let her hand fall. "If anyone should apologize, it's me," she said. She'd started this, after all. She'd started the whole thing by telling Claudia about her parentage. She'd started it by allowing Drew Foster to enter her home. She'd started it thirty-seven years ago by foolishly believing she was in love with Drew.

Bobby's breathing was still ragged, his skin steamy, the sheet bunched around his hips. Despite the dark, she could see the sharp outline of his nose, the angle of his chin.

"Talk to me, Bobby," she pleaded.

"And say what?"

Say you're hurting. Say you're afraid. Say you want to make love to me again, gently this time. Love, not sex. Not anger. But he hated to discuss his feelings, to probe and analyze and bare his soul. For thirty-seven years, she'd been trying to get him to talk, and he never did. "Tell me what you're thinking."

He lay quietly for a stretch, his rib cage rising and falling beneath his skin, his eyes shielded from her. After a while he moved his arm away from his face, but only to stare at the ceiling. "When you build a stone wall," he said, "you've got to pick each stone out and put it in exactly the right place. If you want the wall to be stable, you have to do it right. The size of the stones. The shape."

She wasn't sure what he was getting at, but at least he was talking. She waited for him to continue.

"We didn't lay the foundation down right," he murmured. "We're standing on that wall and it's shaking beneath our feet. It's going to collapse. And we're going to fall."

"We'll get through this, Bobby. I know we will."

He shook his head. "We're falling, Jo. And it's a long way down."

Lying in a bed now cold, with her husband beside her yet a thousand miles away and that awful silence once again settling into the space between them, Joelle wondered how long the fall was and how broken they would be when they landed.

Chapter 4

October 1970

Bobby preferred the part of the cemetery farthest from his mother's grave. When he worked over in her section, near Bailey Road, he found himself lingering at her site, paying too much attention to each weed that dared to poke through the grass, dusting smudges of dirt from her headstone. Reading the stone: *Claudia Ricci DiFranco, February 27, 1930—May 6, 1964. Beloved wife and mother. She is with the angels now.* As if he didn't have the damn thing memorized. As if there was any question in his mind where she was.

Where she wasn't was with him and his brother, Eddie, who were certainly no angels. And she wasn't with their father, who had as much angel in him as the headstone had diamonds.

It was better when he was mowing the lawn on the Jackson Street side of the cemetery. He didn't have to think about angels and his mother as he tidied up the landscape around the older graves, some of them dating back to the late 1800s. Old families in Holmdell had designed little family parks within the cemetery, with the graves all clustered and marble benches where visitors could rest. People rarely left flowers on the old gravesites, although the town always planted a little American flag by each veteran's grave on Memorial Day, the Fourth of July and Veteran's Day. Bobby had had to clear away all the American flags twice this season, but he would be gone by the time Veteran's Day rolled around, on his way to becoming a veteran himself.

Autumn was late arriving in southern Ohio this year. The midafternoon air was hot and heavy, but he wasn't allowed to remove his shirt while he worked. A bare chest was disrespectful to the dead, his boss had scolded him when he'd yanked off his T-shirt and looped it around his belt one scorching afternoon a couple of months ago. He'd learned to bring an extra bandanna with him—one to use as a headband and the other to mop the sweat off his face.

Only two more hours and he could punch out for the day, he thought as the mower's engine made a stuttering noise and spewed some black smoke out the exhaust pipe. Only ten days and he'd be done with this job and on his way to Fort Dix in New Jersey.

He paused under an oak dense with summer-green leaves and pretended the shade was cooler than it actually was. Staring down the hill toward the more recent graves, he saw a few people ambling along the paths. Thursday afternoon wasn't a busy time at the cemetery. Funerals were usually held before noon so that afterward the mourners could eat heartily or drink heavily, depending on how they felt about the dearly departed. Bobby was sometimes assigned to fill in a grave after a funeral service, although that was supposed to be a union job, not a task for the kid who mowed the lawn and pruned the shrubs. But when his boss was shorthanded, or if it was raining and the interment had to be done before the hole filled with muddy water, he wound up shoveling.

He spotted a visitor heading up the hill toward him, walking in long, purposeful strides. Sun-streaked blond hair swung below her shoulders and her white peasant blouse and denim bell-bottoms hung wilted on her slender frame. He knew that walk, that hair. He knew those beautiful blue eyes.

He shut off the lawn mower. If Joelle had come to see him—and she didn't have any loved ones buried in the cemetery, so Bobby figured he was the reason she was here—he could take a break.

He leaned against the tree and pulled a crushed pack of Marlboros from the breast pocket of his faded blue work shirt. By the time he'd shaken out a cigarette she was within shouting distance. Her face was pale and her smile was one of those brave, quivery things women wore when they were about to burst into tears.

He slid a book of matches from where he'd wedged it inside the cellophane wrapper of the cigarette pack. "You okay?" he asked.

"Have you got a minute?"

"Five minutes at least," he said, gesturing toward a memorial bench near the tree. She sat on it and propped her purse in her lap. It was patchwork fabric sack with velvet drawstrings, and she'd told him some time ago that she'd designed and sewn it herself. Bobby was in awe of her talent.

He wondered if she'd traveled here straight from school. She was enrolled in classes at the community college, trying to make something of herself. She had so much going for her—brains, school, a rich boyfriend at Dartmouth and all that gorgeous blond hair—while Bobby cut grass and counted the days until he got shipped overseas. He would have thought that by now she'd have become friendly with her college classmates. She had no reason to hang out with him anymore.

Yet she did. No matter that she was on the path to bigger and better things; she clearly valued their friendship. Just one more reason he loved her.

He lit the cigarette while he waited for her to speak. "I need a favor," she finally said, gazing at the ornately carved headstone of Abigail Charney, who'd died in 1914 and was spending eternity in a grave a few feet from the bench.

"Sure."

She glanced at him, then turned back to stare at the gravestone. "Can you drive me to Cincinnati?"

He almost laughed—that was such a small thing to ask. He'd been expecting something a lot more demanding, given her obvious distress. "You can't borrow your mother's car?"

"No." She shook her head, just in case he hadn't understood her answer. "I could take the bus, but I—" Her voice broke.

Hell. Just as he'd predicted, she started to cry. He pulled the blue bandanna from the hip pocket of his jeans and handed it to her, glad that it wasn't too sweaty. "Screw the bus," he said. "I'll drive you down. When do you have to go?"

Tears rolled down her cheeks. She dabbed at them with his bandanna. "It has to be a weekday. I'm sorry. That probably messes up your work schedule."

"Big deal. I'll call in sick." For Joelle, he'd call in dead.

"It's just that…" She swallowed hard. "I have to see a doctor."

Despite the afternoon's heat, fear rippled like ice down his back. Holmdell had doctors. She must be seriously ill if she had to travel all the way to Cincinnati to meet with one. A specialist, maybe. At one of the big hospitals.

He eased closer to her on the bench and bent so he could peer into her downturned face. "What's wrong, Jo?"

She lifted her chin and gazed at him, her eyes puffy and her cheeks streaked with tears. "I'm pregnant."

She couldn't believe this had happened to her.

Of course, she *could* believe it. This sort of thing happened to girls all the time. And in her case, it was clear Drew hadn't known what he was doing with that damn condom. She remembered the humiliation of having him pry it out of her with his fingers, how nauseating the entire experience had been.

Little had she known then how much worse it would become.

Fresh tears spilled out of her eyes and she squeezed them shut. When the nurse at the college clinic had told her the results of her pregnancy test, she'd managed to hold back her tears until she was outside the building. Then she'd collapsed onto a bench and wept, and thought: *I have to talk to Bobby.* Not her mother, who would immediately view this ghastly mistake as a way to capture Drew. Not even Drew.

Bobby was her friend. They were honest with each other. They trusted each other. In a crisis, he was the one she wanted by her side.

Once she'd calmed down, though, she'd realized she had to tell Drew first. She'd phoned him at his dormitory and forced out the words: "I'm pregnant, Drew. I'm sorry. I'm pregnant."

"Okay. Don't panic, Joelle. I can't talk now," he'd said, though he hadn't explained exactly *why* he couldn't, what pressing matter he had to deal with that was more important than his girlfriend's pregnancy. "I'll get back to you soon, though. Don't worry, okay? We'll deal with this."

He'd gotten back to her, all right. The creep.

Now, belatedly, she'd approached Bobby. She prayed that he would live up to her trust and help her do what had to be done. She could get through this disaster alone if she had to—at least, she hoped she could. But if Bobby could help, if he could hold her hand through the ordeal and offer her a shoulder to lean on... Maybe it wouldn't be quite so bad.

Seated next to her on the bench, he leaned back and dragged on his cigarette. Gray smoke streamed between his lips as he sighed. "What kind of doctor are we talking about?"

"You know what kind," she said, her voice hoarse from her tears.

"Shit, Jo. You don't want to do that."

"Why not?"

"It's against the law."

"Don't lay that on me." She heard the anger in her voice and immediately felt contrite. Bobby didn't deserve her anger. He was only saying what she'd been thinking about nonstop ever since she'd received Drew's letter. "I have the name of a doctor who does this. He's supposed to be safe."

Bobby scrutinized her, squinting as if he thought that would bring her into clearer focus. *Please,* she begged silently, *please don't judge me. Please don't hate me for doing what I have to do.* "Who gave you the doctor's name?" he asked, and she understood his disapproval then. It was aimed at Drew, not her.

He'd obviously guessed, but she answered his question anyway. "I called Drew," she said. "I reached him at his dormitory and told him. He said he'd get back to me, and he did." Her breath hitched from all her crying and she fidgeted with the ties of her purse. "I got a letter from him today. He sent me the name of a doctor and some money. Enough to pay for everything. The doctor and transportation, too."

"I'm not going charge you carfare," Bobby muttered. He rubbed out his cigarette on the sole of his boot. "How much did he send?"

"A thousand dollars."

Bobby flinched. "A *thousand* dollars? What—is he buying you off?"

She had to admit that possibility had crossed her mind, too. "I have no idea what these kinds of doctors charge. Drew sent me a check. I can't cash it in town. Everyone would know. I guess there would be a bank branch in Cincinnati, or somewhere along the way…"

Bobby shook his head and cursed again. "Do you want to do this? Is this your choice, or are you just doing it to make Foster happy?"

"What else can I do?" Her voice began to wobble again. "I can't spend nine months pregnant and then give my baby away. I just couldn't do that. And I can't raise the baby myself. I know what that's like, Bobby. It's the story of my life."

She'd told Bobby years ago about the father who'd briefly, mysteriously drifted through her life. Dale Webber had been a cross-country trucker who used to detour off the highway to avoid weigh stations. He'd met Joelle's mother during one of those detours and they'd gotten involved, enough that every time he was passing through Ohio he'd stop in Holmdell to spend time with Wanda, the cute waitress at the Bank Street Diner. During one of those stops, he'd knocked her up.

Joelle had vague memories of Dale's visiting and bringing her a coloring book and a shabby little doll when she was a toddler. But after a while the visits ended, and when Joelle was about five, her mother had received a letter from a woman who claimed to be Dale's sister in California. The woman reported that Dale had been killed in a highway accident, and she'd enclosed some money from an insurance settlement and they'd never seen Dale again.

Joelle's mother had used the money to buy a car. A Rambler. "It seems appropriate," Wanda had said. "Your dad was a rambling man."

Whether her dad had married her mother, Joelle couldn't say for sure. But one day in fourth grade, Tommy Travers had called her a bastard child. She hadn't even known what that meant, but she'd denied it. She'd stood up to that sniveling bully and told him she wasn't a bastard child, because she understood innately that a bastard child was not a good thing to be.

"I don't want a life like my mother's," she told Bobby now. "And I don't want my child to grow up the way I did."

"So Foster mails you a check and tells you to deal with the problem? He can't even come back and get you through it?"

"He's in college," she pointed out. It was no excuse, but she'd rather defend Drew than admit that he'd given her money with the hope that she'd deal with her problem and disappear from his life.

Bobby pulled another cigarette from his pocket and a book of matches. She watched him bend a match inside its cardboard folder with his thumb and scrape its tip against the flint. It flared into flame and he lit the cigarette, inhaling deeply. "What about adoption?" he asked.

"I can't do that," she said. "Like I said, I can't spend nine months with this baby inside me and then give it away. I just couldn't do that."

He smoked in silence, staring at the sunlight-dappled gravestone in front of them, though his eyes seemed focused somewhere else. He said nothing until his cigarette was gone and he'd stubbed it out. Then he turned to her. "I'll marry you."

She gaped at him, too shocked to speak.

"I'll be your baby's father," he elaborated.

Was he nuts? He would take responsibility for her and a baby that wasn't even his? When she'd screwed up so royally, when she'd pretty much ruined her life with her own stupidity? When she'd told him all summer long that she dreamed of marrying Drew? Bobby was her best friend in the world, but what he was offering went way beyond what anyone should do for a friend. It was crazy.

She couldn't insult him by saying so. Instead she said, "You're about to leave for basic training."

"That's what'll make it work, Jo. It's not like we'd have to live with each other or anything. I'd be away, you'd be my wife, you'd have your baby and then when I got home, we could figure out where we stood."

"Bobby." He couldn't be that generous. Not to her. She didn't deserve such kindness, such a sacrifice on his part.

"If something happens to me in Vietnam," he continued,

sounding calm and logical, "there are widow's benefits. You could use those to support yourself and the kid."

No. She'd been an idiot. She'd gotten pregnant, like some careless, dim-witted slut. Bobby DiFranco was too good-hearted, too decent, to be stuck cleaning up her messes. "Bobby, I—"

"To tell you the truth, having a wife and baby waiting for me back home would help me. It would, you know—keep my spirits up."

That brought her up short. Maybe he wasn't offering to marry her strictly out of charity. He saw something in it for him, too. A wife waiting at home for him. A wife who would write to him, who would send him home-baked cookies and dry socks and reminders of all the good things he'd be returning to once he finished his service. She'd be at home, praying every day for his safety. That might be enough to get him through his year in 'Nam.

"I'd have something to come back to," he explained. "I need that, Jo."

"What about Margie?" she asked. "Aren't you going to come back to her?"

He snorted. "There's nothing there," he said. "We're just… You want to know the truth? We're both just waiting for me to leave so we can break up without going through the fights and the hurt feelings. She thinks she's doing her patriotic duty, going out with me until I leave for basic."

"I'm sure she loves you," Joelle argued, even though she had no basis for that assertion.

He shook his head. "We're already history. Just waiting for Uncle Sam to make it official." He gazed at Joelle's hands, folded tensely atop her purse and then at her face. "I could give your baby a name, Jo," he said quietly. "And then, if I got home and we decided this wasn't what we wanted, we could get a divorce. But your baby would have a name."

Without thinking, she moved her hands to her stomach and pressed. So flat, so smooth. A baby she couldn't even feel was in there, and Bobby was willing to give it his name. Fresh tears welled up in her eyes. "Wouldn't it bother you, knowing that the baby…"

"Was Foster's?" He turned back to stare at the gravestone again. "If we do this, the baby is mine. Your baby would be a DiFranco. Could you live with that?"

She opened her mouth, then shut it. Tears beaded along her lashes and blurred her vision. She didn't deserve this. She didn't deserve him. But as stupid as she'd been two months ago, in the backseat of Drew's father's Cadillac, she wasn't stupid enough to reject what Bobby was offering her.

Had she thought a radio was the best gift she'd ever received? No. *This* was. Bobby's help. His friendship. His hand and his name.

"I would consider it an honor if my baby was a Di-Franco," she said.

Five days later, she stood in her cramped bedroom at the back of the first-floor flat on Third Street one final time. She felt a little queasy, but that was from the pregnancy, not from panic or doubt about what she was doing.

She was running away with Bobby, her best friend, the most trustworthy guy she'd ever known. She was sad, she was grieving over the fact that her life wasn't turning out the way she'd planned—but she had no regrets. For as long as she lived, she would do whatever she could to make sure Bobby never had any regrets, either.

Yesterday morning, she'd mustered her courage and visited the local branch bank. She'd told the teller she was planning to move her account to a bank closer to campus, an explanation the teller had accepted without question. She'd let Joelle empty her account, then cashed Drew's check and counted fifty twenty-dollar bills into Joelle's palm. Joelle had stuffed the money into an envelope, which was now zipped inside an inner pocket of her suitcase.

She'd packed most of her clothing, even though she understood that within a month or two it would no longer fit her. After the baby was born, she hoped she'd get her figure back quickly. If not, maybe she could sell the clothes. The money would come in handy.

She left her prom dress behind, even though she loved it. She left her radio behind because it reminded her of Drew.

One stupid time. She'd given herself to him one stupid, stupid time, and he'd told her it would seal their love. Had he always been such a liar? Had she been dumb enough to love him?

That's the past, she reminded herself. If she looked backward, she'd trip and fall. She had to look forward, to the future, to her baby. Her baby and Bobby DiFranco.

Since she didn't have any classes at the college that day, her mother had taken the car to work. Wanda's absence simplified Joelle's departure. If Wanda hadn't had a shift at the diner, Joelle and Bobby would have had to wait until nighttime to leave, and Joelle would have had to climb out her window—not that difficult, but walking out the front door was a heck of a lot easier.

Still, she lifted her suitcase over the sill and behind the yews that grew beneath her window and then hoisted out the carton of stuff she was sure she couldn't live without—her hairbrush and rollers, her makeup, the polished marble egg Bobby had given her for Christmas, her sewing-pattern books, the teddy bear she'd had as a baby, her flashlight, her jewelry box, which had a built-in music box that played "Edelweiss" when the lid was raised and her college textbooks, which had cost a fortune and might prove handy if she could find a school to attend near wherever she and Bobby wound up.

Passing her belongings through the window was prudent. She didn't want Mrs. Proski to put down her sherry long enough to peer out her living-room window and catch Joelle marching through the front door with a suitcase and a carton.

Bobby arrived at around ten in the morning. While he carried her things down the alley to his truck, she circled her bedroom one last time. It wasn't as if she'd never come back. Of course she would. Her mother would want to see her and the baby. But when she returned to Holmdell, it would be as Joelle DiFranco. Maybe married, maybe divorced—Bobby had seemed pleased by that escape hatch, and if he wanted to leave her, she'd never do anything to stop him—but one way or another, she'd be home again. This wasn't goodbye forever.

She reread the note she'd written to her mother:

Dear Mom,

I'm aware that isn't what you hoped for me, but Bobby DiFranco and I have gone to get married. We wanted to do this before he left for Vietnam. I tried to love Drew, but Bobby is the finest man I have ever known. Please be happy for us. I'll call you once we're settled in. Love, Joelle

It was funny to think of Bobby as a man. Almost as funny as thinking of him as her husband. Thinking of herself as a wife—a pregnant one—was so funny she started sobbing.

She wiped her eyes, blew her nose and left her bedroom. After propping the note against the salt and pepper shakers on the kitchen table where her mother wouldn't miss it, she left the apartment, locking the door behind her.

Neither she nor Bobby spoke until they'd crossed the town line. The morning was cloudless, the sky an intense DayGlo blue. Ahead of them lay acres of pale brown fields, occasionally interrupted by clusters of dried yellow cornstalks left over from the September harvest. Bobby switched on the radio, got static and turned it off.

"You know how to drive a stick, right?" he asked.

"I'll figure it out." *You can teach me,* she thought, although she doubted he'd have enough time to show her how to drive his truck before he reported for basic training.

"I was going to leave the truck behind for Eddie," he said, "but he's got another year before he can get his license. You'll use it for the year, and then when I get back, we'll see."

We'll see. They would see if they still wanted to be married—if they could even stand to be together in the same room. They'd see if Bobby truly wanted to be a father to someone else's baby. In another year, God alone knew who they'd be, what they'd want, how they'd feel. The fate of Bobby's truck was the least of it.

They stopped for lunch at a McDonald's east of Columbus. Joelle's hamburger tasted funny, but pretty much everything had tasted funny ever since the nurse at the college clinic had told her her urine test had been positive. Bobby apparently had no trouble wolfing down two burgers and a sack of fries. He paid for lunch, as if the two of them were on a date.

All summer long, she'd had no trouble talking to Bobby while they'd nibbled on fries at the A&W. But now she didn't know what to say, what they were to each other. Seated across from him on a bench at a redwood table with a big plastic umbrella over their heads, she struggled to force down at least half her burger while she stared at him. His thick, dark hair would soon be gone—the very thought of some army barber shearing him like a sheep was enough to make her want to weep. They'd train him to kill and dress him in khaki and then ship him halfway around the world. *We'll see,* she thought, realizing for the first time that the next twelve months might change him a lot more than they changed her.

What if he was shipped home maimed? What if he came back deranged? The news was full of stories about soldiers coming back to the states crazed or strung out on drugs. What if the Bobby DiFranco who returned to her after a year in Vietnam was someone she couldn't love?

She would love him anyway. That was her vow to him. She hadn't spoken the promise, but she'd stitched it into her heart. Bobby had offered her this chance to be a mother, to keep her baby and give it a home. Whatever he wanted—if she could do it for him, she would.

A group of teenagers drove into the parking lot in a rumbling Camaro. The windows were open and music blasted out of them, Led Zeppelin whining, "Way, way down inside…"

The song made her scowl. The singer whined about giving some woman a whole lotta love, but the loud, thumping music wasn't what love was about—at least, not in her mind.

She peered at Bobby and told herself love was about *him*, his dark, brooding eyes and his hard jaw and his broad shoulders. She told herself that giving his name to another man's baby was a whole lotta love.

He ate without speaking. She wondered if he was having second thoughts, regretting the whole thing, resenting her. He could have stayed home a few more days, spent a few more nights with Margie...

Unless he'd agreed to marry Joelle to get away from Margie. And his dad.

"Did you tell your father what we're doing?" she asked.

The sound of her voice seemed to startle him. He wiped his mouth with a napkin and lifted his cola. He took a long drink, then shook his head. "I told him I got a call from the draft board asking me to show up earlier for basic."

"I left a note for my mother. She'll be phoning your father soon enough."

Bobby emptied the final fry from the paper wrapper and popped it into his mouth. "My father'll be relieved that he didn't have to dress up in a monkey suit and spend a morning in church watching me get hitched. Your mother'll yell at him until he hangs up on her."

"My mother's going to blow a fuse." She would, too. She'd be devastated that Joelle wasn't marrying Drew. If only Joelle had played things more shrewdly, she could have had a big wedding in the Episcopal church—no matter that Joelle and her mother were Catholic—and a reception at Green Gates Country Club, and then Wanda's little girl would be set for life, free of Tubtown and poverty forever.

"What's up?" Bobby asked as he gathered their trash. "You look worried."

"Do you think we're doing the right thing? Or are we just two dumb-ass kids?"

He swung his long legs over the bench to head to the waste bin with their trash, and his eyes darkened. "Who the hell knows?"

They drove straight through Pennsylvania, pausing only to buy gas, use the bathroom and eat a quick supper at a rest stop along I-80. By ten at night they'd reached the outskirts of Trenton. Bobby pulled in to the parking lot of a motel with a vacancy sign glaring in pink neon in the office window. He parked and shut off the engine.

They'd hardly spoken all day and now they were faced with spending the night together. Bobby cleared his throat. "It's not like we're legal or anything yet," he said, addressing the windshield more than her. "I mean, Joelle, I—"

"Call me JoJo," she said. She longed to have her friend back, not this quiet, brooding boy.

He glanced at her. "This marriage…once we do it, it's for real."

She nodded. "That's how I see things, too."

"You'll be my wife. It's not going to be like it used to be with us."

She suffered a pang in her soul. She had treasured Bobby's friendship for so many years. She had no desire for their relationship to change. But it would. Once she was his wife, maybe they wouldn't be friends anymore.

"I think—" he gazed past her "—I think we should wait until we're married, if you know what I mean."

Oh. She noticed the flush reddening his face—they were too far away from the vacancy sign for her to think its glow had caused him to blush. Once they were married, they'd share a bed. They would sleep together. Have sex together.

Sex with Bobby. God, she'd always loved him; he was her best friend—but sex?

Grow up, Joelle, she scolded herself. If he wanted sex, of course they would have sex. That was what marriage was all about, right? Sharing a bed.

"I think we should wait, too," she agreed, hoping he didn't hear apprehension in her voice, hoping that once they shared a bed he wouldn't hate her, or hate himself for having married her.

They had plenty to talk about during the next couple of days, but mostly it involved logistics: blood tests performed at a clinic in Trenton, papers filed at city hall, a futile search for an apartment for Joelle. Bobby mentioned that there might be base housing at Fort Dix, but she couldn't imagine anything more depressing than living on an army base, especially once Bobby had shipped out. "Don't worry, I'll find something," she said, sounding more positive than she felt.

They bought rings, the cheapest they could find. The store wouldn't engrave them—their skimpy width offered no surface to engrave on—but they were genuine fourteen-karat gold and they came in pretty plastic boxes lined with velvet. Finally, the day before Bobby had to report to Fort Dix, all the paperwork was done, the blood test results were normal and she and Bobby returned to city hall to get married. She would have liked to buy a new dress for the occasion, but she couldn't fritter away her money on a dress that wouldn't fit her by December. So she wore a ribbed white turtleneck and a short gray skirt.

Bobby wore his cleanest jeans, a button-front shirt, an ugly striped tie and a brown corduroy blazer. "I stole the jacket from my father's closet," he confessed. "He never wears it, anyway."

Over Joelle's protests, he'd insisted on buying her flowers. Nothing big, nothing like what a real bride would carry, but a small bouquet of daisies and carnations. She broke the stem of one of the carnations and tucked the flower through the buttonhole in his stolen jacket's lapel. Then they entered city hall. When they emerged an hour later, it was as Mr. and Mrs. Robert DiFranco.

They ate dinner at an Italian restaurant a few blocks from city hall, a small place with red-and-white checkerboard table-cloths and mandolin music piped through ceiling speakers. Bobby assured her they could afford a restaurant meal, and she wouldn't deny him a hearty dinner when, starting tomorrow, he'd be stuck eating army food for the next year.

He seemed cheerful. Joelle wasn't cheerful at all. When she gazed across the table at Bobby, with his long, shaggy hair and his drooping boutonniere, she felt…dread. She was *married* now. To *Bobby*. Oh, God, what had she done? Was this an even bigger mistake than giving in to Drew in the backseat of his father's Cadillac two months ago?

"Eat," Bobby ordered her. "You're supposed to be eating for two."

She occupied herself coiling long, marinara-soaked strands of spaghetti around her fork. "I wish you didn't have to leave tomorrow," she said.

"Don't worry." He smiled gently, then tore a hunk of Italian bread from the straw basket and smeared butter onto it. "I'll be back soon enough."

"I don't know, Bobby, I just—"

"JoJo." He set down his bread and reached across the table, covering her right hand with his left. She stared at the gold band circling his finger. The ring looked so delicate in contrast to his labor-roughened hand. "Yeah, this whole thing is crazy. But we can make it work. I'll go, I'll come back, I'll get a job. We'll be a family."

Moisture gathered along her lashes—pregnancy made her much too weepy—but she batted her eyes to keep the tears from falling. They were tears of gratitude, not joy. Wasn't a woman supposed to feel joy on her wedding day? What was wrong with her? Why did she feel as if she'd lost something terribly precious today?

During the rest of their dinner, he reviewed everything she had to do once he was gone: find a place to live, find a doctor to monitor her pregnancy, find a job. "I think there are some colleges in the area, if you'd like to take some classes," he said.

"I can't afford college."

"Well, it was just a thought. Remember—the gas gauge in the truck isn't always accurate. The minute that needle points to three-quarters empty, fill the tank. Otherwise you might wind up getting stranded somewhere."

"Okay."

"And the clutch pedal is tight. You have to press real hard on it."

"Okay."

He continued talking about the damn clutch pedal the whole drive back to their motel. Honestly. He would be leaving tomorrow, shipping off to Vietnam in a matter of weeks, and they'd just gotten married, and all he could do was babble about his stupid clutch pedal. She wanted to scream at him to shut up.

He parked the truck in front of their door near the rear of the motel and she swung out, inexplicably furious. She fumed while he unlocked the door and shoved it open—and then he surprised her by hoisting her into his arms.

She let out a gasp.

"Isn't this how it goes?" he asked, one arm securely under her knees and the other under her back, leaving her no choice but to wrap her arms around his neck. "I carry you over the threshold, right?"

"I guess." That was when she realized she wasn't furious at all. She was petrified.

The truth settled deep into her bones. This was their wedding night. Bobby DiFranco, her buddy, her confidant, her dearest friend, was carrying her over the threshold and into her new life as his wife. Their room had two beds in it, but tonight they would be using only one of them.

She steadied her breath. She could handle this. It would just be one night, and then he'd leave. She could figure out how she felt after he was gone.

Besides, sex with Bobby couldn't possibly be as awful as sex with Drew Foster had been. And it was too late for her to worry about getting pregnant. And this was the deal they'd made: once they were married, the marriage would be real.

He kicked the door shut behind them, carried her across the small, stale-smelling room and lowered her to her feet next to one of the beds. His smile melted away as he gazed down at her. "You okay?" he asked, evidently struggling to read her expression.

She nodded and bit her lip. *You can do this,* she lectured herself.

"A little nervous, huh," he guessed.

"A little."

"Me, too." He smiled then, and brushed her lips with his. "Relax, Jo. I'm not going to hurt you. I would never hurt you. You know that, don't you?"

Yes, she knew that. Hearing him say the words convinced her, not in her brain but somewhere else, some part of her where knowing was a visceral thing. When Bobby kissed her again, a little less gently, she closed her eyes, parted her lips and let him in.

She had never been kissed like this before. She hadn't kissed all that many boys, but none of them had kissed like Bobby. His mouth was so strong, so sure. His tongue was so aggressive. She felt his kiss through her entire body, which felt as if it was unfolding inside, opening like a flower's petals to the sun, warming and softening and wanting.

He undressed her first, and then himself. His body was different from Drew's—bigger, more massive...*older*, somehow. He had hair on his chest; not much, but it made him seem like a man. So did the thickness of his shoulders, the swells of muscle in his arms and legs, the contours of his torso.

When he urged her onto the bed and then lay down beside her, he didn't go straight for her crotch. Instead, he kissed her neck, her shoulders, her breasts. He ran his hands all over her, every now and then murmuring her name. He caressed her feet, her knees, her belly, and when he finally touched her between her thighs, she was embarrassed by how wet she was there.

He didn't seem embarrassed at all. He only murmured her name again and then climbed onto her and pressed her hand to his erection. She stroked him the way she used to stroke

Drew, until he covered her hand with his and slowed her down, showing her how he liked it.

She desperately wanted to please him. Whatever he wished, she would do it. This was Bobby, and he hadn't made fun of her for being so wet or for stroking him the wrong way. This was Bobby, who'd done her the immeasurable favor of marrying her.

This was Bobby, her husband.

When at last he entered her, it didn't hurt at all. It felt... good. Better than good. He moved in a steady, seductive rhythm, and his stomach rubbed hers and he sighed her name again and again. She thought she would die from the sweet sensations surging inside her. "Oh, Bobby..."

"Yeah," he whispered.

Lush pulses swept through her, endless spasms wrenching her and then soothing her. She closed her eyes and sank into the soft mattress, astonished by what she'd just experienced. Above her Bobby thrust hard, then groaned and trembled and lowered himself into her arms. Given his size, he should have crushed her. Yet his weight and warmth felt as good as everything else he'd done.

Was *that* what sex was supposed to be like? So intimate, so tender, such an excruciatingly lovely mix of glorious sensations still throbbing deep inside her, wringing her body and massaging her soul, filling her with the urge to laugh and cry at the same time?

If being Bobby DiFranco's wife meant experiencing sex like this, she yearned to spend the rest of her life in his bed.

She opened her eyes and gazed up at him. His hair fell forward to brush her cheeks and his eyes were dark and beautiful as they searched her face.

Her husband. Dear, God, he was her husband.

"I don't want you to go," she said.

He kissed her. "I'll come back," he vowed.

Chapter 5

"Hey, Dad?"

Bobby slammed his desk drawer shut and glanced up. He'd been staring at an old photo of Joelle that he kept stashed in the top drawer, the picture he'd asked her to pose for before the senior prom. In it she was radiant, her hair rippling around her face, her eyes bluer than the blue dress she wore. He'd carried that photo with him through Vietnam and pretended, whenever he'd looked at it, that she'd been his girl the night she'd worn that blue prom gown. He'd pretended that she'd loved him. In time, she'd sent him other photos—of herself pregnant, of herself *very* pregnant, of herself holding Claudia, a little pink peanut of a girl. But the photo of Joelle before the prom had been his treasure.

The color had faded from it over the years. Three of the corners were bent, the fourth torn. It didn't matter. Some important part of him was in that picture, a slab of his life, his memory, his dreams.

But he didn't want Mike to catch him mooning over it and wondering whether Joelle was any more his girl today than she'd been the night that photo had been taken, thirty-seven years ago. He shaped a smile for his elder son. "How's it going?"

"Good. We're ahead of schedule on the Griffin job."

"Great." He continued to gaze at his son, continued to fake a smile. At twenty-six, Mike resembled Bobby, with thick dark hair a bit curlier than his father's and dark, deep-set eyes. Those eyes were studying Bobby. "It's four-thirty, Dad. What do you say we quit early and celebrate the job you nailed this weekend."

Bobby had spent most of the day making arrangements for that job: a conference call with a swimming pool company he worked with, an order placed with a granite quarry, more calls to area nurseries, a review of his staff assignments to determine who'd be available when, plenty of paperwork and number crunching. As much as he enjoyed outdoor work, he also enjoyed the mental demands. Until he'd taken business classes, he'd never known he had a gift for negotiating and strategizing.

He'd gotten a lot done that day—an amazing amount, considering what a train wreck his personal life was. Bobby had learned how to focus, how to ignore distractions. In 'Nam, distractions could kill a soldier, so he'd developed the ability to tune them out.

Mike wasn't a distraction, though. He was Bobby's son, and if he wanted to celebrate, Bobby would put on a happy face and do his best.

He locked his desk and followed Mike out of the office, which occupied a corner of the small warehouse building that housed trucks and equipment and supplies. Most of what he needed—construction materials and plants—was shipped directly from suppliers to work sites, cutting down on DiFranco Landscaping's storage requirements. But the trucks and tractors had to be parked somewhere at night.

Exiting to the gravel parking lot outside the building, Bobby blinked in the glaring late-afternoon sun. "The Hay Street Pub shouldn't be too crowded," Mike suggested. "Why don't you meet me there."

"Sure." The Hay Street Pub was a relatively subdued place where the TVs were adjusted to a low volume and young singles didn't crowd the place, prowling for pickups. Bobby would steer the conversation toward Mike and survive the next hour without revealing the mess his life was in. He'd gotten through worse; he could get through a drink with his son.

As Mike had predicted, the pub was calm and not too busy and they were able to snag a quiet booth along the back wall. A lamp with a stained-glass shade hung above the table, casting half of Mike's face in red and half in amber.

"I'll have an iced tea," Bobby told the waitress who materialized before them.

"Oh, come on, Dad. Live a little. Have a beer."

Bobby reluctantly ordered a Bud. He enjoyed beer, liked the foam and the sour flavor. But growing up the son of a drunk made him cautious around liquor, so he rarely drank it.

Mike requested a microbrewery lager Bobby had never heard of, and the waitress departed to get their drinks. Bobby gazed at his son through the wash of colored light from the stained-glass lamp. Mike wore a dark green polo shirt with

DiFranco Landscaping stitched in white above the breast pocket. All the employees wore those shirts except for Bobby. Collared polo shirts weren't his style. They looked like something a man would wear on a racquetball court or a sailboat, or at the Green Gates Country Club.

"So, would you like to hear about this English-garden job?" he asked.

Mike's smile faded. He tapped his fingers together, then let his hands rest on the table. "As a matter of fact, no. Dad…" He took a deep breath. "Gary called me yesterday."

The waitress chose that moment to reappear with their drinks, denying Bobby the opportunity to bolt for the door. Not that he could run away from his son. The truth lay squirming on the table between them. It had to be dealt with.

He waited until the waitress was done arranging cocktail napkins, beers, frosted-glass mugs and a bowl of pretzels on the table. He watched her walk away, not because she was worth looking at but because he needed a minute to collect his thoughts. He and Mike shouldn't be having this conversation alone. Joelle ought to be a part of it. Revealing the truth to Claudia had been not his idea but hers—hers and Foster's. Let her do the heavy lifting.

She wasn't here, though. Bobby would have to struggle through it himself.

"Did you talk to Claudia?" he asked.

Mike shook his head. "Gary said she was too upset."

"How about Danny? Did you talk to him? Did Gary mention whether he—"

"Danny's been up at Tanglewood all weekend. Lauren got them tickets to some symphony thing."

"And he went?" Danny's current girlfriend had grown up

in Manhattan, surrounded by museums, theater and Lincoln Center. "He really must love her."

"Either that or she's good in bed," Mike muttered cynically. He was between girlfriends right now. Maybe he wished that, like his younger brother, he had a woman in his life willing to drag him off to symphony concerts. "I saw him for ten minutes this morning, before he headed down to Trumbull for that strip-mall job. We didn't really talk." Ignoring the mug the waitress had brought him, he hoisted his bottle to his mouth and drank. Then he set the bottle down and leaned forward. "What the hell is going on, Dad? Is this for real? Some other guy is Claudia's father?"

"Yes." Bobby took a sip of beer, hoping it would keep him from choking.

"I can't believe it." Mike shook his head. "How could you—" Apparently the question stymied him, because he left it dangling.

"How could I what?"

"Raise Claudia like she's your daughter."

"She *is* my daughter. I love her every bit as much as I love you and Danny. You're my children. All of you."

"Right. She's my *sister*. I can't believe you let her live her whole life in ignorance about this."

Bobby sighed.

"And me and Danny. We're her brothers. I mean—my God, what she must be going through right now…"

"It's not easy, Mike." As hard as it was for Claudia, it was every bit as hard for Bobby. He didn't want to come across as self-pitying, though, so he silenced himself with a sip of beer.

"So…what's the deal? Mom had an affair?"

"She was pregnant when I married her," Bobby said. He could

have argued that what had happened all those years ago wasn't any of Mike's business. But telling Claudia about her parentage had been like poking a hole in a dam. Once the truth started leaking through, it flooded everything and everyone in its path.

Besides, if Gary had called Mike, it had to be because Claudia wanted to share the news with her brothers. "Your mother didn't have an affair."

"You knew she was pregnant with some other dude's baby?" Mike looked appalled.

"That's why I married her, Mike. I loved her, and she was in trouble."

"Jesus." Mike shook his head again and drank his beer. So did Bobby. "I guess back in the days of hippies and free love, the details didn't matter."

Mike's sarcasm rankled. "It wasn't like that," Bobby retorted. "We were young. She got in trouble. Stuff happens."

"But you married her. Even though her baby wasn't yours. What were you—a candidate for sainthood or just a chump?"

Anger bubbled up inside Bobby, spraying in so many directions he wasn't sure where it came from or what it was aimed at. "Mike. This is your mother you're talking about."

"And my sister, who I love. And who, it turns out, is actually the sister of some other guy we never even heard of." He plucked a pretzel from the bowl, flipped it over in his hand a few times, then tossed it onto his napkin. "Do you know Claudia's father?"

More anger, spinning faster. "*I'm* Claudia's father."

"I mean, her *real* father."

Too enraged to speak, Bobby chugged some more beer. It slid down his throat, cold and bitter. "I think we're done, Mike."

"No, we're *not* done. This is my family, too. You and Mom kept this secret from us for all these years. It's *our* family—Claudia's and Danny's and mine. How could you not tell us? How could you let us all live a lie for so long?"

Bobby drained his bottle in two long swallows. He'd known the aftershocks from telling Claudia the truth were going to be bad. He just hadn't realized how much hurt there was to go around, or how wide it would spread. He hadn't realized how much trust would be lost between him and his children, between him and Joelle. Between him and the whole freaking world.

"Here's all you have to know," he said, his voice muted. "You and Danny are my sons. Claudia is my daughter. The past is the past."

"Great," Mike muttered. "If that's the past, I'm afraid to think what the future is."

Joelle had cooked lasagna for Bobby. As if she could make things right by fixing one of his favorite dishes for him.

Sunday had been wretched for them both. She'd arisen early after a restless night and told him she was going to church, something neither of them had done in aeons. She'd asked him to join her. He'd said no. She'd really hoped he would go with her, but she wouldn't beg him. Partly pride, partly fear of making him feel even worse than he already did—she left the house without him.

Morning mass at Our Lady of Lourdes hadn't helped. The local priest was a bland suburban type, so careful to avoid offense or controversy he wound up coming across as plastic and remote. She couldn't imagine asking him for his counsel. Still, she'd prayed—not for herself but for Bobby, for her children and for a young man named Adam Foster, whom she'd never met but who was critically ill. Her prayers seemed to bounce off the vaulted ceiling rather than passing through the rafters and up to God.

When she'd returned home, the house was empty. Bobby had stuck a Post-it note to the mudroom door, saying he'd gone fishing. He didn't even own a rod and tackle, but she accepted his statement as an indication that he needed some time alone.

She'd spent the day doing the housecleaning that had never gotten done yesterday. She'd scrubbed the bathroom floors until her knuckles were chapped. She'd pulled out the refrigerator and vacuumed behind it. By the time Bobby came home—carrying a pizza rather than a fresh-caught trout—the house was cleaner than it had ever been.

When she'd asked him what she could do to make him feel better, he'd said nothing.

She'd decided to make lasagna today after the flowers had arrived. A spiffy young man in a green uniform had delivered them shortly after Bobby had left for work, and they'd sat on the kitchen table all day, a magnificent array of roses, orchids and lilies, ferns and baby's breath in a curving glass vase. Bewildered, Joelle had opened the card that accompanied them:

Joelle and Bobby,
   I can't tell you how grateful I am that you let me into your home on Saturday. I'm aware my visit might have been difficult for you. I hope and pray you can forgive the mistakes of the past and find the compassion in your hearts to help my son. Sincerely, Drew

She must have reread the card a dozen times throughout the day. The flowers were an apology, a peace offering—maybe a bribe. But the callous, selfish Drew Foster she'd remembered, the boy who had mailed her a check and the name of a doctor in Cincinnati, had been replaced in her mind by the sad, desperate man who'd appeared at her front door Saturday morning. He was a father and his son was dying. He'd sent these flowers with the best of intentions.

She hoped Bobby would view them that way, too. But just in case he wouldn't, she'd decided to prepare one of his favorite meals.

She'd bought fresh vegetables for a salad at a local farm stand and a loaf of Italian bread at a bakery in town. All afternoon, as she'd browned the meat and mushrooms and whipped eggs into the ricotta and crushed cloves of garlic for the bread, she'd thought of Bobby, of pampering him, assuring him that she loved him and so did Claudia. He was hurting and she yearned to ease his heartache.

She also hoped a day of productive work at DiFranco Landscaping would cheer him up, or at least remind him that their life today was a universe away from their lives back in 1970, when she'd found herself pregnant and Bobby was heading off to war. They'd believed in each other back then, she recalled. They'd believed no mistake was so bad that doing the right thing wouldn't help. Was fixing this feast the right thing to do? Had cleaning the house yesterday been the right thing? Had telling Claudia the truth been the right thing?

Telling Claudia had definitely been right. So why did the truth leave so damn much pain in its wake?

She heard the rumble of the automatic garage door opening and raced to the first floor bathroom to check her reflection in the mirror. A flushed, sweaty face gazed back at her. It wasn't as if she hoped to entice Bobby with her beauty, which had lost its youthful gloss long ago, but she fussed with her hair anyway and splashed some cold water on her cheeks.

She was surprised to hear Mike's voice rather than Bobby's echoing in the mudroom. Why had Bobby brought Mike home with him? She had more than enough food to feed an extra mouth, but after her visit with Claudia on Saturday night, she wasn't sure she was ready to deal with her sons.

She was even less ready to deal with what Mike brought her. "He's drunk," he said, steering Bobby ahead of him into the kitchen and handing her Bobby's keys.

"I'm not drunk," Bobby growled. His eyes looked bleary, his posture unnaturally rigid.

Joelle had never seen him drunk. He didn't *do* drunk. She fell back a step. "How much did he drink?"

"Not enough," Bobby snapped, then shoved past her and headed for the stairs.

She leveled an accusing gaze at Mike. "A beer," he said.

"One beer?"

"And three whiskies. I drove him home because I didn't think he should drive himself. He's really pissed."

Joelle didn't need Mike to point out the obvious. Her husband was pissed, he was drunk—and as the son of an alcoholic, Bobby would rather smash his head through a pane of glass than drink to excess. If he'd gotten himself blitzed, things were worse than she'd imagined.

"Where's your car?" she asked.

"I left it at the Hay Street Pub. I can take Dad's truck home and pick him up for work tomorrow. Somewhere along the way I'll get my car."

Mike's voice was cold and clipped, his gaze filled with contempt. She realized he must have heard about Drew Foster. Perhaps Bobby had told him between his second and third whiskey. Or perhaps Claudia had brought Mike up to speed.

It didn't matter. He knew the truth and it filled him with hatred. He was her son; she could read him easily.

"I'll drive you over to the pub so you can get your car," she said, not yet ready to confront Bobby.

"That's not necessary."

"Your dad will be using his truck tomorrow. I'll drive you." She turned off the oven so the lasagna wouldn't burn, then grabbed her purse and keys from the storage table near the mudroom and preceded him out to the garage.

The pub was less than ten minutes away in the center of Gray Hill. Ten minutes of silence would be unbearable. Mike clearly didn't wish to speak to her, but that didn't mean she couldn't speak to him.

"How could you let him drink like that?" she asked. "He never drinks. Why didn't you stop him?"

"He's a big boy. He wanted those drinks, so he had them."

A potent blend of sorrow and fury churned inside her. "Your father never wants drinks."

"Yeah, I used to think that, too." Mike's voice reeked of hostility. "Funny how the truth is sometimes completely different from what we used to think."

"I gather you and your father discussed Claudia," she said in as level a tone as she could manage.

"Yes, we discussed that particular subject."

"Life is not always black and white, Mike. There are things you don't know about your father and me."

"Here's what I do know. Our family is a lie. Everything I assumed, everything I thought we were… All a lie."

She wondered whether he really believed that or was just trying to bait her. Either way, his words sliced deep. "I wish you didn't feel like that, Mike. Your father and I love you and we love Claudia. We did the best we could under some difficult circumstances."

"Keep telling yourself that, Mom," he grunted. "Maybe it'll make you feel better. It doesn't do much for me."

She'd barely braked to a halt in the parking lot before he had the door open. Not bothering to say goodbye, he swung out of her car and slammed the door behind him.

She remained in the parking lot, watching him cross the asphalt to his own car, climb in and peel away. A shudder wrenched her as she considered her beloved elder son. She'd been so worried about how Claudia would respond to the truth, she hadn't even considered how the boys would react. Claudia was their sister. This was their family. Their parents had lied for thirty-seven years, and their father had for the first time in his life gotten drunk and everything she valued in the world was dissolving into dust.

With a shaky sigh, she ignited her engine and drove out of the lot. Who was the moron who'd said "The truth will set you free"? The truth had set her daughter and at least one son free to hate her. It had set her husband free to stonewall her, hiding behind his sullen silence and three glasses of whiskey. Saturday night in their bed, the truth had brutalized them both, even as they'd made love.

Right now, she considered the truth a pretty nasty business.

She drove home, her head aching and her ribs weighing heavily on her lungs, making each breath an exertion. Entering the kitchen, she found the flowers scattered across the floor and broken pieces of the vase lying in puddles of water. Drew's note lay crumpled in a ball beside the trash can.

Her instinct was to curl up on the floor, close her eyes and howl. But she'd been through too much in her life to give in to such impulses. When there was a mess, you cleaned it up. Closing your eyes didn't solve anything.

With a ragged sigh, she gathered the crushed blossoms and tossed them into the trash. She picked up the shards of glass carefully to avoid cutting herself and then mopped up the water. By the time she was done, she became aware of the sound drifting down from upstairs, a muffled moan.

She raced up the stairs, hurried through the master bedroom and found Bobby in the bathroom, hunched over the toilet. His shirt lay in a heap in one corner, and the broad, muscular expanse of his back glistened beneath a sheen of perspiration. He held a damp washcloth in one hand, and he took deep, rasping breaths.

All right. He'd drunk himself sick. He'd shattered the vase and destroyed the flowers. He was crocked and he was violent and he was puking. If he were sober right now, he'd be horrified. He'd see how close he'd come to acting like his father.

She was horrified, too—frightened more for him than for herself. She eased the washcloth from his fist, rinsed it out in the sink and ran it gently over his face, which had a grayish cast. "You shouldn't drink like that," she said quietly. "Your body isn't used to it."

"I shouldn't drink at all." He shut his eyes and leaned away from the toilet so she could reach the rest of his face. Then he flushed the toilet, rose shakily to his feet and moved to the sink. Joelle sat on the ledge of the bathtub, watching while he brushed his teeth and scrubbed his face. He avoided her gaze as he grabbed for a towel. Only when he was dry did he look at her. "That son of a bitch sent you flowers."

"He sent them to both of us."

"Yeah. Flowers are the quickest way to *my* heart."

"Bobby. He meant them as a peace offering."

"A peace offering." Bobby hung the towel back on the rod and bent over to pick up his shirt. The movement must have hurt his head, because he paused before straightening up. A few long seconds passed before he turned to her. "They were very nice flowers. Expensive. Top of the line."

"Bobby—"

"Remember the first time I gave you flowers? A two-dollar bouquet on our wedding day."

"That bouquet was beautiful," she said.

"It was cheap. It was all I could afford." He limped toward the door, then halted, gripping the doorjamb as if afraid he might stumble. "You could have done better for yourself, Joelle. You could have held out for a guy who could buy you fancy flowers."

"I didn't want fancy flowers, Bobby. I wanted you."

"Right." Disbelief underlined that terse syllable. "Flowers were a better bet." Bobby swayed in the doorway, then pushed himself out of the bathroom. She listened to his footsteps, heard the creak of the bedsprings and knew he had lain down. She considered joining him in bed, just holding him, stroking his head and reassuring him—but what reassurance could she offer? Could he even bear to have her in bed with him?

He was *drunk,* damn it.

After all these years, after all she and Bobby had endured, all they'd shared, he had done something he'd vowed never to do: he'd acted like his father. He'd gotten drunk and broken things.

Her soul felt as splintered as the glass vase she'd found in pieces on her kitchen floor, as dead as the flowers Bobby had crushed.

Chapter 6

May 1971

The air was like a stew, hot and wet and heavy with the smell of seething plant life. For once Bobby didn't notice the oppressive atmosphere. He was too busy staring at the photo in his hand.

Joelle. Joelle holding a football-sized parcel of pink in her arms. *I named her Claudia,* she'd written. *I hope you don't mind.*

He settled back on his cot and gazed at the photo. His sheets were wrinkled, his blanket lumpy. He recalled how obsessed with tight sheets the commanding officers had been during basic training, but no one gave a damn about tight sheets in-country.

He'd written to Joelle that life in Vietnam was boring. That was half-true. When life in 'Nam wasn't boring, it was terrifying, but he saw no reason to alarm her. He wasn't much for letter writing, and when he wrote, he kept it simple. "I made twenty bucks playing poker last night," he'd tell her, or, "The food sucks," or, "This country doesn't need soldiers. It needs air conditioners."

Yesterday had been one of the terrifying days. His platoon's assignment was to keep a road passable, a task that reminded him of cutting grass. You cut grass, and it grew back again. Then you cut it, and then it grew back. His platoon's job was almost the same, except instead of cutting grass, they had to scout for snipers. They'd kill or capture a few, then go back to base. Then a few days later, someone would get shot at and they'd have to go out and beat the bushes for snipers again. No matter how many snipers you got rid of, more always arrived to replace them. Like well-watered grass, they kept growing back.

Unfortunately, while Bobby and his buddies were visible on their patrols, the snipers stayed hidden, so they got off better shots than the Americans did.

But the platoon had done their sweep yesterday, and today was one of the boring days, a day to relax under the sagging canvas roof of the tent that Bobby had called home for the past six months. A fine, hot drizzle fell from the stone-gray sky. The tent's walls were rolled up to allow in any breeze that stirred the air, and those too-rare breezes brought the dampness in with them.

This place was worse than hell.

But Bobby had a daughter and he didn't care.

A few feet from him, Deke Jarrell and Ramón Ruiz were playing chess, using a footlocker for a table. Two cots down, Joe Kelvin was listening to *Workingman's Dead* tape for the millionth time. "We've got some things to talk about…" the Grateful Dead sang, their harmonies too buoyant for the hot, murky air. A couple of guys sat on the plank floor, divvying up the contents of a plastic bag of weed.

Mail call had occurred three hours ago, but Bobby wasn't done with this letter yet. This letter and this photograph.

Labor wasn't bad, Joelle wrote. *I had the midwife and all my housemates with me.*

After he'd left for basic, she'd taken up residence in a house with a bunch of women. Bobby didn't get it, but she'd insisted the setup was perfect. They all chipped in on expenses, took turns cooking and watched out for one another. Two of the women were attending college full-time, and Joelle had managed to squeeze in a class along with her hours as a teacher's aide at a nursery school. She'd told him how much she loved working with little children—a lucky thing, given that now she had her own little child to work with.

Her living arrangement sounded kind of like a hippie commune to him, with heavy overtones of feminism, but if it made her happy, he wouldn't complain. He actually liked the idea that she wasn't all alone, pregnant and struggling to make ends meet.

The midwife, however… Joelle had been entitled to hospitalization through the army, but she'd claimed that since her pregnancy was progressing well, she saw no reason not to give birth at the house with a midwife. He didn't approve, but he was twelve thousand miles away and couldn't do a hell of a lot about it.

It didn't matter now. She'd delivered a healthy baby girl. A beautiful girl, as he could see in the photo one of the women she lived with had taken with her Polaroid camera. A girl Joelle had named after Bobby's mother.

"Hey, DiFranco, you wanna take the winner?" Ruiz called to him from the footlocker, where the chess game seemed to be racing toward checkmate.

"I'm a father," he called back. He couldn't think of anything else to say, anything that had meaning. The only words he seemed capable of pronouncing were: *I'm a father.*

"Wow! No shit?" Ruiz shouted above the eruption of voices. "Hey, DiFranco!"

"Far out!"

"Girl or boy?"

"Watch it," Bobby warned as the guys jostled one another around his cot in order to view the photo. "Don't touch it. This is the only picture I have."

"Oh, man, she's a heartbreaker," one of the guys said, then sighed. Bobby wasn't sure if he was talking about Joelle or the baby.

"Pink. Must be a girl."

"Man, that thing is tiny! You sure it's not a doll?"

Bobby laughed. Someone slapped his right shoulder. Someone socked his left arm. "We need cigars. Go find Sergeant Weaver. He's always smoking those things."

"His cigars smell like turds, man."

"They look like turds, too."

"No cigar for me," Bobby said, raising the photo above his head, out of reach of the grasping fingers swatting at it. With his free hand, he groped in the breast pocket of his T-shirt and pulled out his cigarettes. "Here, who wants these?"

"That ain't no cigar," Deke complained.

"I'm not smoking anymore," Bobby said. "I'm quitting. Do something with these." He tossed the pack at Deke. "Give 'em away or smoke 'em yourself."

"Hey, gimme one of those," Ruiz demanded, and the swarm abandoned Bobby's cot for Deke's, where they wrestled for possession of his cast-off smokes.

No more cigarettes for Bobby. No more weed. No more sips of that swill Schenk kept in a rusty canteen—Bobby had no idea what that stuff was or where Schenk got it, but it smelled like paint thinner and knocked a guy flat on his ass after one good swallow.

Bobby wasn't going to drink that stuff anymore. He was a father now. He had to live right, be strong—be the man his own father had never been. He had to keep his lungs healthy, his body whole, his mind clear.

He had to stay alive. He had to get through the boredom and the terror, the steamy days and the sticky nights, the explosions and the even scarier silence. He had to survive, because there was a baby girl waiting for him back in America.

Joelle and Bobby hadn't discussed names for the baby—just one of many things they hadn't discussed—but names were important. Joelle had written him a letter a couple of months ago in which she'd asked if he had any preferences. Two weeks later she'd heard back from him, a single tissue-thin sheet of paper telling her about how muddy the base was from all the rain they'd been having.

She'd grown used to his ignoring her questions. Some of them he probably couldn't answer—"What is your mission? Is it dangerous?" Some he likely didn't want to answer—"The newspapers report that everyone's doing lots of drugs over there. Is that true?" He'd developed the habit of writing whatever was on his mind rather than responding to the issues she'd raised.

With no input from Bobby, she was on her own in naming the baby. If she had a boy, would Bobby like her to name him Robert Junior? She couldn't imagine naming a boy Louis, after Bobby's father, since Bobby hated his dad. Nor would she name a son Dale after her own father. She loved the name Michael, but would Bobby approve?

Boys' names went forgotten when, after ten hours of labor—which had seemed like a century to her, but the midwife said was quite fast, especially for a first child—Joelle gave birth to a perfect little girl. Surrounded by her housemates in the rickety old Victorian a mile from the Rider College campus, Joelle wept as the midwife placed the damp, squirming infant in her arms. Gazing into that scrunchy pink face crowned by a tuft of pale hair, she murmured, "Claudia." The baby gazed back at her, and Joelle swore she saw a smile on those puckered little lips.

Bobby's mother had never made a vivid impression on Joelle. Claudia DiFranco had been a vague presence in the background when Joelle was playing in Bobby's backyard, a tangled lot of weeds and scruffy shrubs and old tires that had seemed like a magical world compared with the tiny, fenced-in square of yellowing grass behind her own duplex. Bobby's backyard had trees to climb and junk to explore, room to move—and his front yard had a bathtub shrine.

Occasionally Mrs. DiFranco would stick her head out the kitchen door and say, "How about some cookies?" As they clambered up the back-porch steps, she'd say, "Wipe your feet before you come in." That was pretty much the sum of Joelle's contact with her.

The winter Joelle and Bobby were in sixth grade, his mother grew gaunt and her skin appeared waxy. "She's got cancer," Bobby confided to Joelle. "Don't tell anyone." Joelle wasn't sure why he should keep his mother's illness a secret, but she honored his request.

Claudia DiFranco died in May. With her death, Bobby's secret became public knowledge. Dozens of sixth-graders showed up at St. Mary's Catholic Church for the funeral. Bobby sat in the front pew with his father and his younger brother, Eddie, three sad, solemn figures in dark jackets and ties. Bobby's and Eddie's classmates filled the rear half of the church. Some cried openly. Joelle wondered if they could possibly have known Bobby's mother better than she did, but then she realized those kids were crying because they were thinking of their own mothers, of how horrible it would be to lose a mother to cancer.

Bobby missed a few days of school afterward, and when he finally showed up, no one dared to mention his mother. Joelle asked once how he was doing and he said fine, but his tone was clipped and forbidding. It was clear he didn't want to talk about his mother and his grief, and Joelle would never press him. In art class, she painted a sunset with watercolors and gave it to him, hoping it would cheer him up. He took it and said thanks, and then never mentioned it again.

One night at around ten, just days after school had ended for the summer, Joelle heard a tapping on her window screen. Her room was dark, the air too hot and stagnant for her to fall asleep. She'd been lying in bed, listening to the cricket song through her open window and wondering if she might die from the heat.

She heard the tapping again. She sat up, glanced toward the window and saw a shadow through the thin voile curtains, Bobby's silhouette backlit by the moon. "JoJo?" he whispered.

"Yeah, I'm up." She slid out of bed, tiptoed to the window and drew open the curtains. She didn't care if Bobby saw her in her nightgown. It fell nearly to her knees, and besides, this was Bobby, not some creepy boy who'd go around boasting that he'd seen Joelle Webber in her nightie. Not that there was anything worth seeing. She was skinny and flat chested, her arms and legs too long and her hips nonexistent.

Through the screen she heard Bobby breathing hard, as if he'd run all the way from his house. Once her vision adjusted to the gloom, she made out his face. His eyes were wild, his T-shirt stained. Who washed his clothes now that his mother was dead?

"I'm in big trouble," he confessed. "I have to run away."

Forcing herself to keep her voice as soft as his, she asked, "What happened?"

"I hit my dad. I…I hurt him, Jo."

"Oh, God."

"I didn't want to." A sob seemed to clog Bobby's throat, but he wasn't crying. Just struggling to get the words out. "He was beating on Eddie. I couldn't let him do that."

"Why was he beating on Eddie?"

"I don't know. He was drunk and Eddie's little. I was just trying to get him to stop. I think I broke his nose. Or maybe worse." In the silver moonlight, she glimpsed the shine of tears in his eyes. "There was blood everywhere. If they catch me, I'll go to jail."

"No, you won't," Joelle promised. As if she was any kind of a legal expert. "You were just protecting your brother."

"When my mom was around, he didn't touch us. She wouldn't let him."

Bobby had never before told Joelle that his father was violent. He'd mentioned that his father liked to drink, that he usually started getting loaded when he arrived home from work—unless he went straight from work to the Dog House Tavern and got loaded there—and his temper would flare and his mother would steer him into the bedroom to cool off, or he'd fall asleep in front of the TV. But she'd never heard anything about beatings.

"We don't have my mom anymore." Bobby was still breathing hard—from his emotions, probably. He should have recovered from his run by now. "She used to protect us. If they arrest me, who's gonna protect Eddie?"

"They won't arrest you," Joelle insisted. "You're just a kid. And anyway, all you have to do is tell them he was beating your brother."

"Then they'll take us away from him and put us in an orphanage or something."

Joelle wondered if that might not be an improvement over living with a father who beat his kids. But she didn't want Bobby sent away—either to jail or to an orphanage—because he was her best friend. "Is your father still at your house?"

"I don't know."

"Maybe you should go back and find out if he's okay. Maybe he wasn't hurt as bad as you think."

"He was hurt bad. There was so much blood… What if I killed him? I can't go back there. The police could be waiting for me."

She thought some more. He looked so scared. "I'll go with you," she resolved. "You can hide while I try to find out what's happening. If the police are there, we'll figure out what to do then."

"Okay."

"Close your eyes," she ordered him, then hurried across her room to her closet and removed her nightgown. She trusted Bobby not to look.

She donned a pair of shorts, a T-shirt and her canvas sneakers. Then she crept back to the window and unhooked the screen. Bobby hinged it away from the window frame so she could climb out. The moonlight struck the back of his right hand. His knuckles were swollen and bruised.

How hard had he hit his father? What if he really had killed him?

She refused to consider that possibility. After nudging the screen back into place, she and Bobby scrambled over the fence and through the adjacent backyard and the one after that, down an alley and across another tiny yard. They couldn't risk showing their faces out on the street at this hour.

Bobby's house was only a few blocks away. No police cars lined the road. The driveway held only Bobby's father's old truck, with its dented rear fender and rust scabs and bug-crusted windshield.

They sneaked past the truck and around to the backyard. Bright yellow light spilled through the kitchen windows and the screen door and voices could be heard—Bobby's father and another man. *Please, not a cop,* Joelle silently prayed.

Bobby hunkered down in the shadows of an overgrown forsythia while Joelle inched closer to the back porch, straining to make out what the men were saying. She heard a burst of laughter. If Bobby had hurt his father that badly, he and the other man wouldn't be laughing, would they?

She crouched as she approached the porch, then straightened enough to spy through the vertical slats in the railing. "So, I'm thinking that sumbitch owes me a raise, one way or the other," Bobby's father was saying. "I work harder than he does, don't I? So— Ouch! No more ice."

"It'll keep the swelling down," the other man said.

"The hell with it." She heard the thump of a glass against the table.

Gripping the railing, she inched higher, hoping to peek through the window. Unfortunately Bobby's father saw her as soon as she saw him. His nose was covered with white gauze and tape. "What the hell?" he muttered, rising from the kitchen table and crossing to the porch, his friend right behind him. Both men wore sweat-stained undershirts and work pants worn to a shine at the knees and frayed at the hems. Both were unshaven, and both had tousled hair. Louie DiFranco also had a puffy cheek and a purpling eye and all that bandaging on his nose. "Who is that?" he demanded, swinging open the screen door.

Joelle hadn't heard Bobby come up behind her, but he said, "It's me, Dad. Me and Joelle Webber."

"Bobby?" Louie seemed to falter for a moment. Then he managed a feeble smile. "What are you doing out this late? Ya missed all the excitement, buddy."

"Your daddy walked into a door," his friend said, then laughed. "Looks like the door won, huh?"

Bobby and Joelle exchanged a glance. Apparently Bobby's father hadn't told his friend how his face had gotten busted up. If he wouldn't tell his friend, he sure wasn't going to tell the police.

"It's kinda late for you kids to be running around, don't you think?" Louie asked. "A little past your bedtime?"

More than a little. "I gotta take her home," Bobby told his father. "Then I'll go to bed."

Something flickered across Louie's face—anger, maybe resentment that Bobby hadn't apologized for being out late and then meekly entered the house. Maybe fear. But he said, "Fine, you take your friend home and then you get your butt up those stairs and into bed."

Neither Bobby nor Joelle spoke as they walked back to her house. No need to run—Joelle's mother never checked up on her after she went to bed, and now that they knew Bobby's father hadn't called the cops, the urgency of the night had vanished. Bobby hadn't killed his father, he wasn't going to jail and in all likelihood no one but Bobby, his father, his brother and Joelle would ever know what had happened that night. The rest of the world would be snickering about the night Louie DiFranco drank too much and collided with a door.

Unlike the DiFranco house, the first-floor Webber apartment was dark and quiet when they reached Joelle's bedroom window. Bobby jiggled the screen loose from the frame, then let his hands drop to his sides and turned to Joelle. "Thanks."

His voice had deepened this past year. It was still a boy's voice, but lower and thicker than it used to be. When he whispered, he sounded almost like a man.

"Will you be okay?" she asked.

He nodded, but his eyes said no. Joelle opened her arms and he let her hug him. Surrounded by the hot summer air, the screech of crickets and buzz of mosquitoes, she held him tight. She felt his rib cage and spine right through his shirt, through his skin. His shoulders had begun to widen, but he was only an inch or so taller than her, and not much broader.

She couldn't tell if he was crying. She hoped he was. He

needed to and he didn't have to be embarrassed in front of her. She would never tell anyone.

For a long time they just held each other. Eventually he leaned back. His cheeks were damp, and she knew if she touched her hair she'd feel his tears in the strands. "I miss my mom," he murmured, his voice hoarse.

"Of course you do."

He let out a broken sigh. "She wasn't—you know, beautiful or funny and she didn't talk a lot, but... She believed in me."

"I believe in you."

He searched her face, then turned to stare at the moon. "Sometimes I don't know how I'm gonna survive without her."

"You're strong, Bobby," Joelle assured him. "You'll survive."

"What if my dad starts in again?"

"You're almost as big as he is," Joelle pointed out. "He can't push you and Eddie around. You showed him that tonight."

"He breaks things," he told her. "When he gets mad, he breaks things."

"They're just things. As long as he doesn't break you and Eddie, you'll be okay." She reached up to wipe a stray tear from his cheek. He ducked his head away, but not quickly enough to avoid her touch. His skin was warm and fuzzy, like suede. In another year or two, he'd be shaving. "If he tries to hurt you or Eddie, grab Eddie and come here. We'll figure out what to do."

"This isn't your problem."

She shook her head. "I'm your friend, Bobby. That's all that matters."

He peered down at her. Another tear streaked down to his

chin, and she brushed her hand against his face. "Yeah," he murmured, then lifted the screen. "You better go in."

She hoisted herself over the windowsill. Bobby held the screen in place while she hooked it shut inside. Then he sprinted across the small backyard to the fence and vaulted over it.

She stood at her window, watching the night outside. The dampness of Bobby's tears lingered on her palm.

Gazing at the squirming bundle of pink in her arms, she remembered that night. Bobby never mentioned his father hitting him or Eddie again, but sometimes she'd sensed a tension in him. And every now and then, when they were hanging out at the A&W or some other place, he'd have Eddie with him. No explanation, no discussion about why a kid three years their junior was tagging along. Joelle suspected that those were nights when Bobby's father had drunk too much and was breaking things.

She had learned that night how much Bobby's mother had meant to him. Maybe the woman had been quiet, maybe she'd made no more of an impression on Joelle than a passing breeze, but she'd protected Bobby and his brother. She'd kept them safe for the years it took Bobby to grow up, to become big enough to fight back. Joelle didn't really believe in guardian angels, but if they existed, she liked to think Claudia DiFranco was watching over Bobby now, keeping him safe while he faced dangers greater than his father's fists.

She was only vaguely aware of all the bustle around her—Maggie, the midwife, gently washing her off with warm, wet cloths, Joelle's housemate, Lucy, snapping photos with her camera, Suzanne—at forty, the owner of the house and the grande dame of their community—gathering towels and linens into a laundry basket, Renee combing Joelle's hair back from her sweaty, teary cheeks and Lenore giggling and cooing and generally being useless. "Try giving her a breast," Maggie advised. Before Joelle could respond, Renee and Lenore eased down the strap of Joelle's nightgown to free her breast.

She lifted her squirming little daughter and guided her nipple into the baby's mouth. With an eager tug, the baby started to suck. It was all such a miracle—this glorious little girl feeding from Joelle's body. Joelle a mother. This precious life. This tiny angel.

"Claudia," she whispered. "You'll be my Claudia." *Our* Claudia, she added, praying that Bobby would accept her as his daughter, that he would return from Vietnam and still wish to be Joelle's husband. What if he looked at Claudia and saw Drew Foster in her pale, feathery hair, in her round, gray-brown eyes, her little pink hands and her fingernails like tiny seed pearls? What if, when he confronted the reality of what he'd done, he decided to flee? He'd been the one to point out that they could always get a divorce.

He'd also been the one to say this baby would be his, a DiFranco.

Maggie approached Joelle with a clipboard. "Oh, she's nursing so well! She's probably not getting full-strength milk yet, but that'll come soon. I hope she does everything as beautifully as she does this."

"So do I." Joelle was unable to look anywhere but at the baby in her arms, her cheeks pumping and her feet kicking eagerly against the soft cotton blanket in which she was wrapped.

Maggie picked up the clipboard. "We have to fill out a few forms for her birth certificate. Father's name?"

Joelle drew in a deep breath and said, "Robert Louis DiFranco. Capital D, capital F."

The midwife left about a half hour later. Suzanne went downstairs to fix dinner and Lenore volunteered to run a load of laundry. Lucy left a stack of instant photos on the bedside table and Renee, at Joelle's request, brought her stationery box over to the bed. Claudia had already emptied one breast and was drinking from the other, although a lot less enthusiastically. Her eyelids fluttered and her legs didn't move so much. All the excitement of getting born and eating seemed to have tired her out.

She had the most delicate eyelashes Joelle had ever seen.

"Would you like to rest?" Renee asked.

The peace in the room, after all the tumult of the birth, soothed Joelle. She suspected moments of peace would be rare now that Claudia was in her life. "Thanks," she said, nodding at Renee.

Renee left the room, one of five cozy bedrooms in the rambling Victorian. Through the floorboards Joelle could hear the sounds of her housemates moving around downstairs, the muffled drone of the TV, Lenore's giddy laughter. In her arms, Claudia made a slurping sound, then nestled her head into the bend of Joelle's elbow. Her eyes were shut—she was obviously asleep, although her mouth kept making sucking motions. Maybe she was dreaming about milk, Joelle thought with a smile.

Trying not to jostle the baby, she grasped with her free hand for her stationery. She also gathered up the photographs. A couple were blurred and one hadn't developed very well. But one showed her and Claudia clearly. She set it aside, then took a sheet of letter paper from the box. *Dear Bobby,* she wrote, *I gave birth today to a baby girl. I named her Claudia. I hope you don't mind.*

Chapter 7

Bobby knew more about gardens than Joelle did, but after thirty-seven years of marriage, she'd learned a few things. A few years ago, she'd asked him to help her plant a vegetable garden in the backyard. He'd carved her a plot with as much care and professionalism as he would for any DiFranco Landscaping project. He'd cut a nice-sized rectangle, surrounded it with marigolds and trimmed it with scalloped wire fencing buried deep enough to hinder burrowing critters. He'd filled the enclosed area with enriched loam. He'd supplied her with frames to tie her tomato vines and some sort of organic antigrub soil treatment.

When her children were young, her summers had been filled with mothering. She'd spent every July and August shuttling the kids to day camp, Little League, swimming lessons and play dates. When they'd grown older, she'd chauffeured them to assorted summer jobs.

But now they were gone and Joelle's summers were her own. A lot of teachers picked up supplementary income working as camp counselors or tutors, but Joelle and Bobby didn't require the extra money. And since summer was his busiest season, she was happy to spend those months free of paying work and available to take care of chores he had no time for. She sewed, she puttered, she grew fresh vegetables and she fixed special meals to greet him with at the end of his long days.

Like lasagna, she thought churlishly, recalling the over-cooked meal she'd wound up throwing away last night.

Gardening wasn't merely a hobby today. It was therapy. She needed the grit of the warm soil against her knees and between her fingers. She needed the hot sun roasting her. She needed the satisfying rip of roots as she tore weeds from the dirt. She needed something to tame, something to inflict her anger upon.

How could Bobby have gotten drunk last night? How could he have come home and smashed a vase? Was her family as broken as that vase? Had she demolished the family by telling Claudia the truth about her birth, or had the lie, the basis of her marriage, been like a flaw in the glass, an invisible crack just waiting to split apart?

Lost in her ruminations and drugged by the morning heat, she wasn't at first sure she heard Claudia's voice: "Mom?" Silence, and then she heard it again. "Mom."

She glanced over her shoulder and saw Claudia standing on the patio, using her hand to shield her eyes from the sun's glare as she gazed at Joelle. She wore white cotton shorts and a lime-green camp shirt and she was alone.

Where were the children? Did Claudia intend to deny Joelle

access to her grandchildren because of what she'd done so many years ago? If she did...Joelle would die. Without her beloved grandbabies, she couldn't imagine how she would go on.

She stood, tossed down the garden claw she'd been using to loosen the weeds' roots and dusted the dirt from her knees. "Hello, Claudia." No sound of Jeremy's or Kristin's laughter drifted from the side of the house. Not that Claudia would have let them out of her sight if she'd brought them with her. They would have been standing right beside their mother on the patio—or, more likely, racing across the grass to Grandma, arms outstretched as they clamored for hugs.

Claudia must have read her question in her eyes. "I left the kids at a neighbor's house," she said. "This isn't a friendly visit."

Of course not. Joelle supposed that meant she shouldn't hug Claudia, either. Clearly Claudia meant to punish her for...what? Giving birth to her? Marrying a man who promised to be a father for her? Raising her and loving her and sending her off into the world?

"I want to know about my father," Claudia said.

"He's at work right now," Joelle said, her voice taut. "You have his number." *Maybe you can meet him for a beer and a few whiskies after work,* she thought bitterly. *Maybe you can get him so drunk he'll get sick, the way your brother, Mike, did, and by the time I join him in bed he'll be passed out.*

"I meant my birth father," Claudia said quietly.

Joelle sighed. She heard an undertone of worry along with indignation in Claudia's voice. Sadness, too, and fear. "What do you want to know?"

"I tried Googling his name," Claudia told her, then laughed

dryly. "*Drew Foster*. I got thousands of hits about foster programs for children, plus a few that seemed to be about drawing pictures and a couple about duels."

"Duels?"

"People drawing their guns. Maybe I would have found some information about him online if his name was weird—Vladimir Binglehoffer or something." Claudia's lingering smile, although faint, gave Joelle a touch of hope. Her joke was a door opening a sliver.

Joelle dared to smile back. "He was one of the rich kids in town," she explained. "A purebred Wasp with a Waspy name." Leaving her tools, her gloves and the bucket of weeds by the garden, she strode across the lawn to the patio. "What do you want to know? I'll tell you everything I can."

Claudia ruminated. Evidently she didn't know what she wanted to know. Finally she asked, "Was he smart?"

"He was a good student. He went to Dartmouth College. People at our high school were so excited about his going there. Ivy League colleges were a big deal in those days."

"They still are." Claudia's eyes remained on Joelle. "Did he have any talent? Was he musical?"

Joelle realized Claudia was trying to figure out what gifts Drew's genes might have bestowed upon her. "I don't recall him playing any instruments," she said. "He played tennis, though. I remember he played soccer, too. Our school had a team, but it wasn't such a popular sport back then. Not the way it is now."

"What did he look like?"

Joelle struggled to conjure a picture of a teenage Drew. Whatever memories she'd had of him from high school had been overtaken by his appearance inside her house a few days ago. He'd looked prosperous and middle-aged that morning, not like the boy she'd fallen for in high school. "I've got my Holmdell High School yearbook somewhere," she said, swinging open the back door into the kitchen.

Claudia followed her inside. The kitchen was pleasantly cool after the oppressive heat of the backyard. Joelle paused at the sink to wash her hands and face. She toweled herself dry, then headed for the basement door.

Bobby had finished a rec room in the basement a few years after they'd bought the house, once he'd had the rest of the place in reasonable repair. The rec room was nothing fancy—Sheetrock walls, cheap brown carpeting covering the concrete floor, built-in shelves and drop-ceiling fluorescent lighting. It had been a haven for the kids, a place for the boys to scatter their toys and play video games, a lair where Claudia and her teenage friends gathered for sleepover parties. By the time the boys were in high school, Joelle had added some style to the decor, painting the walls a cheerful yellow, spreading a few braided rugs on the floor and sewing new slipcovers for the sofa and chairs. Last year Bobby had splurged on a wide-screen TV. Joelle considered most TV shows just as inane in wide-screen as on the old set, but Bobby adored the oversized screen. So did Mike and Danny, who spent many Sundays in the fall watching football with their father. If the TV lured her kids home for visits, she was glad Bobby had bought it.

The carton she was searching for was in the unfinished half of the basement, where the furnace and the hot-water tank, Bobby's tool bench and a wall of steel storage shelves were located. The shelves were stacked with boxes of Christmas decorations, old athletic gear, luggage, tax records and junk that, for whatever reason, Joelle wasn't yet ready to discard.

She shoved a few boxes around until she located the carton at the back of one of the shelves.

She lugged the carton into the rec room, Claudia shadowing her. After dropping the box onto the coffee table, Joelle settled on the couch. She wrinkled her nose at the sour scent of the dust that rose from the flaps as she pulled them apart.

She hadn't opened this carton since the family had moved to Gray Hill, and she told herself its contents no longer meant anything to her. But when she lifted out the polished marble egg Bobby had given her for Christmas so many years ago, in high school, she felt a pang so painful it brought tears to her eyes. "Oh, God," she said, her hand molding to the smooth curves of the egg. "This was a present from your dad."

"My birth father?"

Joelle started. "No. Your *real* father." She held the egg up for Claudia to see.

Claudia frowned. "What is that?"

"An egg. A marble egg. There was this little head shop in town that sold them."

Claudia took the egg from her and studied it, her frown deepening. "What were you supposed to do with it?"

"I don't know. Display it. Hold it." She sighed. "There was no 'supposed-to' about it. All I cared about was that Bobby DiFranco gave it to me."

"Even though you were in love with some other guy," Claudia said, her tone laced with suspicion.

"I always loved your father," Joelle insisted, silencing the quaver in her voice. Last night when Bobby was lost in a drunken slumber, had she loved him? Had she loved him when she'd thrown away the ruined flowers and the broken glass and the dinner he'd never eaten? Why couldn't he have stayed calm and reasonable and *talked* to her? Why, when they were both so sad, did he get to act out, while she got stuck cleaning up after him?

Sighing, she reached back into the carton and pulled out her old jewelry box. She opened its lid. The box was empty— the few pieces of jewelry she'd owned before she left Holmdell with Bobby had since been moved to a much nicer jewelry box, which sat on her bedroom dresser. After all these years, she hadn't really expected the old box to start playing "Edelweiss," but the silence jolted her.

She flipped the box over and cranked the key protruding from the underside. Then she righted the box and opened it again. The crystalline notes of the song emerged.

"Hey." Claudia's eyes grew wide as she sank onto the sofa next to Joelle. "I know that song."

"It's from *The Sound of Music,*" Joelle said.

"No, I mean—I *know* it." She eased the music box out of her mother's hands and placed it on her knees, letting the music rise like a vapor in front of her. "I know this music box."

"It's been stored away forever," Joelle said, gesturing toward the carton.

Claudia frowned, shook her head and twisted the key to make the music continue. "When I was really little, before we lived here, Daddy would play this music box for me. He'd sit me on his knee and open the lid. I thought it was magic, the way the music just rose out of the box like that."

Daddy. Claudia wasn't referring to Drew Foster now. Her daddy was Bobby, the man who'd raised her, who'd made her believe in the magic of a music box.

Joelle didn't remember Bobby playing the music box for Claudia, but the early years of their marriage had been filled with a lot of tag-team parenting. She'd worked while he was in physical therapy. Or she'd brought Claudia with her to the preschool where she was employed. Or he'd cared for Claudia in the evenings while Joelle attended college. Those first few years after Bobby came home from the war were a blur of exhaustion, determination and discovery. They'd had to learn how to be a husband and wife at the same time they were learning how to be parents. They'd had to learn how to create a family while actually doing it.

Apparently during those times when Bobby and Claudia were on their own, Bobby had amused his daughter with the music box. Together they'd experienced things that Joelle had never been a part of.

If Claudia could remember "Edelweiss," her relationship with Bobby couldn't be torn apart by the intrusion of Drew Foster into their lives. It simply couldn't.

While Claudia opened and shut the music box, lost in her own memories, Joelle dug deeper into the carton. There was her old childhood piggy bank, long empty. There was her teddy bear, which she'd let Claudia keep until she'd had enough money to buy her a brand-new stuffed animal. And there, underneath the black plastic folder holding her high-school diploma, was her yearbook.

She hoisted out the heavy album and nudged the carton away so it wouldn't cast a shadow on the glossy pages. Claudia set down the jewelry box and lifted the yearbook onto her own lap. "I don't think I've ever seen this," she said, spreading the book open across her thighs. She sped through the first part of the book, full of candid shots and faculty photos, and then slowed when she reached the portraits of Joelle's classmates. "Foster," Claudia murmured, flipping past the *A*s, the

*B*s, the *D*s so quickly Joelle didn't even glimpse Bobby's picture.

Claudia halted at Drew's page. The photo resembled him as much as any yearbook photo would: a black-and-white portrait of a young man gazing dreamily just past the photographer's shoulder, his eyes aimed at some supposedly glorious future. His hair was neatly combed and not particularly long for 1970. He wore a dark blazer, a white shirt and a dark tie. His face was smooth and boyish.

"That's him?" Claudia asked, her voice a whisper.

"Yes."

She scrutinized the picture, as if trying to discern his character from that one artificial pose. She traced the photo with her fingertips, as if she could feel the shape of his nose, the curve of his chin. She stared, sighed, drank him in.

"He doesn't look like that now," Joelle reminded her. "He was eighteen when that photo was taken."

"I know, but… It would have been right around when you became—I mean, this is what he looked like when you conceived me."

Unsure what to say, Joelle remained silent. Claudia seemed both horrified and enthralled by the photograph. Joelle was mostly just horrified by it. She'd believed she loved that boy— a boy so selfish, his way of dealing with his pregnant girlfriend was to send her a check and the name of a doctor. Why had she agreed to help him now? He'd been a son of a bitch, just as Bobby said.

His son, she remembered. She was doing this for his son.

For her daughter, too. Observing the intensity of Claudia's expression as she studied the man whose sperm had created her, Joelle had to believe she'd been right to tell her daughter the truth. She couldn't let herself believe anything else.

After several long minutes, Claudia thumbed back a few pages, into the *D*s, until she found Bobby's photo. Unlike all the other students on the page, Bobby lacked the traditional tentative yearbook smile, and he stared directly at the camera, not at some goal hovering just above the photographer's right shoulder. His dark hair was long and wild with waves, his eyes dark and burning, his mouth set firmly. He wore a blazer—a corduroy blazer, Joelle realized as she leaned in to study the photo. His father's jacket, the one he'd stolen when he and Joelle had fled to New Jersey and gotten married.

Claudia had wedged her finger into the book to hold Drew's page, and now she turned back to that page. She inspected Drew's photo, then flipped back to Bobby's page and grimaced. "Dad was so cool. Why didn't you go out with him?"

Studying Bobby's photo, Joelle had to agree that he'd been handsome. But she'd known him so long, she'd hardly even *seen* him by the time they were high-school seniors. When she'd looked at him, she'd seen their shared history. She'd seen his wicked grin, his sense of humor, the smell of his cigarettes, the grief darkening his eyes at moments when he didn't realize she was watching him. Grief over his mother's death, she'd assumed, or over his father's drinking, or over the fact that kids like him were denied the opportunity to escape their fate. No wonder he wasn't gazing into the future in his yearbook photo. The future he'd imagined for himself back then wasn't one he'd wanted.

Objectively, though, he'd been gorgeous. His hair, his eyes, the stubborn set of his jaw, the fierce defiance in his gaze… Definitely gorgeous.

"I didn't date your father because he never asked me out," she answered.

Claudia eyed her dubiously.

"We were friends, but he dated other girls."

"Who?" Claudia began thumbing through the pages. "Who did he date?"

Quite a few, Joelle recalled. Bobby had made the rounds of available Tubtown girls throughout their high-school years. He'd always been popular. He'd dated one in particular toward the end; he'd been going with her when he'd asked Joelle to marry him. "Margie something," she recollected. "I think her last name began with an *N*. Newland, maybe?"

Amid the *N*s, Claudia found Marjorie Noonan's photo. "Her?" She scowled in disapproval.

Claudia looked at Margie's photo. Joelle looked, too. She'd forgotten how beautiful Margie was, with her long black hair, her round cheeks and her large, almond-shaped eyes framed in thick eyelashes. Her lips shaped a perfect pout as she focused on the space beyond the photographer. Why hadn't Bobby stayed with her? She was much prettier than Joelle.

"She was nice," Joelle told Claudia.

"She's tarty. He could have gone out with you."

"He wanted to go out with her," Joelle said simply. The emotion that welled up inside her wasn't simple, though. Bobby had gone out with Margie and other girls because he'd wanted to—and he hadn't wanted to go out with Joelle. Surely if he had, he would have asked her out. Surely if he had, she would have said yes.

But he hadn't loved her, not that way. She'd been his pal. Not the girl of his heart. Even when he'd married her, she'd been aware of that.

And it hurt. After all these years, it still hurt to admit that Bobby hadn't loved her the way he'd loved all the girls he'd been involved with in Holmdell. He'd married her out of friendship and charity, nothing more. Crazy though it was, she suffered a pang of jealousy for all those girls he'd dated, all the girls he'd chosen. He'd never really *chosen* her. She'd been his good deed, nothing more.

"So he was dating her, and you were dating…" Claudia returned to Drew's photo amid the *F*s. "Drew Foster."

"Drew was very nice," Joelle defended him. "He was smart and handsome and considerate." *Until the end,* she added silently. *Until he found out I was pregnant and sent me money.*

"He looks rich."

"He was."

Claudia raised her eyes to Joelle. "Is that why you dated him?" she asked.

"Of course not," Joelle said automatically, then pressed her lips together. Hadn't she told her daughter enough lies for one lifetime? "I didn't mind the fact that he was rich," she confessed. "He lived in a neighborhood called the Hill, where all the rich people lived. It's been so long since you've been in Holmdell, maybe you don't remember. But the part of town where Dad and I grew up, where Grandma Wanda lives and Papa Louie used to live, was where all the poor kids lived. And Drew lived up on the Hill, on the other side of town, in a big house on two acres, with cars and a huge allowance and a membership in the country club. I was dazzled, Claudia. I couldn't believe a boy like him would be interested in a girl like me."

"Did you love him?"

Joelle lowered her gaze back to the yearbook page. "At the

time, I thought I did," she conceded. She *had* thought she loved him, and not because he was rich. Because he had confidence. Because he had two parents. Because he knew who he was and where he belonged and what he was entitled to. To a bastard child from Tubtown, his life seemed like a fantasy.

Claudia continued to study Drew's photo, as if trying to memorize it. "You had sex with him?" she finally asked, her gaze trained on the yearbook.

"Obviously."

Claudia sighed and shut the book. "Why didn't you marry him?"

"He…" It pained Joelle to admit the truth, almost as much as it pained her to acknowledge that Bobby hadn't loved her like a girlfriend. "He wasn't ready for marriage and fatherhood. He was in college. He sent me money to get an abortion."

Claudia shrank from Drew's photo. "God."

"He was frightened," Joelle said, although she had no good reason to defend him. "He wasn't ready to be a father."

"And you were ready to be a mother?"

Joelle laughed sadly. "I was so unready. But I wanted you, Claudia. In spite of how young I was, and how unprepared, I wanted you. And your father—your *real* father—wanted you, too. So we got married."

"Dad's name is on my birth certificate," Claudia said. At Joelle's nod, she asked, "You lied on the birth certificate? Is that legal?"

"You're the one married to a lawyer," Joelle reminded her. "You'd have to ask him. I guess we figured that as long as no one probed, what difference did it make? Your father loves you, Claudia. You are his daughter. The reason I never told you about all this—" she gestured toward Drew's yearbook photo

"—is that I was afraid it might make you feel differently toward him. Maybe you'd stop loving him. That would kill him, Claudia. If he lost you, he would die." Or at least, he would drink and break things and stop being the man he was.

Claudia digested this, then steered her attention back to the yearbook. Her face registered revulsion as she stared at Drew's photo. "So this boy wanted you to get rid of me. And now, all these years later, he comes back into your life and says he's my father?"

"He's grown up, Claudia. He's not the kid he once was." Joelle sighed. "God knows, he could have found me years ago and insisted on being a part of your life."

"But he wanted me dead," Claudia argued, still staring at Drew's photo, as if trying to imagine him capable of wishing such a terrible thing. "He wanted you to get rid of me. And now he claims he has a right to—to what? My bone marrow?"

"I don't think he believes he has a right to anything, Claudia. He only has hope."

"And you kept all this from me because you didn't want me to stop loving Dad." She shut the yearbook and shoved it off her lap, onto the coffee table. "Did it ever occur to you that maybe I ought to know who my father is?"

"Yes." Joelle sighed and rubbed her face with her hands. "Claudia, Dad and I were so young then. We were only trying to do what was best. It wasn't like we sat down and said, 'Let's keep this secret from Claudia. She doesn't need the truth.' We only wanted you to grow up happy and loved, with two parents who were crazy about you. Who never, ever wanted you dead."

Claudia's shoulders trembled, as if she were shaking off a chill. "I feel cheated."

"I'm sorry." Those words sounded so feeble falling from Joelle's mouth. "It's my fault, Claudia. I made a mistake. I got into trouble. Your father rescued me. I was a fool and he was a saint. If you want to hate someone, hate me. Your father…" Her voice faltered and she cleared her throat. "He's afraid he's lost you, Claudia, and he doesn't deserve that. Please don't hate him." Tears beaded along her lashes. She ducked her head so Claudia wouldn't see.

"I don't hate him." She sighed. "I hate this man, this Drew Foster…but he's my father. I'm not sure what I'm supposed to think, how I'm supposed to feel."

Once again Joelle ached to touch her daughter, to wrap her arms around her and heal her pain with a kiss, the way she used to use mommy kisses to heal Claudia's childhood scrapes and mosquito bites. But Claudia was an adult, and what was troubling her now couldn't be kissed away.

"Maybe you could feel a little forgiveness, honey," she said. "You're stuck with a bunch of people who did the best we could a long time ago."

"A long time ago," Claudia echoed, raising her eyes to Joelle. "What about now?" She was on the verge of tears, too. Joelle opened her arms, but Claudia leaned away. No, mommy kisses weren't going to cure anything today.

Suffering the sting of her daughter's rejection, Joelle stood and started stuffing things back into the carton. Her musical jewelry box. The marble egg. The book containing photos of a long time ago, of the people who'd made devastating mistakes with the best of intentions.

Bobby's head ached and his tongue felt like a strip of sandpaper inside his mouth. He'd been drinking water all day, and he'd managed to consume some saltines and half an apple at noon. But the heat and glare of the sun assaulted his brain. Too bad he couldn't spend the day in his air-conditioned office, but a bluestone patio had to be installed around a free-form pool in Arlington, and Bobby was better than any of his employees at cutting the stone slabs to mesh with the pool's amorphous shape. So he was at the job site, exposed to the elements.

The two crew members working with him were sweating like marathoners, their faces red and shiny. Bobby considered telling them they could take off their shirts, but the customer was home, no doubt spying on them through the windows that overlooked her backyard. Bobby thought having the guys work shirtless might be disrespectful. He had never forgotten the lecture he'd received when he'd removed his shirt while mowing the cemetery lawn in Holmdell.

If he could keep his shirt on, so could his crew. They were good kids, college boys working for DiFranco from mid May through the end of August. They could probably hold their liquor better than he could, too.

He lifted a twenty-pound slab of stone from the pile, carried it over to the pool and laid it on the sand-and-pebble bed he'd groomed as the patio's bottom layer. He appreciated the weight of the slab, the way it tugged at the muscles in his back and arms. Sweat burned his eyes. He told himself that a little exertion, a little suffering, might make him less aware of his headache.

As if his throbbing skull was the only thing bothering him. Hell, his hangover was nothing compared with the *real* demons gnawing at him.

Joelle must despise him. Last night he'd turned into someone he'd sworn to himself he would never become: his father. He'd gotten ripped, he'd smashed a vase, he'd crushed a bunch of flowers. He'd let his rage blind him.

Yet he'd been unable to apologize. Last night he'd felt too ill. He'd fallen asleep sometime before eight, and he'd regained consciousness at six that morning, much too early to wake Joelle. He'd remained in the shower a long time, but she'd still been sleeping when he was washed and dressed, so he'd left for work without talking to her.

He wouldn't have known what to say, anyway. "I'm sorry I got drunk yesterday, but I'm not sorry I destroyed those damn flowers."

"I'm sorry I made myself sick, but after all these years, we should have left the past alone. We shouldn't have torn away all the scar tissue and let the old wounds start bleeding again."

"I'm sorry, Joelle, but it's killing me that that guy, the big love of your life, can march into our house and make you see things his way."

In his jeans pocket his cell phone vibrated. He nestled the stone into place, straightened up and dug out the phone. A glance at the tiny monitor informed him it was Mona, his office manager. He flipped the phone open. "Mona?"

"Hi, Bob. You got a call here at the office."

He shrugged. Mona's job was to take messages, not to interrupt him at work—unless the call was an emergency. "From Joelle?" he asked. His anger went forgotten. Was she all right? Had she been in an accident? Had something happened to Claudia or the babies?

Of course, if Joelle faced an emergency, she could have phoned him directly. She knew his cell number. But maybe after last night, she was afraid to call him. Maybe she was annoyed about his sneaking out of the house that morning while she slept, instead of waking her up and having it out with her. Not that he knew what the "it" he was supposed to have out with her was. Apologies? Recriminations? Accusations? Howls of outrage?

"No, it wasn't from Joelle. That's the thing." Mona hesitated. "It was from a woman and she said it was personal. I just—it's none of my business, but you were in a kind of a mood this morning, and…I thought I should let you know about this call."

A woman? Personal? He might have hit a pothole with his wife—or maybe plunged into an abyss—but he couldn't think of another woman who would phone him with something personal.

"She said her name was Helen Crawford," Mona informed him, "and it was important and it was personal. She requested that you call her back. I stuck the message in the top drawer of your desk. I didn't think it should be lying around on your blotter where someone might see it."

"I don't know anyone named Helen Crawford."

"Whatever. I'm just passing the message along." Mona hesitated. "Something's going on with you, and to tell you the truth, I'd rather not know. But I don't want to be taking these kinds of messages, okay? Tell her to call you directly."

Mona could be a sweetheart. She could also be a prig. Right now, she was being a bitch. "I don't know what *kind* of message this is. I've never heard of Helen Crawford. So stop implying things."

"I'm not implying anything," Mona said, sounding put upon. "I'm just telling you I decided it was best not to leave this message lying on your desk in full view."

"Thanks." He flipped the phone shut, wondering whether she thought she deserved his gratitude for having insinuated that he'd gotten a phone call from... What? A girlfriend? A mistress? A customer who'd hired him for more than just landscaping?

Honest to God. Not only did he have fissures in his relationship with his wife and his daughter, but now the third most important woman in his life—his loyal officer manager—thought he was screwing around with someone named Helen Crawford, whoever the hell she was.

He'd figure it out later. His life was already a disaster, possibly beyond redemption. If his mystery caller wanted to mess things up even more, let her try.

But not now. He had to finish building a patio. He had to get one thing right in this long, hot, miserable day.

Chapter 8

August 1971

By the time she finally heard from Bobby, she'd already received an official letter from a medical officer:

Dear Mrs. DiFranco,
*   This is to inform you that your husband, P/FC Robert L.*
DiFranco, was wounded in the line of duty during a routine
patrol. He was brought to a field hospital to be stabilized and
then evacuated to a military hospital in Hawaii for further treat-
ment. If you have any questions…

She'd had questions, tons of them. But when she'd dialed the phone number provided in the letter, the woman at the other end of the line had offered no answers. "I'm sure you'll be kept informed about his condition," the woman kept saying. "I'm honestly not sure about the extent of his injuries, but the doctors will be in touch."

The doctors weren't in touch. Joelle had no idea what had happened to Bobby, how serious his injuries were—the words *stabilized* and *evacuated* scared the hell out of her—or what would happen next. She drifted through her days in a trance, feeding Claudia, changing her diapers, feeding her again, laundering her smelly little outfits, rocking her, singing to her and all the while wondering whether she would be a widow before she ever saw Bobby again.

He'd told her, when he'd offered to marry her, that if something happened to him, she could use her widow's benefits to support herself and the baby. Now something had happened to him. She didn't want benefits. She wanted *him*. She wanted him home. She wanted him well. She wanted him to be Bobby D, with a cocky smile and a swagger, lecturing her about his truck's sticky clutch pedal and blasting his Doors albums. She wanted him to know she had a daughter—*they* had a daughter. Had his "routine patrol" occurred before he'd received her letter about Claudia's birth?

At least that question was answered when a letter from him arrived a couple of weeks after the letter notifying her that he'd been wounded in action. He must have left his letter behind when he'd gone on his "routine patrol," and someone had eventually found it and mailed it to her.

Like all Bobby's letters, it was brief. Writing wasn't his thing. He scribbled:

Dear Joelle,

I got the photo. You are both so beautiful. I wish I could be there with you and hold the baby in my own arms. Take care of her for me. Take care of yourself, too. Thank you for naming her Claudia.

He didn't sign his letter *Love, Bobby.* He never signed his letters with love. Neither did Joelle. She figured he was avoiding the word for a reason and she'd best avoid it, too. Maybe the idea of love scared him. Or maybe he just didn't love her. She believed she loved him—but they'd spent less than twenty-four hours as a married couple before he'd left. Did she love *him* or did she love what he'd done for her? Did she love him as a friend, a husband or the father of her baby? Did definitions matter when she felt guilty for devoting more time to worrying about him than about Claudia?

She loved him. She felt so many things when she thought of him, but add them all together and they equaled love. She couldn't expect Bobby to love her, but that didn't matter. What mattered was that she loved him.

The weeks dragged. She fretted that she was a terrible mother, so tired all the time, her breasts leaky and aching, her eyes scratchy from fatigue. When she sang to Claudia, the lullabies were out of tune. When Claudia awakened in the middle of the night for a feeding, Joelle staggered to the crib she'd bought for fifteen dollars at the Goodwill thrift store, lifted Claudia out and plugged a breast into her mouth. She didn't coo to her. She didn't babble and nuzzle her daughter's soft, sweet belly. She was too weary, too frazzled… too afraid of what Bobby would be like when he got home. *If* he came home.

Thank God the preschool where she worked gave her a maternity leave. She could barely manage her own child, let alone nine others. Her housemates spoke in murmurs and handled her chores when she neglected them. When day after day passed with no word from Bobby or his doctors, they hugged her and assured her that everything would be all right.

Then, at last, he phoned. The call came at 10:00 p.m. She'd already bathed Claudia, dressed her in one of the terry-cloth sleepers she'd stocked up on at Woolworth's and was trying to get her to nurse before bed when Lenore hollered up the stairs, "Joelle! Hurry! Bobby's on the phone!"

Joelle nearly tripped racing down the stairs. Bouncing against her shoulder, Claudia fussed and whimpered. They skidded into the kitchen, where Lenore held the receiver of the wall phone while Suzanne pulled a chair from the table closer to the wall so Joelle could sit while she talked. She grabbed the phone from Lenore, settled Claudia into the crook of her arm and drew in a deep breath. "Hello?"

"Jo?" He sounded faint. But he was alive. He knew who she was. Whatever his injuries, they hadn't affected his mind.

"Bobby." She said his name just to taste it, to savor the fact that he was connected to her. She wanted to chant it over and over, to croon it, to cheer it—but that would waste precious time. "Where are you?"

"Hawaii."

"You're still in the hospital?"

"Yeah. I can't talk long. A nurse rigged this call. I just…" Claudia began to fuss again, mewing like a kitten. "Oh, God," he said. "Is that her?"

"That's Claudia." Joelle's cheeks were as damp as Claudia's, but she laughed, too. "That's our baby."

"Oh, God," he said again, softly, like a prayer.

"How are you?"

"I'm okay."

"What happened to you?"

"I can't…" Long-distance static filled the line. Then he spoke. "I'm okay. Making progress."

"Did you—" she couldn't think of a tactful way to ask "—did you lose anything?" She watched the news and read the newspaper. Lots of soldiers arrived home missing limbs, in wheelchairs, paralyzed, damaged beyond description.

"A body part? No."

She started breathing again.

"My leg is f—screwed up," he said, considerately editing out the obscenity. "I had surgery. They put me back together again. They're gonna send me home once I'm vertical."

"Vertical?"

"Walking. Or crutching, I don't know. You'll have to find us a place to live with no stairs. I've got to do rehab before I can deal with stairs."

"All right."

"Call Fort Dix. Someone there'll help you with housing."

"Are you in a lot of pain?"

"It's not too bad." He chuckled. "They give me drugs."

She was desperate to know more. What did "screwed up" mean in regard to his leg? What kind of rehab would he need? What drugs was he taking?

If he'd wanted to go into detail, he would have. Clearly, he didn't wish to. "Should I contact your father?"

The laughter left his voice. "And tell him what?"

"That you were hurt?"

"No." His tone was gentler when he added, "I'm okay, Jo. I'm gonna make it, and I'm gonna come home. All right?"

"Come home," she said. Claudia was sobbing now. So was Joelle. She didn't care if Bobby could hear her tears in her voice. "Just come home."

"I've gotta go. Give Claudia a kiss for me. I'll see you soon." She heard a click, and then dead air.

She should have told him she loved him. Maybe he didn't love her, maybe he didn't want to think about love, but she should have said what was in her heart.

Over the next several weeks, Bobby sent her a few short, cryptic notes: *They've got me doing some exercises. The dizziness is gone.*

What dizziness? she wondered.

My hearing's starting to come back.

His hearing? He'd been deaf? If so, how had he been able to talk to her on the phone?

Guy in the next bed is in really bad shape. I'm so lucky, Jo.

How lucky could he be if he'd had to spend months in a hospital, dizzy and deaf and horizontal? When would he be vertical? When would he get home?

He would get home in early September. She spent most of August searching for a first-floor apartment she and Bobby could afford, signing a lease and furnishing the place on pennies and ingenuity. Her housemates helped. She couldn't imagine how she would have coped without them, and she was reassured when Suzanne was able to find a college student arriving in September who could take over Joelle's room and her share of the expenses.

Anxiety unraveled Joelle's nerves as Bobby's arrival date

drew near. Renee had urged her to buy some sexy underwear for the occasion, but she was still breastfeeding Claudia, and while she'd lost her pregnancy weight, her breasts were fat and the skin of her tummy was still loose and puckered. She hoped Bobby wouldn't be repulsed by the sight. She also hoped she wouldn't be repulsed by the sight of him. What if he was scarred? How could she be fretting about her bloated breasts and baggy tummy after what he'd been through?

How could she be worrying about appearances, at all? When he'd left her, nearly a year ago, he'd been her best friend. Now…she didn't know. He'd fought in a war and she'd become a mother. Would they even recognize each other?

The day before his homecoming, she drove his truck through a car wash and filled it with gas—he'd warned her never to let the needle drop too close to empty. At the grocery store, she splurged on a porterhouse steak and fresh strawberries and Suzanne bought her a bottle of red table wine because Joelle was still too young to buy that herself. The morning he was due, she made the bed with brand-new sheets, gave Claudia a bath and dressed her in her prettiest outfit—a pink dress and matching pink socks that Joelle's mother had sent from Ohio. Despite her swollen breasts, Joelle was able to fit into a sundress she'd sewn last year, a simple sheath hemmed several inches above her knees.

Swallowing her nerves, she drove to McGuire, the air force base adjacent to Fort Dix. A dozen soldiers were scheduled to arrive on the same plane, and an officer corralled Joelle and the other waiting relatives into a fenced-in area near the tarmac. The sun beat down on Claudia in her stroller, and Joelle lowered its canopy to protect her.

The other waiting relatives all seemed joyous. None of them appeared to be wrestling with dread the way she was. But then, the other young wives had probably been married for longer than a day before their husbands had left—and they probably were safe in the knowledge that their husbands loved them.

The plane landed on a distant runway, then taxied over. Someone wheeled a stairway to the door. A woman in uniform opened it and the soldiers emerged, clad in their dress uniforms, many of them with medal ribbons pinned to their shirts. Next to Claudia's stroller, a boy of about five waved an American flag. A few people snapped photographs.

The last soldier to emerge was Bobby. She absorbed the sight of him, framed by the plane's doorway. He was standing. His hair was longer than she'd expected, but she supposed he hadn't needed a buzz cut while he'd been in the hospital. He handed a pair of crutches to the soldier in front of him, who headed down the stairs, leaving Bobby to maneuver the descent alone, his hands gripping the railings for support. His left leg was strapped into a metal brace that resembled a medieval torture device. He extended that leg in front of him and hopped down the stairs on his right foot. At the bottom of the steps, he took back the crutches, said something to the soldier who'd been holding them and then gazed at the fence. At Joelle.

All the other soldiers ran once they spotted their loved ones. Bobby couldn't run. Joelle wished she could run to him, but the relatives had been ordered to stay behind the fence. So she only watched him as he made his laborious way across the asphalt.

As he neared, she searched his face. No obvious scars, but his appearance had changed. His eyes were darker, more wary.

His easy smile was nowhere in evidence. Maybe he wasn't happy to see her.

He passed through the gate and hobbled over to her. The bone slid in his neck as he swallowed. "Bobby," she murmured, then mustered her courage and rose on tiptoe to kiss his cheek.

"Jo." He didn't kiss her back. His gaze was on the stroller. "Pick her up," he said.

She folded back the canopy, unstrapped Claudia and lifted her so Bobby could see her. He stared at her and his eyes grew misty. She stared right back, then reached out and tried to grab his nose.

He allowed himself a smile as he ducked his head, evading her pudgy little hand. "Hey, there," he whispered. "Hey, little girl. You know who I am?"

Claudia issued a cheerful gurgling sound.

"I'm your daddy," Bobby said. "I'm your dad." He bowed and brushed her cheek with his, then leaned back and met Joelle's eyes. His smile didn't completely disappear, thank God. He'd saved a little of it for her. "Let's get out of here," he said.

Someone lugged Bobby's duffel to the truck. Someone else folded the stroller and put it in the flatbed while Joelle strapped Claudia into her baby carrier. The truck's front seat would be crowded with all three of them crammed in—especially since Bobby had his crutches and couldn't bend his leg. She supposed that was what a family was: everyone crowded together.

The drive back to the apartment passed in silence, and Joelle's nerves frayed until they were nothing but ragged threads. When she glanced at Bobby, she saw him gazing out the window, his face blank. Maybe viewing New Jersey's sub-urban sprawl was a shock to him after Vietnam and more than two months in a hospital. Or maybe she and Bobby just didn't know how to talk to each other anymore.

His expression remained inscrutable as she led him into the apartment. It wasn't grand, but she'd knocked herself out to make it as pretty as she could on a budget of zero. She'd picked daisies growing along a roadway and stuck them in an empty Coke bottle to create a centerpiece for the coffee table in the living room. She'd sewn curtains for the windows and throw pillows for the couch. She'd bought a small black-and-white TV with a rabbit-ear antenna at the St. Vincent de Paul store. She'd set up a corner of the bedroom as a nursery area, squeezing in Claudia's crib and the changing table she'd created out of an old kitchen table and a colorful plastic pad. When Claudia had been born, the women at the house had bought her a mobile of butterflies, which Joelle had fastened to the crib railing so the colorful butterflies floated above her when she slept.

Bobby thumped around the apartment on his crutches, saying nothing.

"Is it all right?" she asked. "For what we could afford, I—"

"It's fine," he said.

They ate their steak dinner. Bobby didn't want any wine, so Joelle skipped it, as well. He watched TV while she got Claudia ready for bed. Once she had the baby down for the night, she joined Bobby on the couch. "Can you tell me about your leg?" she asked.

He forced a grim smile. "They had to use some bolts to pin the bones together. I'll have another surgery to remove those once it's healed."

"But it *will* heal." She asked more than said it.

"That's what they tell me."

"And your hearing?"

"It's back."

"Anything else?"

His gaze was haggard as he glanced her way. "I don't want to talk about it."

"Okay." She dared to touch his wrist. "If you change your mind, I'm here, Bobby."

He didn't move his arm away, but he didn't twist his hand to capture hers, either. They sat for another hour, her fingers resting on the back of his wrist, and watched *The Mod Squad*. Then he went off to the tiny bathroom to shower, insisting he didn't need any help.

While he was in the bathroom, she undressed, setting aside her boring underwear and putting on the prettiest nightgown she owned, thin white cotton with flowers embroidered on the front and the shadows of her body visible through the fabric. She turned down the blanket and brushed her hair a hundred strokes and prayed that she and Bobby would connect in bed, even if they hadn't connected on the couch. Their wedding night had been so wonderful. She wanted that closeness again. She wanted Bobby back.

He crutched into the bedroom, clad in sweatpants and a clean T-shirt—olive drab, army issue. His hair was wet, and the spicy scent of his shampoo nearly overpowered the sweet perfume of baby powder that filled the air. He made his way to the bed, dropped his crutches on the floor beside him and unstrapped his brace. Then he lay down.

Joelle hurried into the bathroom. It was humid and smelled of soap and toothpaste, of Bobby. She washed, inserted the diaphragm the midwife had urged her to buy—"People say you can't get pregnant when you're nursing, but that's not true," she'd warned—and returned to the bedroom. He'd turned off the lamp on his side of the bed and pulled the covers up to his waist. If he'd noticed the pretty new sheets, he didn't mention them.

She climbed into bed next to him, switched off her bedside lamp and waited. Nearly a year had passed since they'd been together. Nearly a year since they'd been intimate. Maybe he'd visited prostitutes in Vietnam—soldiers did that—and he'd realized that he longed for a more experienced woman. Joelle knew next to nothing about lovemaking, and even after bathing she smelled like baby's milk, and Bobby had been around the world and he'd probably been with all kinds of sexy, worldly women who could satisfy him so much better than Joelle could.

Still, she was his wife.

He made no move toward her. She wondered whether he was in pain, whether his leg just didn't work well enough. Drawing again on every ounce of courage she possessed, she rose and leaned over him. Even in the dark, she could see his face. She touched her lips to his.

He kissed her back, gently, softly. He lifted his hand to her cheek, dug his fingers into her hair and closed his eyes. A shudder passed through him, and she felt him withdraw. Even before he let his hand drop, she realized she'd lost him.

"Bobby—"

"Don't," he whispered. She heard his sigh, and the steady rhythm of Claudia's breathing as she slept across the room. "I don't know where I am yet. I need..."

"Time?" she said helpfully.

"Yeah."

"Okay."

"I'm sorry."

"No, Bobby—don't be sorry. It's okay. Really."

He said nothing more, but shifted on the mattress, retreating.

She rolled away from him and squeezed her eyes shut to keep from crying.

The next day, Bobby and Joelle drove to a used-car lot and traded in his beloved truck for a five-year-old Chevy Nova with eighty thousand miles on it. It had an automatic transmission, so he'd be able to drive it without a functioning left leg. Joelle had never been enamored of the truck, but Bobby's wistfulness was obvious as he signed the paperwork and handed the truck's keys over to the salesman.

Once he had a vehicle he could drive, he concentrated on organizing his life. Three days a week, he would attend physical therapy sessions at the V.A. hospital. The other two days, Claudia stayed home with him. He carried her around in a pouch Joelle had fashioned from an old knapsack, and together they ran errands and visited the playground. Bobby rigged a device out of pieces of an old bicycle's handlebar that enabled him to push Claudia's stroller with his chest while he propelled himself along on his crutches.

Joelle was impressed by his determination and focus, and pleased that he was no longer smoking. "Did they make you quit at the hospital?" she asked when he'd been home for nearly a week and she hadn't seen him light up once.

"I quit for Claudia," he said. He didn't elaborate, and Joelle didn't press him. Whatever the reason, she was glad he'd kicked the habit.

He might have demonstrated good judgment about the

smoking, and he was without question a devoted father. But still, a wide emptiness gaped between him and Joelle. He loved perching Claudia on his lap and letting her tug on his fingers, which would cause her to squeal with joy. He never gave his hand to Joelle to hold, though. Sometimes he smiled at her, sometimes he patted her shoulder as he maneuvered around her in the apartment's cramped, dark kitchen and once, while playing one of his Doors albums on the portable record player she'd found at a garage sale, he'd smiled at her and crooned, "'Come on, baby, light my fire'" along with Jim Morrison.

But when he climbed into bed, clad in sweatpants and a T-shirt... Nothing. He wouldn't reach for her. He wouldn't talk to her. He wouldn't touch her.

One night in late September, Suzanne invited them over to the house for dinner, claiming everyone missed Claudia and wanted to meet Bobby. He was a good sport about it, even though Joelle guessed an evening spent with a group of women wasn't his idea of fun. Suzanne made lasagna, thank God, and not one of her lentil-and-bean casseroles. Everyone but Bobby drank wine. Joelle wondered whether he was declining alcohol because of the painkillers he still occasionally took. That she didn't know—that her husband wouldn't discuss with her why he refused to drink wine—only proved that their marriage was a farce.

She drank enough for both of them, figuring she could indulge since he'd be driving them home. Bobby bore up well as her old housemates peppered him with friendly questions. The student who had taken over Joelle's room when she'd moved out tried to explain to him why the Vietnam War was a bad thing, but he was more knowledgeable about the subject than she was, and he didn't need her lecture. "I got drafted," he explained. "Don't blame me."

After dinner, he and Claudia settled in the living room with a few of the women. Someone turned on the stereo and strains of Joni Mitchell seeped into the air. Joelle suppressed a chuckle. Joni Mitchell was such girlie music. Listening to her sweet, trilling soprano as she sang about heartache and romances gone sour was probably torture to Bobby.

Suzanne asked Joelle to keep her company in the kitchen while she cleaned up. Joelle refilled her glass with wine and gathered some plates from the table.

"I think everyone here has a crush on him," Suzanne said. "He's really cute."

"I know." He no longer appeared as drawn as he had the day he'd limped off the plane. His hair continued to grow in, black and thick with waves and he smiled a little more often. He'd always had a strong physique, but propelling himself around on crutches had built up the muscles in his arms and shoulders. As for the rest of his body, she couldn't say. She hadn't seen him undressed since the night they'd gotten married, close to a year ago. He'd been thin when he'd hobbled down the steps from the plane at McGuire; she suspected he'd gained a few pounds since he'd gotten home, which he'd desperately needed.

"You, on the other hand, look like hell," Suzanne said as she squirted dishwashing soap into the deep-basin sink.

"Thanks." Joelle smiled feebly. "I'm just tired, Suzanne. Between work and the baby and taking care of Bobby—"

"Does he want you taking care of him? For a guy recovering from some serious injuries, he seems to be doing pretty well."

"He is. But…" Joelle shrugged and drained her wineglass, then busied herself wrapping the leftover garlic bread in aluminum foil.

Suzanne eyed her sharply. "But what?"

Joelle adored Suzanne. The woman had been the big sister she'd never had, the surrogate mother she'd needed over the past year. Yet how could she tell her the truth—that her husband didn't desire her anymore? That their marriage had never been real, that they'd entered into it with the understanding that they could divorce each other once Bobby's military service was done? That he'd married her only because she'd been in trouble and desperate to keep her baby, not because he loved her?

"It's an adjustment," she finally said, because she had to say something.

"There are marriage counselors," Suzanne reminded her. "And don't tell me you can't afford them. I bet the army provides free counseling. You're not the only couple separated by the war and having adjustment problems." Suzanne shook the water from her hands and clamped them on Joelle's shoulders. "Talk to someone, Joelle. Get this worked out. If you love him, it's worth the fight."

Suzanne's words echoed inside Joelle as she and Bobby drove back to their apartment in the dark New Jersey night. Claudia lay strapped into her seat between them, pulling on one of her bare feet and making gurgling noises. "Bobby," Joelle called across the seat to him.

His gaze remained on the road. His profile could have been carved from granite it was so still.

"Maybe…maybe we ought to see a counselor."

In the glow from an oncoming car's headlights, she noticed a muscle ticking in his jaw. "I don't need a shrink."

"Not a shrink, Bobby—"

"You think I'm a head case?"

"No." She put more force into her voice. "I didn't mean *you* should see someone. I meant *us*. I was thinking of a marriage counselor."

He shot her a look, then turned back to the road. He said nothing.

Was he insulted? Hurt? She knew he wasn't given to deep introspection. She wasn't big on that, either—but their marriage was a disaster. Either they had to fix it or they had to quit.

His silence convinced her he'd just as soon quit.

It's worth the fight, Suzanne had said. If only Joelle had some idea about the right tactics. She wasn't the soldier in this car. She was nineteen years old, a mother, living in the amorphous center of suburban New Jersey because that was where an army base happened to be, not because it was her home. She was married to a man who had proposed to her with the promise that they could get out of this marriage if they wanted, no hard feelings.

"Do you want us to be married?" she asked, hoping he didn't hear the quiver in her voice. She was trying to be strong, tough, fighting for the man who was her husband.

He shot her another look. "Do we really have to have this discussion?" he asked. "You've been drinking wine all night."

"I'm not drunk. And all I'm asking—" *is for you to love me.*

Claudia chose that moment to start crying. Her outburst gave Bobby an excuse not to respond to Joelle. He winced at Claudia's wailing and steered in to the parking lot of their apartment complex. Joelle rubbed Claudia's belly, hoping to soothe her. But Claudia continued to howl all the way to their assigned parking space outside the door of their building.

Bobby shut off the engine and Joelle unstrapped Claudia. She took the baby onto her shoulder and rocked her. "Something happened to you in Vietnam—"

"No kidding," he muttered.

"And now, I just... You said we could split up when you got back. Is that what you want?"

"Joelle." He practically had to shout to be audible over Claudia's shrieks. "Why are we screaming at each other in the car?"

"Because you won't say what's going on with you!" She felt as frantic and frustrated as Claudia. "You never talk to me, Bobby. You never tell me what you're going through, what you're thinking. You won't even tell me what you went through over there."

"I don't want to talk about that."

"Yeah, I've figured that out. You don't want to talk about anything that matters. I'm your wife, Bobby—at least, I am right now. And you won't even—I mean, when you were wounded... You don't act like a husband. You don't..." She was too embarrassed to ask him why he wouldn't kiss her, gather her into his arms, make love to her the way he had on that lumpy motel bed a year ago. "You don't do what a husband does," she finished feebly. "I can't help wondering if maybe, when you were wounded..."

"Were my balls blown off?" His hands gripped the steering wheel so tightly she was afraid he might crush the plastic. "No."

Then the problem was her. He just didn't want her.

Too hurt to respond, she shoved open her door and swung out of the car. Getting out of the car took Bobby longer; his leg didn't move well and he had to retrieve his crutches from the floor of the backseat. Joelle didn't wait for him. She stormed into the building, silently howling along with Claudia.

Inside their apartment, she marched straight to the bedroom, to Claudia's changing table. The baby's diaper was full of poop, and once Joelle had her cleaned up and snapped into a sleeper, she subsided. A few minutes of nursing, and she fell into a peaceful slumber.

Joelle didn't feel peaceful. She couldn't imagine falling asleep. But it was nearly eleven, and she wasn't going to stay awake and chat amiably with Bobby, who had remained in the living room the whole time she was dealing with Claudia. She shut herself up in the bathroom, washed, changed into a nightgown and bundled under the covers, even though the room was too warm for a blanket. The sheets smelled of fabric softener. She laundered them every week, despite the fact that not enough life existed in their bed to warrant that much laundering.

After a while, Bobby joined her. As always, he wore sweatpants and a T-shirt. As always, he remained on his side of the bed. He might as well have been in Ohio, for all the distance between them. He might as well have been in Vietnam.

He lay motionless, his respiration growing deeper and more regular as he sank into unconsciousness. She stared into the darkness, too agitated even to close her eyes. What should she do? If they got a divorce, where would she go? She couldn't move back to Suzanne's house; her room there was occupied by that new college student. And she sure as hell couldn't go back to Holmdell.

Nor would Bobby pay her alimony if they divorced. She was earning more money than he received from the V.A. Maybe he was staying with her only because of her salary.

"Shank," he mumbled.

She turned to look at him. Her eyes had adjusted to the gloom, and she could see his face contorted, his body twitching.

"Shank. Shank."

What was he talking about?

He flinched, deep inside a nightmare. "Oh, Jesus—Shank?"

She sat up and leaned toward him. He might not love her—he might even hate her—but the humane thing was to awaken him from his terrifying dream. "Bobby…"

She reached out to shake his shoulder. His body thrashed, his arms flying. Before she could duck, his fist connected solidly with her cheekbone.

She screamed.

Bobby opened his eyes in time to see Joelle leap out of bed and run out of the room. From the crib rose a thin, anxious wail. He cursed. His body was damp with sweat, his head throbbing, his bad leg rattling with pain.

Just when he'd thought he couldn't do any more damage, couldn't cause more destruction, couldn't ruin Joelle's life more than he already had, he'd hit her. That he'd been asleep at the time didn't matter. He'd hit Joelle and he'd hurt her, and he wasn't sure how he was going to live with himself.

He'd had lots of nightmares during his months at the hospital, but they'd tapered off since his discharge. Sure, he continued to suffer from flashbacks, tremors, black memories, but nothing so fierce it made him flail and punch people. Why he'd done that tonight he couldn't say, unless it had something to do with Joelle's accusations in the car.

An evening drinking wine with her girlfriends had given

her the courage to take him on, and she'd slammed into him hard. Every word she'd said was true—except when she'd denied thinking he was a head case. He was. The war had messed with his brain, and he was afraid to tell her, afraid for her to think he really was insane.

Maybe he ought to leave, let her go, give her the chance to find someone better than him, someone who wasn't all busted up inside and out. Someone able to love her the way she deserved to be loved.

Claudia had revved up to a full-throttle roar. Bobby reached for his crutches and eased himself to his feet, not bothering with the brace. Two hops brought him to the crib's railing. Leaning against it for balance, he lifted Claudia onto his shoulder. He'd noticed that she liked big shoulders. She calmed down a lot quicker when he was holding her than when Joelle was.

Eventually Claudia wound down, sniffled, pressed her moist, overheated face against his neck and let out a breath. A few more minutes and she was asleep.

He lowered her into the crib, then pivoted and observed the empty bed. The blanket was rumpled, the sheets untucked.

Steeling himself for the likelihood that Joelle had fled the apartment, he hobbled out of the bedroom and into the living room. Relief swamped him when he saw her seated on the couch, pressing a lumpy dish towel to her face.

He worked his way over to the couch, lowered himself beside her and nudged the towel away. The lumps, he realized, were ice cubes. The skin where she'd been holding the compress to her face was cold and imprinted with the towel's texture. A faint red mark along her cheekbone told him where he'd hit her. He'd bruised her. Hell.

"I'm sorry," he said.

"You didn't know what you were doing." Refusing to look at him, she directed her words to her knees. "You were sleeping."

"I'm still sorry." That faint red mark might as well have been a gushing wound. He'd promised her, the night they'd gotten married, that he would never hurt her. Add a broken promise to all the other reasons he was no good for her. "What you said earlier—if you want to leave me—"

"I don't want to leave you," she retorted. "I want you to..." She drew in a deep breath. "Touch me," she whispered, still staring at her lap. "I know you don't desire me. The pregnancy made me all pudgy—"

"Oh, God, Joelle." He closed his eyes, as if not viewing her would make him want her less. But even with his eyes closed he saw her, her soft golden hair, her soft body, her soft blue eyes. He had been watching her since the moment he'd spotted her behind the fence at McGuire, wearing a sleeveless minidress that showed off her graceful arms and legs. He watched her when she washed dishes, her fingers glistening with soap, and when she entered the apartment after a day working at the preschool, her hair disheveled and a smear of fingerpaint on her shirt. He watched her when she fed the baby. She always tried to cover herself with a cloth or the edge of her shirt when she nursed, but he could see. The sight of her nursing Claudia was so beautiful it pained him.

Everything pained him. That was the thing. His body ached, his mind ached, his soul ached. Joelle was lovely, untouched by anything mean and ugly and violent, and he was scarred, so grotesque he couldn't bear for her to get close to him.

And damn it, he *had* touched her—in a mean, ugly way. The bruise below her eye was smaller than one of Claudia's hands, but it was there.

"Why were you talking about a shank?" she asked.

His eyes opened. "When?"

"In your dream. You kept saying 'shank, shank.'"

"Schenk," he corrected her, then closed his eyes again and leaned away from her.

"Schenk?"

"One of the guys in my platoon." His voice went paper thin.

"Tell me what happened, Bobby. Tell me about your dream."

He sighed. If she wanted to know—if she really wanted to know why he'd been such a crappy husband, such a poor excuse for a human being—he would tell her. "Schenk always had a canteen full of booze with him, even during the day, when we were out in the field. He'd share it if you wanted some, but it was vile stuff. He was…kind of wild, but a good guy. He'd give you the shirt off his back. Or the rotgut out of his canteen."

Joelle twisted on the couch, tucking one foot under her other thigh and facing him. Her expression was solemn, expectant.

"We were on patrol, and he was taking a hit from the canteen and he tripped a wire. I was maybe three, four feet away from him. All I saw…" A wave of nausea swept through him and he swallowed, wishing he could speak the memory without living it. "All I saw was red. There was no more Schenk."

She didn't fall apart, thank God, or do anything to indicate she pitied him. She only nodded.

"I was shouting—only, I couldn't hear my voice. I started running toward him—only, I wasn't moving. In my head I was running and shouting, but I was just...just lying there, seeing red."

She reached for his hand, but he drew back. She hadn't heard the worst of it yet.

"It wasn't just my leg. The explosion ruptured my left eardrum, but that healed. I had shrapnel embedded in my back, my side. The shrapnel didn't only come from the mine, Jo. It..." Another wave of nausea hit him, but he fought it off. "It came from Schenk. Pieces of his canteen. Pieces of his rifle, his helmet... Pieces of *him*."

She reached for him again, this time snagging his hand before he could pull it away. Her fingers were cool and smooth and gentle. He felt tears sting his eyes; he didn't deserve her gentleness.

"Did they get all the shrapnel out?" she asked.

He shook his head. "They don't remove it surgically, unless it's in an organ. If it's just in your skin, they leave it. It comes out on its own over time." His nausea seemed to fade, mostly because Joelle wasn't grossed out. She appeared sad, even anguished, but not disgusted. "It's still coming out, Jo. I can't let you see my body. Can you understand that?"

"I can understand it," she said, "but I'm your wife. If you want this marriage to work, you can't hide from me. I'm your wife, Bobby." She rose onto her knees, released his hand and freed his T-shirt from the waistband of his sweats. Jaw set, lower lip caught between her teeth, she shoved the shirt up, over his head and off.

He watched her while she scrutinized his torso, the mosaic of sores and scars along his side. Some of the wounds had closed into ropy pink scar tissue. Others were scabbed. He knew how grotesque he looked. He inspected himself in the mirror every day after his shower, searching for bits of shrapnel that had worked their way to the surface of his skin, reading his wounds as if they were some kind of obscene graffiti.

Joelle didn't recoil. She ran her hand lightly over his side, then shifted to view his back. Even the nurses in Hawaii hadn't ministered to him as gently as she did. "Does it hurt?"

"No." Not physically. Emotionally it was excruciating.

"I want to see your leg," she said.

"That's not so pretty, either." The grueling physical therapy was only just beginning to rebuild his wasted muscles, and he had surgical scars running like train tracks near his ankle and knee and along his thigh. But he couldn't bring himself to stop her as she untied the drawstring and eased his sweatpants out from under his butt and down his legs. There he was, naked, mutilated. Not the man she'd married. Not the man he'd been before Vietnam had done a number on him.

Her hand glided the length of his legs, moving her fingers lightly across the scars on his left leg, tactfully not mentioning that the calf of that leg was a good three inches smaller in circumference than its mate. Her palms floated, glided. They were cool, but they made his skin burn. As she skimmed her hands up his thighs, the burning traveled with them. By the time she'd arrived at his groin, he was practically in flames.

She raised her face to him, then inched one hand around his dick and stroked. Slow and tight.

She'd seen him and she hadn't run away. If he hadn't already loved her, he would have fallen madly in love right now, just because she was there, touching him, accepting what he was.

He gripped her shoulders and pulled her to him, sinking into the cushions and bringing her with him. He kissed her, kissed her with everything he had, every bit of strength, every bit of trust and yearning and love the war hadn't wrung out of him. She kissed him back, matching his passion, his desperation.

By the time she broke the kiss and gulped in a breath, he was ready to burst. "The bed might be more comfortable," she murmured.

"It's a friggin' nursery in there," he argued. He wasn't even sure he could make love to her when his leg wasn't working. He sure as hell couldn't make love to her with Claudia snoring just inches away from them and the air smelling like baby powder.

Joelle smiled hesitantly, a little nervously, then leaned back and lifted her nightgown over her head. A surge of lust ripped through him as he gazed up at her. "You are so beautiful," he whispered.

She made a face. "I've got stretch marks, and my breasts are too big—"

"No such thing as too big," he argued, filling his hands with her breasts. He caressed them, then slid his hands down to her belly, to her crotch. She was already wet, and he was dying for her. Clamping her hips, he urged her down onto him.

As bad as he'd been feeling for far too long, that was how good he felt now, inside her. From nightmare to dream, from hell to heaven, it was a change so swift he felt a whiplash in his spine.

She seemed uncertain, and he realized she'd probably never been on top before. What was her experience, anyway? One night with him, and one other guy he refused to think about.

He used his hands to guide her, moving her up and down. His body strained, pressed, wanted. He wasn't going to last—

he knew that. His first time with Joelle in nearly a year, his first time since his world had come apart, and she was so soft and warm and snug around him, her skin like velvet, her hair spilling down into his face. He had no willpower, no staying power, nothing. Nothing but the pulse pounding in his head, the fire in his balls, the tension in his muscles as Joelle rode him. Nothing but gratitude and fear and love.

He tried to slow her down, but she was rocking on her own now, emitting hushed, throaty sounds. He wedged one hand between them, and when she rose, he found her with his fingers. She let out a cry, and that was it. He was gone, his body wrenching, emptying, spilling into her.

She collapsed on top of him, light and limp. He closed his eyes, closed his arms around her and willed his heart to stop hammering in his chest. He didn't deserve a woman as good as she was, a woman so sexy, a woman who could accept his ravaged body, who could accept him when he'd shut her out for so long, when he'd been so sure she would reject him. He didn't deserve this.

But it was his, at least for now, and he'd take it.

Chapter 9

Joelle looked at the shrimp, on skewers, swimming in teriyaki sauce and ready for the grill. They'd been marinating for hours, far longer than necessary. Right now, she was ready to throw them into the trash.

She heard a rumble in the garage, the truck's engine echoing off the concrete walls, idling and then shutting off. The understanding that Bobby was finally home caused her hands to clench so tightly her fingertips tingled. Her gaze rose to the clock on the wall oven's facade: seven-thirty.

Would he be drunk this time? Would he break things and puke and act like a jerk? Had she been a fool to spend hours fussing with her shrimp, measuring rice and water into a pot, hoping that her having prepared yet another of his favorite meals would soften him up? Her lasagna hadn't made a difference. Her rosemary chicken hadn't. Nor had her rib-eye steaks.

Grilled shrimp teriyaki? While he'd been out doing who knew what?

She listened to the door opening, and then the clomp of his boots in the mudroom. *Don't throw a tantrum,* she reminded herself. *Don't jump down his throat the instant you see him.* Her willpower was in short supply, though. She'd been building up to this moment ever since she'd gotten that phone call an hour ago. She wanted to scream, to flail, to force that fool husband of hers to tell her what the hell was going on.

He swung into the kitchen, his hair windswept, his skin darker than it had been just a week ago. He'd been working outdoors a lot, building a patio in Arlington and consulting on a plaza at a college down in Bridgeport. Unlike her, he wasn't fair-skinned. A few days in the summer sun and his complexion turned brick-brown.

He didn't seem drunk. But that was the least of her worries.

Without a word, he crossed to the sink and twisted on the faucet. He washed his hands, using soap, lathering up past his wrists. What was he washing away?

"Who is she?" she asked when she couldn't stand the silence anymore.

He gazed over his shoulder, scowled, then tore a few squares of paper towel from the roll. "Who is who?"

"The woman you were having a drink with," she said, her nerves cutting through her voice like jagged bits of broken glass.

He shot her an unreadable look.

"Harriet Briggs from down the street saw you go into the Hay Street Pub with a woman. She followed you inside. You and that woman were at a table for two."

"And then Harriet raced outside and phoned you," Bobby muttered. "She's a bitch. She's always trying to stir up trouble."

"She can't stir up trouble unless there's trouble to stir up." Joelle leaned against the counter and crossed her arms over her chest. That position forced her to relax her fists before her nails drew blood from her palms.

She wasn't jealous by nature. Early in her marriage, she'd been envious of other women—women whose husbands had married them for all the right reasons, women certain that their husbands loved them, women who understood sex in ways she didn't. She'd wondered whether Bobby might have been with other women while he'd been in 'Nam. True, he'd been a married man, but their marriage had barely existed when he'd left her. Just one night, and then he'd been gone.

But he'd come home, and they'd stuck together and her schoolgirl insecurities had gradually faded.

They were back now. Drew's invasion into their lives re-awakened all her anxieties, her worries about whether she was good enough, whether she should still feel beholden to Bobby for having married her. And he was obviously so angry with her now. If he could get drunk like his father, what else was he capable of doing?

"The woman," he said slowly, his frown aging his face, "was Helen Crawford."

That name meant nothing to Joelle.

"You don't know her," Bobby continued, parceling out information as if it were more precious than gold. "She's Foster's wife."

Drew's wife? Bobby had been having a drink with Drew's wife? Joelle struggled not to launch herself at him, grip his shoulders and shake him until the whole truth spilled out.

"She called and said she wanted to meet me. So I said okay, and she drove up to Gray Hill."

"And you took her to a bar?"

"I had iced tea. She had a wine cooler." He tossed the paper towels into the trash and turned back to Joelle. "She looks a little like you. Foster must have a thing for blondes."

How could he act so calm, so aloof? Didn't he realize their marriage was disintegrating? He was the one who'd said they were perched on a stone wall that was about to collapse. That was last Sunday. Now it was Thursday, and the stones were scattering and slipping. She and Bobby were in a free fall with no soft place to land.

And he chose to talk about Drew Foster's taste for blondes?

"Why didn't you call me?" she asked. "I would have met you there."

"Helen didn't want you there. She wanted to talk to me alone."

Joelle stared at him. Even across the room, he seemed to loom above her, tall and sturdy. He hadn't removed his boots, and their thick, ridged soles added an extra inch to his height.

Had Drew Foster's wife noticed what a handsome man he was? Did the women Drew had a thing for have a thing for Bobby?

"Why did she want to talk to you alone? Am I allowed to ask that?" She wished she could behave as detached as Bobby, but she couldn't. Panic churned inside her, searing her stomach with acid.

Bobby didn't comment on her sarcasm. He crossed to the refrigerator, swung open the door and pulled out a can of ginger ale. He snapped the top, took a sip, then dropped onto a chair by the table. That made him seem a little less imposing, at least.

"She said she and I were…how did she put it? The outer corners of a trapezoid."

"What?" Joelle would have laughed if she hadn't been so upset.

"There are four people involved, so we can't be a triangle. But we're not a square, because we've got different investments in this situation. So we're a trapezoid." He must have sensed Joelle's bemusement, because he shrugged. "I'm just quoting her."

"Yes, we aren't a triangle," Joelle said. Besides, a triangle would imply there was something going on between her and Drew.

He shrugged again. "She said she was still in shock from the news that her husband had fathered a child out of wedlock. She just learned about it a few weeks ago."

"So did he," Joelle pointed out. "Until he hired that detective to find me, he had no idea that I hadn't used his money to get an abortion."

"He knew he'd knocked you up," Bobby reminded her, his voice taking on an edge of its own. His words were cold and bitter.

"So...what? His wife decided to get together with you and plot against Drew?" *And against me?* she almost added.

"We didn't plot anything." He swallowed some ginger ale and leaned back in his chair. His eyes were tired, his mouth grim. "She wants her son to have a chance. I felt sorry for her. Her kid is critically ill and her husband is a freaking son of a bitch. So she wanted to drink a wine cooler and vent a little. No harm in that."

Like hell. Bobby had given this poor grieving woman his shoulder to lean on, and all the while Joelle had been home, exerting herself to prepare yet another special dinner for him while she fretted about how to mend their marriage. "You could have called and told me you'd be late. I was worried. I didn't know where you were."

"Yes, you did. Harriet Briggs told you." He drank some more soda. "I had a drink and a conversation with a woman, and you automatically assumed the worst."

"Bobby—"

He peered up at her and she noticed more than weariness in his eyes. "What did you think? I was doing something wrong with this woman? Having an affair? What?" His gaze was stormy. "You have that little faith in me?"

"Of course I have faith in you," she said, but her voice wavered and she averted her eyes. Yes, she'd assumed the worst. Given the current state of their marriage, given that the last time Bobby had touched her she'd instigated it and he'd wound up pounding into her like someone crazed, she'd assumed the absolute worst.

At one time she'd had faith in Bobby, in herself, in their marriage. But tonight...the faith wasn't there.

"What have I done that would make you stop trusting me?" he challenged her.

"Three days ago you came home drunk."

He scowled. "Lots of men come home drunk every day. My father did."

"And I haven't been able to talk to you. There's all this anger. You resent me."

"What makes you think that?"

"It's there, Bobby. In the silence. In everything you don't say, everything you won't tell me. All I feel coming from you these days is hostility."

His scowl intensified, making her feel even more hostility.

"Maybe we should get counseling," she said, then braced herself for his response.

As she'd expected, it wasn't positive. He hammered his fist against the table. "I'm not going to bare my soul in front of a total stranger."

"But we can't talk anymore. Maybe a therapist would help get us talking."

"We're talking now."

"And saying nothing. Nothing that matters. You're stewing inside, Bobby. It's like when you came back from the war and you had all this rage inside you, and you wouldn't let it out. That's what you're like now."

"Who needs a counselor when I've got you?" he snapped. "You've got me all figured out, Jo. Why waste time talking?"

"You consider talking a waste?"

"Talking about this is." He thumped his hand against the table again. "What should I say? All Claudia's life, I was her father. Now I'm not. That's all there is to it."

That wasn't all there was. "What about our marriage?" she asked. "Isn't that about more than Claudia?"

"You married me because you had to," he reminded her, his voice taut and low. "You married me to protect Claudia. Now she doesn't have that protection anymore. The reason we got married—it doesn't exist anymore."

"But our marriage still exists, Bobby. You're saying there's no reason for that?"

He eyed her sharply. "I was Claudia's father, and you took that away from me."

Joelle's legs faltered beneath her. Her vision blurred, then sharpened into painful focus on the man seated at the table in the center of her kitchen. Was that really how he felt, after all these years?

She knew he hadn't married her out of love. Marrying her

had been an act of enormous kindness and generosity on his part—and she'd done her best to show her gratitude over the years. She'd confided in him, cooked for him, argued with him, goaded him, cheered him on. She'd shared his bed.

Now their bed was cold and barren, a reflection of their marriage. It was no longer a haven where they could shut out the world and open to each other. It had become a place she dreaded.

"When we got married," she said, struggling to keep her voice level, "you said we'd go into it with the understanding that we could always get a divorce. Now you're saying the reason we got married doesn't exist anymore. Do you want to cash in? Play your get-out-of-jail card?"

"I didn't say—"

"You said I married you only because of Claudia. *You* married *me* only because of Claudia. Now that reason is gone." Could he hear the tremor in her tone? Could he tell she was struggling not to shake? "What's left? What is this marriage really about?"

He turned to stare out the window, avoiding Joelle. "God only knows," he muttered.

"Then what do you want from me? A divorce?" Maybe if she said the word enough, she might begin to accept its weight.

"I want…" He looked at her. "I want what we had before. And I can't have that anymore. You took that away from us. It's gone."

Bobby so rarely allowed her to glimpse his soul. Opening him up was like chiseling through solid stone. When he'd been ravaged by injuries and nightmares after the war, she'd had to drag his feelings out of him. He never would have told her if she hadn't forced him.

She'd forced him now, and his feelings lay plain before her. The foundation of their marriage had vanished, and he blamed her for it.

Holding her face immobile, refusing to let him see the devastation he'd inflicted on her, she carried the tray of shrimp to the refrigerator and slid it onto a shelf. Then she walked out of the kitchen, away from her husband. Away from the man who felt their marriage no longer had a reason to exist.

He made a point of driving home early the next day.

Their bed had turned into hostile territory, as ominously quiet as patrol in 'Nam. He and Joelle slept side by side like strangers. Every night he lay awake, holding himself motionless, wondering where the mines were and how close he was to tripping one. And sometimes not even caring if he did.

Things couldn't go on this way. He had to find his way back to Joelle. Tonight was Friday, and they had a weekend ahead of them. They would talk. Talking—*real* talking, personal talking—didn't come easily to him, but he'd try.

He'd been an idiot last night. He should have phoned Joelle and told her he was getting together with Foster's wife after work. When Helen Crawford had said she wanted to meet with him alone, because he and she were the two "outsiders" in this situation—whatever the hell that meant—he should have said no, that Joelle ought to be included. But Helen had shown up at his office, slim and pretty and as fresh as an ocean breeze, her face unnaturally smooth and her blond hair containing not a single strand of silver, and when she'd said, "Let's go somewhere and talk," he'd said sure. As they'd left his office, he'd felt Mona's eyes on him, as suspicious as any wife, and he hadn't cared.

Helen had dominated the conversation; he'd mostly listened. She'd told him about how shocked she'd been to learn of Claudia's existence. "Thrilled and appalled at the same time," she'd explained. "Thrilled that my son might have a chance to beat his leukemia, but appalled that Drew had been so careless and thoughtless all those years ago. He'd been young and foolish, of course, but it's one thing to be young and foolish and another to impregnate a girl and then leave her to fend for herself."

Bobby hadn't had an argument for that.

"At least you knew the truth all along," she'd gone on. "I was the only one who had no idea what had happened way back when in your little Ohio town."

Not true. Claudia hadn't known, either. The boys hadn't known. But he'd let Helen vent, let her babble, let her lean toward him and murmur that she was sure he could appreciate why she felt the way she did, that certainly he understood her feelings in a way her own husband couldn't begin to grasp.

She'd been coming on to him. Subtly, not openly, but he'd picked up on it. He wasn't interested—women whose faces were stretched tighter than a bedsheet on a barracks cot weren't his type—but he was a man, and when a classy New York City lady sent signals, he would have had to be dead not to feel a little flattered.

Helen Crawford was distraught. She was resentful. If it made her feel better to flirt, who was he to stop her? He hadn't encouraged her, hadn't reciprocated, but given how unpleasant things were at home, he'd allowed himself to enjoy the moment.

Today he felt guilty. Last night he'd fumed in silence at the fact that Joelle didn't trust him, and today he was prepared to admit that maybe she'd been right not to trust him. He didn't like dredging up old crap, probing his emotions, analyzing things to death, but if Joelle wanted to talk to him tonight, they'd talk.

He'd take her out to dinner. He'd massage her shoulders and neck, if she'd let him. He'd fight his way back to her. This had been the angriest week of his life—worse than any week he could remember in 'Nam, even after he'd gotten blown to shit. It was time to assess the damage, time to reset the broken bones and start rehab.

Joelle's Prius was gone from the garage when he got home, and a note was waiting for him on the kitchen table:

Dear Bobby,

I need some time to myself, to clear my head and think things through. If the kids have to reach me, I've got my cell phone. The shrimp I was going to cook last night is in the fridge. Fire up the grill and lay the skewers on. When the shrimp is pink, it's cooked. It shouldn't take more than five to ten minutes on each side.

Not a word about where she'd gone or when she'd be back. Just cooking instructions.

He read the note again, crumpled it into a ball and hurled it across the room. Then he retrieved it, grabbed his reading glasses from atop that morning's newspaper on the kitchen table, smoothed out the note and read it once more. His glasses didn't alter a word of her message. She was gone, and he should grill the shrimp.

He crossed the room to the cordless phone and punched

in her cell-phone number. After four rings, her taped voice answered: "Joelle can't talk right now. Please leave a message."

A message, he thought frantically. There were plenty of things he wanted to say. Like, *Jesus Christ, Joelle—where are you? How could you run away like this? Here I am, ready to talk.*

All he said, however, was, "Come home. Please."

He knew why she'd run. Four days ago, he'd stormed into the house drunk from a binge, broken a vase on the floor and thrown up. He'd gotten crocked and acted violently. Shamed by his behavior and infuriated by Joelle's refusal to pity him, he'd withdrawn. He'd been nowhere, nothing, way out of reach. More accessible to Foster's wife than to Joelle.

Of course she'd left. Why would she want to hang around with a screwed-up asshole like him?

He swung open the refrigerator and found, along with the tray of shrimp skewers, a few bottles of microbrewery beer. Joelle kept them on hand for when the boys dropped by. They liked gourmet beer, which Bobby considered a contradiction in terms.

He pulled out a bottle and carried it out the back door to the patio. The evening sky was the pink of a dogwood blossom, pale in parts and more richly hued where thin clouds streaked above the horizon. He sprawled out on one of the lounge chairs, tapped his palm against the bottle's cap but didn't twist it off, not yet.

Where would she have gone? She was still close to that woman Suzanne, the senior member of the communal house she'd lived in while he'd been in 'Nam.

Suzanne was living somewhere in the Southwest. She and Joelle still exchanged Christmas cards. He wondered if they kept in touch with e-mail, too.

E-mail. If he could open Joelle's account, he might find evidence of where she'd gone. He had no idea what her password was, but he could probably figure it out. Her maiden name, maybe, or one of the kids' names.

No, he couldn't hack into her software. She'd left him because she didn't trust him anymore. He wasn't going to win her back by doing something untrustworthy.

He lifted the bottle again. Its brown surface was slick with condensation. He closed one hand around the cap to twist it off, then hesitated and balanced the unopened bottle on the arm of his chair.

Damn it, JoJo.

The coppery sun rode along the spiked tips of the pine trees that edged the horizon beyond his yard. Purple shadows stretched across the grass and reached into Joelle's vegetable garden. Her tomato vines were covered in yellow flowers, her zucchini shaped a tangle of dark green along the ground and her chard looked like miniature shrubs leafing out from the soil. He'd created that garden for her. He'd bought the house and rebuilt it for her. He'd bought her the damn Prius she'd run off in because she wanted to save the environment. Everything he'd done, everything he'd become—it was for Joelle. He'd given her everything he could.

Apparently everything wasn't enough. The one thing he couldn't give her was marriage to the man she'd loved.

Thirty-seven years. He and Joelle had had good times, great times, tender times, but the knowledge that he wasn't the man she'd been in love with burned like a pilot light inside him, never extinguished. She'd married Bobby only because she'd had to, because the alternatives had been worse. Bobby DiFranco had been her second choice, her desperation choice.

He sat outdoors long after the light faded from the sky, after the crickets began to chirp and the mosquitoes to bite, and the air cooled down and filled with the pure scent of evergreens and grass. He sat listening to the emptiness of the house behind him and wondering whether marrying Joelle had been the smartest thing he'd ever done in his life, or the stupidest.

Finally, after slapping a mosquito dead on his cheek, he rose from the lounge chair and went inside to wash the bits of bug from his hand and face. He put the unopened beer back into the refrigerator.

Drinking wasn't going to help.

After hours of insomnia, he rose from bed early the following morning. His forehead felt tight, his throat was dry and his empty stomach grumbled. He threw on an old pair of shorts and a T-shirt, staggered down the stairs and entered the kitchen. Opening the refrigerator, he saw the skewers of marinated shrimp and lost his appetite again.

Joelle's absence was like an invisible beast. All night long, lying in their bed alone, he felt that beast's hot breath against his neck. Never in his life had he felt so alone.

He put up a pot of coffee to brew, then wandered into the living room and crossed to the hutch that held their stereo equipment. Doors, he thought—he needed the Doors. He slid four Doors CDs onto the carousel, punched the "shuffle" button and returned to the kitchen to get some coffee.

Damn. He had an appointment to meet with a potential client that morning. Joelle was supposed to dust and vacuum and scour the sinks, and Bobby was supposed to traipse around yet another estate with yet another proud new home owner and promise to create yet another weekend paradise of flowering shrubs and hot tubs and stone walls.

He couldn't even bring himself to shave. Dealing with a new customer was way beyond him.

Mike could handle it, he decided, grabbing the phone in the kitchen. He punched in Mike's number, apologized for calling so early, said he wasn't feeling well and asked Mike to walk the property with the prospective client and write up his specs. "Bring Danny with you," Bobby suggested. "Between the two of you, you'll get it right."

"Danny's with Lauren," Mike said.

The symphony girl. "Are they at Tanglewood again?"

"No—I think they're at his place."

"Then it's not a problem. He can go with you." Being one half of a couple didn't mean you stopped doing what you were supposed to do.

Being one half of a couple when the other half had vanished, however... That was enough to stop Bobby dead.

"Have you been drinking, Dad?" Mike asked.

Great. His wife was gone, and now he had Mike distrusting him, too. "No," he said coldly. "I only drink when I'm with you."

"Right." Mike sounded just as cold.

"I'm not hungover, if that's what you're asking. I'm just..." *All alone and scared to death.* "Not feeling well. Take the client for me, would you?"

"Sure."

He said goodbye to Mike, listened as Jim Morrison ordered him to break on through to the other side and lifted the phone's handpiece again. He entered Joelle's cell-phone number, then pressed the phone to his ear. Four rings and her taped voice requesting that he leave a message.

He'd already left the only message he had for her. *Come home.* He disconnected the call and lowered the phone to its base.

He poured himself a cup of coffee. He'd made it too strong, and it scorched the length of his digestive tract.

He knew he should eat something. Instead he returned to the living room with his Number One Dad mug, sank onto the overstuffed sofa, rolled his head back and closed his eyes. The music washed over him like a warm tide. He wished it would lift him up and carry him to some other, happier shore. A golden beach where Joelle would be waiting for him, smiling, her arms spread wide.

The sound of the doorbell jarred him from his trance. "Riders on the Storm" had been playing, slow and bluesy and mournful. He didn't want to drag himself off the sofa. He didn't want to see anyone. But what if it was the police? What if they were here to tell him something awful had happened to Joelle?

He forced himself to his feet, strode across the living room to the entry and opened the door. Claudia stood on the porch, holding the morning newspaper he'd never bothered to bring inside. "What's going on?" she asked, shoving past him and across the threshold.

"Why are you here?" he retorted, too tired to bother with manners.

"Mike phoned and said something was wrong. He and Danny had to go meet with a client because you said you were sick. Where's Mom?"

Claudia was as brisk and focused as he was hazy. He watched her poke her head through the living-room doorway before stalking down the hall to the kitchen, calling for her mother.

Reluctantly, he followed her into the kitchen. She stood in the middle of the room, hands on hips. "Where's Mom?"

What was the point in pretending? "She left," he said.

"She left? What do you mean, she left?"

He moved to the counter and located the wrinkled sheet of paper with Joelle's note on it. "I mean she left," he said, handing the note to Claudia.

She read it, her brow furrowing. "When did she leave?"

"She was gone when I got home last night." He sipped his coffee. It had cooled off, but its bitterness scorched his throat.

"Did you phone her?"

"Twice. She won't answer."

Claudia pursed her lips. "She's got caller ID on her cell, right? Let me try her from my phone. Maybe she'll take my call." She set her purse down on the table and rummaged through it. "Have you eaten anything?"

"I'm drinking coffee. Don't baby me."

Her lips pursed harder, compressing tighter than a kiss. She dug out her cell phone. "Any idea where she might have gone?"

"She took her car. How far do you think she'd drive?"

"The airport isn't that far," Claudia pointed out. "She could be anywhere." She tapped her thumb against the buttons on her cell, then held it to her ear. After a few seconds, she started talking. "Mom? It's Claudia. Where are you?"

Bobby dropped onto one of the chairs. He no longer had the strength to refill his mug. The comprehension that Joelle would accept a call from Claudia but not from him cut through him like a stiletto, so sharp it took him a minute to realize how badly he was bleeding.

"Okay, I understand," Claudia said into the phone. "It's just…" She glanced toward Bobby. "No, he's fine," she said, and Bobby closed his eyes and nodded his thanks. "He says he tried to phone you."

"Tell her I want her to come home," Bobby murmured.

"He wants you to come home," Claudia told her mother, then listened some more. "All right. Yes. I'll tell him. I'll talk to you again later." She folded her phone shut, then regarded her father sternly. "She said she needs a little time to herself to think things through. She also said to let you know the Prius got excellent mileage on the highway."

"Where is she?"

"Holmdell." Claudia lifted the coffee decanter, studied the gravy-thick sludge inside it and emptied it into the sink. She rinsed it and prepared a fresh pot. Then she walked to the re-frigerator, opened it and pulled out a package of English muffins and a tub of butter. Without a word, she slid two split muffins into the toaster oven and turned it on. While the muffins browned, she returned to the refrigerator, removed the platter of skewered shrimp and dumped its contents into the trash.

Bobby felt a rush of gratitude that she'd disposed of the damn shrimp. When she presented him with a plate holding the toasted muffins, he felt a little less grateful. "You don't have to feed me," he said. "I'm not one of your babies. Where are they, anyway?"

"They're with their father," she said crisply. She set the tub of butter in front of him. Then she filled his mug with the freshly brewed coffee, poured some into another mug for herself and joined him at the table. "Is this all because of me?"

"What do you mean?"

"Mom's disappearing act. Is it because of me?"

He opened his mouth, then shut it and used the time it took to butter his muffin halves to sort his thoughts. "None of this is because of you, Claudia. I don't ever want you thinking that."

"But if my real—I mean, my biological father hadn't made the scene, Mom would be home right now."

"I don't know." Bobby lifted the muffin, then lowered it back to the plate. He ought to eat something, but he couldn't. He was starving, but he wasn't hungry. "Drew Foster opened a door we used to keep closed," he said. "Whatever was behind that door existed, even when the door was bolted shut. Now it's open. That's all."

"What's behind the door, Dad?" Claudia asked, her voice hushed and gentle.

"I don't think that's your business," he said, equally gently. She meant well, but Christ. She was his daughter.

"It *is* my business. The person who unlocked this door you're talking about was looking for me." She folded her hands on the table in front of her, like a schoolgirl praying to do well on a quiz. She was dressed in a flowery sundress. Claudia was the kind of woman who'd put on a dress at eight on a Saturday morning just to check on her father. There was nothing pretentious about it, no attempt to impress. It was just the way she was.

Her lovely grooming made him feel twice as rumpled. He hadn't combed his hair, his cheeks were covered in stubble, the edges of his shorts were fraying and his bare feet were ugly. Thanks to Joelle, he'd learned not to be self-conscious about his scars, which had faded over the years. Along his side and back was a faint graph of pale lines. As for his legs, he could wear shorts and not care that someone might notice the tracks his surgeries had left on his skin.

But even if he'd been left with huge, ugly scars, Joelle had accepted his body, and that had enabled him to accept it.

He managed to swallow a bite of muffin. "Your mother

married me so you wouldn't be born out of wedlock," he said. "Is that what you wanted to know?"

"I already figured that out."

"Okay, then. You get the picture. We didn't marry for love."

"But you *do* love each other." Claudia studied his face, searching for reassurance.

"I love your mother. I don't think she loves me."

"Just because she went off to Ohio doesn't mean she doesn't love you."

"I'm not talking about this." He gestured toward the note Joelle had left him. "I'm talking about our lives. She married me because she had to, because she couldn't see any other way to keep you. And we made a go of it for a long time because we kept that fact locked behind the door. If you don't think about something, you can pretend it isn't there."

"She told me…" Claudia traced the rim of her mug with her finger. "She told me she would have gone out with you in high school if you'd ever asked her. You never did."

Bobby sat back, surprised. For a moment he regressed to being a teenager, Joelle Webber's best friend and secret admirer. "We were pals," he said.

"You never asked her out. You were dating some other girl. Mom showed me everyone in her high-school yearbook. I don't remember the girl's name. She had black hair and too much eye makeup."

"Margie Noonan," Bobby recollected. Then he shook his head. "Your mother was out of my league."

"She was a kid from the wrong side of the tracks, just like you."

"She was a Tubtown kid, but she wasn't anything like me." He sipped some coffee. It tasted wonderful after the crap he'd brewed earlier. "She was going places. She was destined for greatness. I wasn't about to stand in her way."

"You were destined for greatness, too," Claudia said. "Look at you, Dad. You own your own business. You own a beautiful house on a beautiful piece of land in a beautiful part of New England. You're an American success story."

"I never thought I'd wind up like this," he admitted. Even scruffy and agitated, his wife gone and his future threatened, he allowed himself a moment of pride in all he'd accomplished. Then he acknowledged the truth: "Whatever success I've achieved, it was because of your mother. I wanted her to have the life she'd dreamed of. When I came back from the war, I was a mess, inside and out. She had two babies to deal with, not just one. You and me. She deserved so much more—and I've spent my life trying to give it to her."

"That's not the way she tells it," Claudia argued. "She's always told me you were the bravest man she'd ever known."

"There was nothing brave about getting drafted."

"She isn't talking about your service in Vietnam," she clarified. "She's talking about when you came back. Mom said you were in a million pieces and fought your way back to health—and all the while, you were taking care of me. That took a lot of courage." She smiled nostalgically. "She showed me this old music box you used to play for me. Do you remember? It played 'Edelweiss.'"

"Yeah, I remember that." He shared her smile, then grew solemn. Would Joelle really have gone out with him in high school? They'd been such close friends, dating her would have seemed incestuous. "The bottom line was, your mother hoped to marry Drew Foster," he said quietly. "She had to settle for me."

"I think she loves you more than you realize," Claudia said, reaching across the table to squeeze his hand.

"And I think you're a daughter trying to keep her parents together." Noticing a darkness on the inside of her elbow, he frowned. He'd glimpsed it earlier and assumed it was just a shadow, but when she extended her arm he saw more clearly that it was a bruise. "What happened to your arm?"

"Oh, this?" She glanced at the discolored skin just below the crease of her joint. Then she met his gaze. "I went for a blood test yesterday."

"A blood test." His heart pinged, like a car engine with a malfunction.

She squeezed his hand again. "Whatever happened in the past wasn't that boy's fault. I don't know how I feel about everything else, but I can't just turn away and let that boy die. He's my brother."

That boy might die anyway. Claudia might not be a match. And all the pain, all the brutal truths that had rampaged through that door when Drew Foster had forced it open might have been exposed for nothing. If Foster hadn't barged back into Bobby and Joelle's lives just one week ago, they might have gone on happily, forever.

But now Claudia believed she had a brother. Not just Mike and Danny, but another brother. Drew Foster's son.

She broke into his ruminations, as if trying to tear him away from the idea she'd just presented to him. "Seeing a marriage counselor might be a good idea."

"I hate that stuff," he said, not ready to be torn. *He's my brother,* Claudia had said. Foster's kid was her brother.

"Sometimes it's easier to talk your problems out with an objective outsider. You could get it all out in the open. You could say things to the counselor that you can't say to each other."

"Like that's such a great idea," he muttered, then sipped his coffee. "I don't think there's all that much inside me, anyhow. And if there is, maybe that's where it belongs. Inside me. Left alone."

Claudia finished her coffee and stood. Her hair was the color Joelle's used to be before a few streaks of gray had sneaked in, but straighter. It fluttered around her face as she carried her mug to the sink and washed it. After propping it in the drying rack, she faced Bobby. "Either you and Mom can talk to each other and get things out into the open, or you can go back to pretending everything's fine when it isn't."

"We can't go back," he said.

"Right. You can't. Because even if you wanted to pretend everything was fine, you can't pretend that I'm..." She drew in a breath and let it out. "You can't pretend I'm your daughter anymore. I mean, I *am,* but..."

"Yeah. I know." From the living room drifted the sound of Jim Morrison singing, "You're lost, little girl." Bobby considered storming into the living room and shutting off the damn music—or maybe dragging the CD player off its shelf and stomping on it. What more did he need in his life? His wife gone, his daughter telling him she wasn't his daughter and the Doors providing the sound track. And violent urges rising in him. Maybe they'd been behind that door, too, just one more nasty bit of truth, his father's legacy. The door was open and now he was going to become the beast his father had been.

He'd denied Claudia her genes. Maybe he'd denied his own, as well.

"I'd better get back home," she said. "Gary's probably

tearing his hair out by now. The kids can be pretty demanding first thing in the morning."

Bobby nodded. He pushed away from the table, stood and wondered whether he should kiss Claudia goodbye.

She answered that question by crossing to him and kissing his cheek. "Things will work out, Dad."

"You're sure of that?"

She shrugged, then patted his arm. "Promise me you'll remember to eat. I'll call you this evening to see how you're doing."

"I'll be fine," he swore, hoping his words weren't just another lie. "Will you tell me the results of the blood test when you get them?"

"I'm not sure," she said, then turned and left the kitchen.

He should have accompanied her to the door, but he couldn't bear to watch her walk out of his house and away. She was right; he could no longer pretend she was his daughter. *You're lost,* the song reminded him.

As if he didn't already know.

Chapter 10

May 1987

The spring sunlight was like a warm, white bath soaking Joelle as she sat on the stiff folding chair. To her left was her mother, who'd traveled all the way from Ohio for this day. To her right were the boys, Mike flipping through the program and Danny squirming incessantly, kneeling, sitting, climbing down from his chair to get a closer view of an ant plodding through the grass. On their other side sat Claudia, just a couple of weeks short of sweet sixteen and acting as if she had no idea who the two rambunctious little boys beside her were.

Joelle didn't care if the boys were restless. She didn't care if Claudia wished she were seated in another row, a member of another family. She didn't care that Wanda was there—her mother could be a pain, but she'd insisted on coming and then requested that Bobby and Joelle pay her airfare, since she couldn't afford it herself. None of that mattered.

This was truly one of the greatest days of her life.

Twenty rows in front of them, under a white canopy, a man in a long, black robe spoke ponderously into a microphone, his voice distorted by echoes and amplification as it drifted across the field.

"I'm bored," Danny whined.

Joelle dug in her tote bag and pulled out an Etch-a-Sketch. "Here," she whispered. "Play with this—but don't talk. People are trying to listen to the speech."

"It's boring," Danny muttered, although he subsided in his chair, crossed his legs and twisted the Etch-a-Sketch's dials.

Amazing that they'd gotten here, Joelle thought. Amazing that they'd reached this day, this place, this sun-blessed corner of western Connecticut. Amazing that Bobby was graduating from college.

How did people get from point A to point B? she wondered as the orator droned on. How did sixteen years fly by so quickly? It felt like mere days ago that Bobby returned his cane to the V.A. hospital. "I hate New Jersey," he'd said as he'd left the rehab clinic for the last time, walking with only a slight limp. "Let's get the hell out of here."

One of the physical therapists he'd worked with had a cousin who ran a masonry business in Bridgeport, Connecticut. Bobby and Joelle knew nothing about Bridgeport, Connecticut, except that it wasn't New Jersey—and it wasn't Ohio. Bobby phoned the cousin and got himself hired.

Joelle and Bobby decamped for Connecticut and moved

into a two-bedroom apartment they could barely afford. Bobby learned how to do brickwork and stonework for the new subdivisions and office parks sprouting across the region. People hated talking about the Vietnam War, but they seemed happy to hire a veteran. When Joelle suggested to Bobby that she'd like to return to college, he told her to go ahead.

Claudia, fortunately, was an easy child. She loved her pre-school and didn't cling to her mother—probably because she'd spent so much time with Bobby during her first few years. Joelle was able to schedule her classes at Fairfield University in the mornings, so Claudia attended preschool for only a half day, which saved on the tuition. In the afternoons, Joelle played with Claudia and taught her the finer aspects of shopping: "Always use a coupon if you've got one," she'd explain as she pushed Claudia up and down the grocery-store aisles in a shopping cart. "Always look for a Sale sign," she'd instruct in a clothing store. After a while, Claudia began to recognize the letters. *Sale* was the first word she ever read.

Bobby's job healed him as effectively as the surgeries and physical therapy had. Bending, lifting, laying stone and lugging thirty-pound sacks of concrete powder honed his body. He came home every evening filthy and exhausted, but smiling. In the evenings, after dinner, he would play with Claudia while Joelle studied. Seated in the kitchen with her textbooks and notes spread across the table, she would hear Bobby and Claudia chatting and laughing and watching *The Muppet Show* together in the living room. Before bed, Bobby would always read to Claudia. "Make Eeyore's voice," she'd order him as he worked his way through *Winnie the Pooh* with her. "Make it funny, like you did last time."

He would summon Joelle when Claudia was ready for her

good-night kiss. Joelle and Bobby would tuck her in, turn on her seashell-shaped night-light and close her door. And then they'd retreat to their bed.

As expensive as it was, a two-bedroom apartment was worth every dollar it cost them. Back in New Jersey, Joelle had finally moved Claudia's crib and changing table out of the bedroom and into the living room. She'd hated having her baby so far away—and stuck in a room that clearly wasn't a bedroom—but she and Bobby couldn't have sex while Claudia was in the room with them.

And sex with Bobby was a revelation. In the months after his return from Vietnam, Joelle had learned so much about physical pleasure, partly because she'd had so much to learn and partly because Bobby's body was broken. He had no strength in one leg. His balance was off. He was thin and fragile and, despite her reassurances, embarrassed about his scars. The nightmares would strike without warning and he'd shout his friend's name while his body jerked and flinched. Joelle pleaded with him to talk to a therapist, but he hated the idea of opening up to a stranger.

He opened up a bit to Joelle, at least. They would lie beside each other in the dark, and he'd tell her about his platoon's routine patrols, how frightening they were, how pointless they'd seemed. He'd tell her about the bone-deep envy he'd felt whenever one of his platoon mates finished his hitch and got to leave. He'd tell her about the heat and the humidity and the insects as big as a woman's fist. He'd tell her how he would keep his fear of dying at bay by reminding himself that if he died, she and the baby would get widow's benefits, so something worthwhile would come from his death. He'd tell her about the mud and the eerie green cast of the morning light and the sense he sometimes had that he was standing in quicksand and would never escape—until he pulled out the photo she'd given him, taken the evening of the senior prom. And he would gaze at her, looking so pretty, so clean and healthy and lovely, and he'd be reminded that a life was waiting for him back home, if he could only keep himself from getting killed.

These bedtime conversations were as intimate as making love. And when they weren't talking, they did make love. Bobby would ask her to try different positions. When his leg and back were hurting him, he'd move her around on the bed and use his hands and his mouth on her. Their bed was their own magical world, a place of adventure and safety, a place where Joelle believed that everything would work out, that her marriage would last her lifetime.

The clouds that had followed him back to America from Vietnam gradually dissipated. Months would go by without his shouting Schenk's name in his sleep, and then years. A Vietnam veterans' group in southern Connecticut sent him invitations to events, but he never attended. "That's over," he'd say. "It's history. I don't have time for that stuff."

Wanda didn't come to Connecticut for Joelle's college graduation. She was still working full-time at the Bank Street Diner then, and Joelle and Bobby and Claudia had driven out to Ohio during Joelle's spring break less than two months earlier, where they'd spent four hideous days shuttling back and forth between Joelle's mother and Bobby's father. Louie DiFranco had been surly and vicious, reeling from the news that Bobby's brother, Eddie, was gay. "I never shoulda let him go to college," Louie had railed. "Shoulda made him join the military, like Bobby. That woulda made a man out of him."

Eddie had wisely moved to San Francisco, leaving Bobby to receive the brunt of his father's bitterness. One morning, as he fumed about his pathetic younger son, Claudia beamed a smile up at him and said, "I like fairies, Papa Louie. They can do magic." That had shut him up.

At least Wanda didn't have a temper. But she did little to conceal her disappointment that Joelle had married Bobby when, had she only played things right, she could have wound up with Drew Foster. "You say you're happy, so okay," Wanda would mutter. "But honestly, Joelle. For years you had to work to support him, and now that he's finally able to work, he's a laborer. He comes home every night with dirt under his nails. And he limps."

"Hardly," Joelle had defended Bobby. "And he knows how to wash his hands."

Joelle graduated from college with only Bobby and Claudia to cheer for her as she accepted her diploma, and she landed a kindergarten teaching job in Arlington. "That takes some pressure off you," she told Bobby. "I'll be working, we'll have two incomes—things'll get easier."

"Easy is boring," he argued. "I don't mind pressure. I've been thinking, Jo. Now that you'll be earning a steady income and we can get insurance through your job... I want to start my own landscaping business."

Bobby knew bricks and stones. He knew grass and shrubs. But running a business? What did he know about that?

She kept her doubts to herself. "Go ahead and do it," she said.

His boss in Bridgeport mentored him. He went out in search of customers far from the city and discovered communities in the northwest hills where New Yorkers were buying up old properties and hiring contractors to fix them up. He enrolled in an evening class in marketing at the local campus of the state college system. Just to get a little business knowledge, he'd insisted. Just one class.

Eight years later, he'd built DiFranco Landscaping into a thriving enterprise. He'd done extensive renovations on the fixer-upper he and Joelle had bought in Gray Hill. He'd fathered two sons. And he'd completed a degree at Western Connecticut State, majoring in business and minoring in botany.

"This I've got to see," Wanda had said when Joelle told her about Bobby's graduation. He himself hadn't wanted to participate in the commencement ceremony, but damn it, he'd worked so hard to get through college—when he hadn't even had to, given that his business was thriving. No one hired a landscape designer for his educational pedigree. They hired DiFranco Landscaping because the company had an excellent reputation for getting a job done on time and on budget.

But he'd wanted the degree. Something beyond his business had motivated him. Two courses a semester, an occasional summer class… He'd fought for every credit, every B-plus. And Joelle resolved that he would wear a cap and gown and march with his fellow graduates and have the dean of the college place in his hand his very own diploma, rolled into a tube and tied with a ribbon.

The orator in the black robe finally ran out of steam. Joelle glanced to her right and saw that Mike had taken over the Etch-a-Sketch and Danny had curled up like a snail on the seat of his chair and was fast asleep. Claudia sat with her head back and her legs slightly angled, trying to maximize the sun's rays so she could improve her tan.

Joelle felt a slight breeze against her left arm. Glancing in that direction, she found her mother using the commencement program as a fan. She considered suggesting that her mother might be cooler if she removed the jacket of her suit, but Wanda had boasted about buying the outfit new at Beldon's just for this trip. The jacket's shoulders had padding bigger than a linebacker's. "Krystal Carrington on *Dynasty* has a suit just like this," Wanda had insisted.

Joelle opened her own program and smiled to see they'd reached the "conferring of diplomas" portion of the ceremony. She pulled her camera out of her tote and removed the lens cap. She was seated much too far away to get a good shot of Bobby— she didn't have a zoom lens—but she didn't care. Even if all she got was a blur of cap and gown, she would know that blur was Bobby, doing something no one had ever expected of him.

The dean intoned each graduate's name. In alphabetical order, the graduates marched across the platform, accepted their diplomas, shook the dean's hand and then walked back to their seats. They all looked so young. At thirty-five, Bobby was surely one of the oldest graduates.

"They're starting the Ds," Wanda whispered to her.

"I know." Joelle stood and edged past the kids' chairs to reach the grassy aisle. She lifted her camera and waited.

"Robert L. DiFranco," the dean announced.

Joelle snapped three photos. Three blurs of Bobby striding across the platform, his hair straggling out from under his mortarboard and brushing the neckline of his robe. Unlike some of the young graduates, who appeared to be wearing shorts under their robes, and sneakers or sandals, he wore black trousers and dress loafers. He held his head high, and Joelle could see his lips move as the dean handed him his diploma.

She sidled back to her chair and sank happily onto it. "He needs a haircut," Wanda muttered.

"I like his hair that way," Joelle defended him. "So does he."

"Can we go now?" Mike asked in a stage whisper.

"Soon," Joelle promised.

Once the graduation ceremony finally ended, Joelle had to shoot more photos. A photo of Bobby holding his diploma. One of him and Claudia and the boys standing in front of the student union. One of him with a groggy Danny in his arms and the plant studies laboratory in the background. One Wanda clicked of all five of them.

Joelle refused to quit taking pictures until she'd used up the roll of film. Only then, reluctantly, was she willing to leave the campus.

After Bobby returned his rented cap and gown to the student union, they piled into the minivan he'd bought last fall and drove to the Arlington Inn, where Joelle had reserved a table for six. She issued stern instructions to the boys through tight lips as the maître d' led them to a circular table covered in a heavy white linen cloth. "I want your best behavior," she warned. "No wild stuff. This is a fancy restaurant."

"Can I get a hamburger?" Mike asked.

"Yes."

"Can I get choco milk?" Danny wanted to know.

"If they have it, yes."

They had chocolate milk—and also crayons and paper place mats with pictures on them that Danny and Mike could color. Claudia ordered a Seven Up and Wanda insisted on wine for the adults. Bobby reluctantly allowed the waiter to fill a glass for him.

"A toast," Wanda announced, raising her glass. The boys

spiritedly raised their glasses, too, and Joelle, seated between them, steadied their hands before they could spill their drinks. "A toast to Bobby, who now has two remarkable accomplishments to his name. You got my daughter to marry you, and you got yourself a college degree."

Bobby grinned. "Not bad for a Tubtown boy, huh?"

"The degree I can understand," Wanda said. "You always were a smart kid, even if your prospects weren't so hot. How you managed to snag Joelle, though—that's a mystery." She was smiling, teasing him, but Joelle sensed a serious undercurrent in her tone.

"He snagged me just by being Bobby," she said, shooting him an affectionate look. "He didn't have to do anything more than that."

He smiled back, but she could tell from the chill in his eyes that he'd felt the barbs in Wanda's words. He consumed a tiny sip of his wine, then put down the glass and settled back in his chair. "So now that I have a bachelor's degree, does that mean I'm a bachelor?"

"Ha-ha," Claudia muttered, rolling her eyes.

The rest of the meal went smoothly. No more digs from Wanda, no major misbehavior from the boys. Claudia thought one of the busboys was cute and repeatedly visited the ladies' room so she could walk past his station. He clearly thought she was cute, too, since he followed her with his gaze every time she entered his field of vision path. When he came to the table to refill her water glass, he blushed.

Joelle glanced Bobby's way and noticed him observing the flirtation. He turned in time to catch her eye. His eyebrows arched. So did hers.

They were too young to have a daughter old enough to

be interested in boys. But then, they'd done everything too young—left home, gotten married, had Claudia. And they'd gotten their college educations too late, Bobby even later than Joelle. Their timing was abysmal, yet somehow everything had worked out.

After dinner, they drove back to Gray Hill. The evening was mild and dry, and sitting out on the back patio would have been pleasant—except that Bobby hadn't finished building the patio yet. A pile of flagstones stood near the door, awaiting his attention. Now that his schooling was done, he might be able to complete that job.

Joelle sent the boys into the backyard to run around for a little while and tire themselves out. She asked Claudia to keep an eye on them, then went upstairs to make sure Danny's bedroom was ready for her mother. Whenever Wanda visited, Danny's room became the guest room and he moved into Mike's bedroom for the duration. Mike had a bunk bed and he loved the excuse to sleep on the upper bunk.

Danny's bed was made with fresh linens. Joelle left a bath towel and washcloth on the dresser for her mother, then opened the window to allow in some cool evening air. In the twilight, the boys chased each other, shaping their hands into guns and making bullet noises.

She heard footsteps behind her, two sets. Turning, she saw her mother enter the room, followed by Bobby, who was carrying her suitcase. "I'm going to change my clothes," he said as he set the bag down. He nodded at Wanda and then left the room.

"Those boys," Wanda said, joining Joelle at the window. "Where on earth do they get their energy?"

"They're boys," Joelle answered, as if that explained everything.

"I guess." Wanda pushed a shock of hair back from her face. Her hair had naturally been a dark blond shade, but now that she was coloring it it seemed a bit brassy. Her suit had wilted in the heat, but beneath it she still had a decent figure. In her late fifties, she was tenaciously holding on to her looks. "I never had to deal with little boys," she conceded. "I don't know if I'd have the energy."

"They're wonderful," Joelle said. Tiring, yes. Challenging, always. But God, how she loved them.

"They resemble Bobby strongly," Wanda noted. "Both of them. I tell you, you look at them standing next to him, and you don't have to guess who their daddy is. Now, Claudia... there's nothing of Bobby in her at all. Absolutely no resemblance whatsoever."

Joelle stiffened and peered behind her. To her dismay, she saw Bobby lurking in the hall just outside the door. He'd heard Wanda. A shadow flickered across his face.

She spun back to her mother. "Claudia has Bobby's eyes," she said, then looked over her shoulder again, in time to watch him entering their bedroom and shutting the door behind him.

"You think so? I don't see it at all."

"Well, it's there." Joelle hoped her mother didn't hear the belligerence in her tone. More quietly, she said, "I'm going to give Bobby a hand. He can't hang up a suit without getting it all wrinkled. You should have everything you need. Toothpaste's in the bathroom, shampoo in the shower. If you want a hair dryer, I can lend you mine. Claudia is kind of possessive about hers."

"My hair's fine," Wanda said, although Joelle barely heard her. Her attention was on the door Bobby had closed, on the man behind that door.

Entering the master bedroom, she found him standing in front of the open closet door. His jacket was off, his dress shirt unbuttoned and untucked and his tie slung unknotted around his neck as he wrestled his jacket onto a hanger. Hanging the trousers first would be easier, but she didn't give a damn if his suit wound up as wrinkled as a raisin. She crossed the room to him and hugged him from behind, her hands meeting on the warm skin of his chest. She turned her head and pressed her cheek to the smooth cotton of his shirt. "Bobby," she murmured.

"She knows."

"She just made a stupid comment. People say that kind of thing without thinking."

He drew in a breath, then let it out. She felt the surge and contraction of his diaphragm against her palms. "She knows," he said. "Did you tell her?"

"Of course not." Joelle was insulted that he'd accuse her of such a thing. "Nobody knows."

"*We* know," he said. He hung up his jacket, then eased her hands from him and faced her. "If she saw it, other people see it."

"Stop it, Bobby. Nobody knows. Nobody talks about it."

"*We* know," he repeated. "We don't talk about it, but we know."

"It doesn't matter," Joelle said, understanding the truth in the words as she spoke them. They were a family. Bobby was a father, Claudia a daughter.

"It's like…" He gazed past her, as if searching the air behind her for the right words. "It's like a piece of shrapnel that never came out. It's just floating around inside me. I don't feel it. I don't even know it's there. But yeah, it's there, and it could migrate to my heart and kill me."

Joelle shook her head. "Claudia is your daughter." Eager to steer his thoughts in a better direction, she reached around him and pulled a bag down from the closet shelf. "I forgot to show you what I bought," she said with artificial cheer. She slid a picture frame from the bag. "For your diploma."

"You want to frame it?" he asked, eyeing the frame warily.

"It'll look great." She carried the frame to the bed, then grabbed his diploma from the top of his dresser and untied the ribbon.

"You never framed your diploma."

"Where would I put mine? In the classroom?" She twisted the clamps at the back of the frame and removed the backing. "You can hang yours in your office."

"Why would I want to do that?"

She glanced up at him and smiled. "Pride?"

"People come to my office to talk about the price of pine mulch or the delivery date of gravel. They don't come to review my credentials."

She smoothed the diploma against the batting and glass. The parchment was curled, but the frame flattened it. "Well, you can hang it wherever you want, then," she said, displaying the framed document for him. "In the den. In the bathroom. It's beautiful, isn't it?"

Two strides carried him to her side. His chin was harsh, his eyes unfathomable. His hair was definitely not too long. It was just the right length for Joelle to ravel her fingers through it, to stroke it back from his face.

He lifted the framed diploma out of her hands and tossed it onto the bed. "I didn't go to college so I could hang a piece of paper on a wall," he said.

"Why did you go?"

"To learn something. To run the business better." She raised her hand to his face again, but he caught her wrist before she could touch him. "To prove something to myself."

"That you could do it?"

"Yeah."

"Of course you could do it. Anything you put your mind to, you can do," she said, meaning it as much as she'd meant everything else she'd told him in the past few minutes. He could do anything. His diploma was beautiful. He was Claudia's father. No one knew different.

She wished she could make sense of the emotion in his eyes. He seemed uneasy, dissatisfied, not at all proud. Could her mother's idiotic words have deflated him so completely? Did he not know what a fantastic father he was, what a magnificent man?

He lifted her hand to his lips and kissed her knuckles. Then he lowered it to her side and took a step back. "You deserved a husband with a college education," he said, returning to the closet to put away his tie.

She stared after him, unsure she'd heard him correctly. "You mean, because I had a degree?"

"Because you always wanted to be the wife of a college man," he reminded her without looking at her.

Drew, she realized. She'd told Bobby, years ago, when they were just friends, that she'd hoped to marry Drew, who was heading off to Dartmouth. But that was so far in the past. Bobby would never have even thought about Drew if her mother hadn't opened her stupid mouth.

She followed him back to the closet, planted her hands on his shoulders and forced him to face her. "I'm the wife of the best man in the world," she said.

He managed a smile, and when she pulled him down to her, he gave her the kiss she wanted. Then he straightened and turned away, moving to the bureau and taking pair of jeans from a drawer.

Allowing him his privacy as he undressed, she left the bedroom and went downstairs, through the kitchen to the back door, where she could call for the boys to come inside and start getting ready for bed.

Claudia followed the boys through the door. Her hair color lightened every spring, the sun painting streaks of platinum through the blond. The older she got, the prettier she grew. Teenage boys phoned the house constantly.

Joelle was determined not to pressure Claudia the way she herself had been pressured. Claudia would never feel she had to reel in a good catch, as if boys were fish. She would be successful on her own terms, by her own actions. She wasn't a Tubtown kid. She'd grown up secure, close to both her parents, loved by both. No rambling man had passed through her life a few times, left her with a doll and a coloring book and then died in a highway accident.

Claudia knew who she was: the daughter of a woman who would never imply that her worth was based on whom she dated, and the blessed, beloved daughter of Bobby DiFranco.

Chapter 11

The West Side Motor Lodge on Rockwell Turnpike had not aged well. It was clean and the staff was friendly, but Joelle seriously doubted the motel had undergone any significant renovations since she'd left town thirty-seven years earlier. The pattern in the lobby's carpet had faded so badly that the black circles resembled oil stains marring the green background. The trite still-life paintings on the walls were faded. The leaves on the fake potted plants had been bleached by time to nearly white.

The room rate was cheap, though, and the night clerk hadn't balked when Joelle had checked in at nearly midnight last night. She probably should have stopped for the night somewhere in Pennsylvania, rather than driving all the way to Holmdell in one day. But she didn't want to be in Pennsylvania.

She wasn't sure she wanted to be in Ohio, either. All she

had was a vague idea that returning to the place she and Bobby had agreed to get married might help her understand how their marriage had reached this crisis.

She'd considered driving straight to her mother's house last night, but she hadn't even warned her mother that she was coming to Holmdell. If Joelle had rung her mother's bell in the middle of the night, Wanda would probably have had a heart attack. Joelle didn't need that calamity on top of everything else she was dealing with.

So the West Side Motor Lodge had been her home for the night. She'd staggered into the room, taken a quick shower and found herself too agitated to sleep, even though she was exhausted and aching. She'd unpacked her cell phone recharger, plugged it in, then lifted her phone and listened, for at least the dozenth time, to Bobby's message: *Come home. Please.*

The "come home" she could handle. The "please" filled her eyes with tears.

She couldn't bring herself to call him. She'd tried to talk to him all week and he'd shut down on her. Well, now it was her turn to shut down. She'd phone him when she was ready—and she wasn't ready yet.

She'd crawled into the hard motel bed and willed herself to rest. The sheets had smelled of starch and bleach. The air conditioner had rattled like a tin can rolling down the sidewalk. The curtains at her window didn't meet, and through the narrow slit she'd seen the occasional flash of headlights as a car barreled down Rockwell Turnpike, heading toward Indiana.

Eventually she'd drifted off. But the first gray light of dawn to slice through that crevice in the curtains roused her, and by seven-thirty she was seated in the motel's sleepy restaurant, sipping coffee that tasted burned and waiting for a platter of scrambled eggs.

Was Bobby awake yet? Was he eating a decent breakfast? Had he ever grilled the shrimp?

Her phone rang, and she checked the caller ID. Bobby again. Why did he want to talk to her now? Why couldn't he have talked to her before she'd left, when she'd been begging him to open up?

The phone stopped ringing, and she checked to see if he'd left another message. He hadn't. If she'd answered, he probably would have only asked her to come home. Maybe he would have said "please" again.

She didn't want to go home, not until she knew what she was going home to.

She was on her third cup of coffee when Claudia called. As soon as she answered, she realized Claudia was phoning from Joelle and Bobby's house. She heard Doors music in the background—not a listening choice Claudia would make in her own home. Claudia assured her that Bobby was all right and Joelle told her to tell Bobby about the Prius's outstanding highway mileage.

She signed her breakfast bill to her room, then left the motel. More than ten years had passed since she'd last been back in her hometown. It was so much easier to fly her mother to Hartford than to try to haul everyone to Holmdell for a visit, especially now, with Jeremy and Kristin in the family. Since her mother had more or less retired from her job at the Bank Street Diner, she had no real constraints on her schedule and could visit Connecticut without having to negotiate for vacation time.

She still went to the diner a few days a week to run the

cash register, because sitting around her apartment was boring. She had no family in town; she'd told Joelle that her coworkers at the diner were her substitute family and she'd go there when she felt like seeing them. She'd station herself behind the cashier's desk and schmooze with the customers, and most people seemed to think Wanda Webber's presence at the Bank Street Diner meant all was as it should be.

Joelle drove up the turnpike into town and turned onto Bank Street, stopping at the corner where the diner sat, only because a red light forced her. The eatery's windows were cloudy, the interior dimly lit, but the awning shading the windows appeared new, its green-and-white stripes vivid in the pale morning light.

The traffic signal changed and she continued down the street. The sidewalks had been inlaid with bricks in a herringbone pattern, she noted, and a few concrete planters had been installed along the curb, holding clutches of impatiens. Evidently Holmdell had hired the local version of DiFranco's Landscaping to spruce up the downtown area. Although limp in the late-June heat, the flowers were pretty.

She noticed that Fontaine's Beauty Salon was gone, replaced by something called Kwik-Kuts, and Clement's Hardware had been taken over by one of the national retail-hardware franchises. Beldon's Department Store had looked like something out of the thirties when Joelle had been a child; it still looked like something out of the thirties, its limestone facade boasting an art deco flavor and its outer walls stained from decades of auto exhaust. A Starbucks stood next to Harley's convenience store, where Joelle used to work. Even Holmdell had its own Starbucks now, Joelle thought with a smile. The Bank Street Diner had better improve the quality of the coffee it was serving if it hoped to compete.

She passed the bank building, a massive structure with a clock embedded in its front wall. When Joelle was a child, the clock had been round, with ornate hands and gothic numerals. That clock had been replaced by a digital panel that flashed not just the time but the temperature in Fahrenheit and centigrade. The clock was off by eight minutes, and the thermometer claimed it was only sixty-five degrees. It felt warmer than that to Joelle.

She turned off Bank Street and headed toward Tubtown. The gentrification that had improved Holmdell's business district hadn't reached this part of town. The neighborhood was still dreary, houses and duplexes crowded together, sidewalks crumbling or nonexistent, buildings crying out for paint or a new roof. At least every fourth house had a bathtub shrine adorning its front yard.

She steered down one familiar street and then another until she reached the DiFranco house. The last time she'd been here, her goal had been to empty the house and shut it down after Bobby's father died.

Mike and Danny had driven out to Ohio with Bobby and Joelle when they'd received word that a neighbor had found Louie lying dead on his kitchen floor. The coroner wasn't sure how long he'd been there—a couple of days, at least. Fortunately a funeral home had already carted his body away by the time Joelle and the family arrived. All medical evidence had indicated that Louie DiFranco had died of a massive stroke, although according to the autopsy, he'd had a great deal of alcohol in his blood.

Claudia and her new husband had flown in for the funeral.

Eddie had traveled east from San Francisco, leaving his partner behind. Louie hadn't left a will—that would have made things too easy—but his estate hadn't been large or complicated, and Bobby and Eddie had agreed to split whatever was left after expenses. The funeral service at St. Mary's had been sparsely attended. Wanda had offered to pay her respects, but Joelle told her not to bother.

Joelle had felt sadder viewing Bobby's mother's grave than watching Louie's casket as it was lowered into the ground beside her. Bobby had remained expressionless throughout the entire ritual, one hand holding Joelle's and his other arm looped around Eddie's shoulders, as if he still felt he had to protect his baby brother from Louie's fists. There would be no more fists, no more violence.

Joelle and Bobby had sent the boys home on a plane with Claudia and Gary, and then they and Eddie tackled the daunting task of emptying Louie's house. Running fans in the windows, they managed to chase most of the foul, musty smell from the rooms. They threw out empty pizza boxes, bags of stale bread, a plastic container of rice pudding edged in blue mold and all the liquor Louie had left behind, scattered in bottles throughout the house. While Joelle scrubbed the kitchen, Bobby and his brother sorted through Louie's belongings in the rest of the house, stuffing his old clothing into boxes, gathering up the unpaid bills piled on his dresser, filling trash bag after trash bag with the contents of his drawers and cabinets.

Bobby tuned his father's radio to an oldies rock station so they'd have music to distract them while they worked. Above the din of Bruce Springsteen and the Eagles and Pink Floyd, she'd hear Eddie shout, "Hey, look at this!" or Bobby holler,

"Damn—remember this?" When their words were followed by laughter, she'd smile and scrub the stained counters and sing along with whatever was playing on the radio.

After three days of sweaty labor, the house was as empty and clean as it would ever be. Bobby gathered the few items he intended to bring back to Connecticut with him—an old, weathered baseball glove, a ratchet set and a crucifix that had belonged to his mother—and hired a Realtor to sell the place for him and Eddie. Then they'd driven away.

"Are you sad?" she'd asked him.

He'd thought awhile before answering. "I'm sad that I don't feel sadder."

Someone had painted the house yellow since that August day so many years ago, but the place still seemed shabby and mournful. The roof was missing a few shingles, the shrubs were overgrown and the Madonna statue in Bobby's mother's bathtub shrine listed as if she'd been guzzling some of Louie's leftover booze. Joelle knew someone else had bought the house the spring after Louie's death, and maybe more families had moved in and out since then, but the place seemed abandoned. No cars in the driveway, no tricycles or basketballs on the lawn, no plants visible along the windowsills. Joelle parked, strolled up the front walk and knocked on the door. No one answered.

She wandered around to the back of the house. The back porch still sagged and the back door's screen still sat crookedly on its hinges. She recalled a night when light had spilled through that screen door and she'd heard voices coming from inside. Bobby had stood behind her in the shadows, fearing for his life, while she'd peeked through the door into the kitchen and seen Louie with his busted nose.

Oh, Bobby… Maybe one of the things she'd loved about Drew Foster back then was that he'd been so simple. No deaths in his family, no drunks, no father swinging his fists. No ghosts in his soul, no torment in his eyes. Whatever he'd wanted, he'd gotten. He'd had never had to fight for anything.

Bobby had always had to fight. He'd fought here, in this house. He'd fought in Vietnam. He'd fought his own body after a land mine had shattered it. He'd fought to create a viable business, to become an educated man.

And now he was fighting Joelle. He was fighting Drew. He was fighting to hold on to the lie on which they'd built their lives—but he'd already lost that fight.

How could she get him to stop fighting?

Sighing, she trudged back around the house, across the scraggly front yard to her car. Her heart was so heavy it seemed to pull her off balance. When she gazed through her windshield at the bathtub shrine, she wondered whether perhaps the Madonna's heart was heavy, too, and that was why she couldn't stand straight.

Joelle steered away from the DiFranco house, away from the leaning Madonna and the memories and drove back through downtown, past the rivet factory on Bailey Street where Bobby's father had worked; past the cemetery; past the high school, to where the altitude and the economic status were elevated. The houses on the Hill were spacious and solid. No vinyl siding here, no rusty rain gutters, no driveways with weeds growing through cracks in the concrete. No half-buried bathtubs.

The curving roads in this part of town bore names like Cedar Lane and Glenville Terrace and Harvard Street. The air smelled of newly cut grass and sun-warmed roses. The houses featured elaborate stonework, leaded windows and heavy oak front doors with polished brass knockers. The two-car driveways that weren't vacant held Audi coupes and Lexus SUVs.

She cruised down Harvard Street, then veered onto Birchwood Drive. The road arched around the golf course, the rear yards of the houses separated from the fairway by rows of Scotch pine and aspen. When she reached the house where Drew Foster used to live, she coasted to the curb and turned off the engine.

Drew's house, a symmetrical mansion of brick and stone with a peaked slate roof flanked by chimneys on either side, had once seemed like a palace to her. The few times she'd been a guest there she'd felt like a village peasant paying homage to nobility.

It seemed a bit less grand to her today. She'd grown used to the rambling houses of northwest Connecticut—and she'd grown, period. She was no longer a poor girl in awe of her hometown's wealthiest residents. As she gazed at the Foster house, she acknowledged that the Fosters had a grandson who might die too young from a terrible disease. How could anyone envy them?

The front door opened and a slim woman with short red hair emerged. She had on a tank top and cargo shorts, white anklets and sneakers. She might have been dressed to go for a jog, or to clean house. If Joelle were home right now, she'd be dressed much the same way, and she'd be dusting and polishing furniture, pushing the vacuum around, making the bathroom sinks sparkle.

Instead she was in Holmdell, spying on a stranger as she strolled down the slate front walk to the mailbox at the curb. The woman opened it and emptied it of its contents, then marched back up the walk to the house.

Watching as the woman vanished behind the ornately carved wooden door, Joelle acknowledged that the Fosters no longer lived there. They'd probably decamped to Florida or Arizona or wherever rich retirees who no longer wanted to deal with snow lived.

She stared at the house for a minute longer, trying to envision herself living in it, ambling down that front walk past rows of flowering spirea, past a lawn as smooth and green as the surface of a billiards table, to pick up her mail. She couldn't picture it. Even if Bobby hadn't married her, she could not imagine herself living the life of a Foster.

She started her car's engine, U-turned and drove back to Harvard Street, to Glenville Terrace, down the hill, toward town. On Jackson Street, she slowed as the black wrought-iron fence bordering the cemetery loomed into view. Alongside the cemetery's border, she eased to the curb and yanked on her parking brake. Through the fence she saw the rows of headstones, all different sizes, different sentiments. Somewhere up the rise, near an umbrella-shaped oak tree, was a marble bench beneath a tree where she'd found Bobby one September afternoon and asked him for a favor.

Why had he proposed marriage that day? Friendship and fear, she realized. Friendship for her and fear for himself, for what lay ahead of him in Vietnam. "I'd have something to come back to," he'd said.

He'd been coming back to her ever since—from Vietnam, from his injuries, from his nightmares. From work at the end of each day. She'd been there waiting for him, never expecting him to stagger home drunk, to arrive late after spending time in a tavern with another woman.

The day he'd asked her to marry him, she had trusted him

more than anyone else in her life, anyone else in the entire world. She wanted to trust him like that today, but she longed for something more: she longed for him to love her.

He'd never spoken the words. He had never handed her his heart, never offered her his soul. He'd lived with her, made babies with her, created a family with her—but never once, in all the years she'd known him, had he said, "I love you."

Five years ago, when Mrs. Proski had died and her son had put the duplex on Third Street up for sale, Wanda had bought it, with help from Joelle and Bobby. They'd provided the down payment, and she'd paid the mortgage using the rent she collected from the Tranhs, a family of Vietnamese immigrants who'd moved into the upstairs apartment. Unlike the old DiFranco house, the duplex was spiffed up: recently painted, new roof, air-conditioning units in several windows and the old washtub flowerpot gone, replaced by azalea bushes blossoming pink and magenta. Since Joelle and Bobby considered the house an investment, they made sure Wanda was diligent about maintaining the property.

Joelle walked up the neatly edged path to her mother's front door and rang the bell. She half expected her mother not to be home, but Wanda opened the door. She was wearing an old housedress, a loose-fitting thing of thin cotton with snaps down the front, and her hair was unbrushed, the gray roots in need of a touch-up. Seeing Joelle on the front step, she appeared at first thrilled and then stricken. "What happened?" she asked.

"I just…needed a road trip," Joelle said. "Nobody's dying, I swear. Everyone's fine. Can I come in?"

"Of course." Wanda swung open the door and beckoned

Joelle inside. From the living room drifted the babble of a television show, people conversing energetically in saccharine-sweet voices. "I slept in this morning—up late last night. Me and Stan Sherko, you remember him? We went down to the Dog House Tavern to watch the Reds game on the wide-screen TV and have a few beers. And that's all we did," she added emphatically. "We're just friends."

"I didn't say a thing." Joelle stifled a smile.

"I fixed a pot of coffee. Would you like some? It's fresh. You hungry? When did you get to town? Where are you staying? Here, of course," she answered herself. "You're staying here. Where's your suitcase?"

"I got in late last night," Joelle said, following her mother into the kitchen and settling onto a chair at the table. Her mother's high-voltage chatter tired her as much as driving eight hundred miles had tired her yesterday. "I took a room at the West Side Motor Lodge for the night."

"No sense paying them when you've got a comfortable bed here."

Joelle wasn't so sure her narrow childhood bed was all that comfortable. But her mother's coffee couldn't possibly be worse than what she'd been served in the motel's restaurant. "I'll check out and stay here," she agreed.

The kitchen hadn't changed since the day Joelle had propped a note to her mother against the salt and pepper shakers and left town with Bobby. Same Formica-topped table, same vinyl-padded gray chairs, same clock in the shape of a rooster fastened to the wall above the window. Same graduated canisters filled with flour, sugar and tea bags, same two-slot toaster plugged into the wall, same stained porcelain sink.

She thought of her own kitchen, and of the note she'd left

propped up for Bobby yesterday morning. And the note he'd left propped up for her a week ago. He'd said he had gone fishing. Maybe she'd done the same thing. Maybe she was fishing for something here in Holmdell.

Her mother hustled into the living room and switched the television. She moved fast for a woman on the far side of seventy-five. All those years waitressing had kept her reasonably fit. Age had left is marks all over her—skin hung loose from her bony arms and her upper lip was pleated like a fan. But she remained light on her feet as she glided to the counter, filled two cups with coffee and carried the cups and saucers to the table without splashing a drop.

"So," she said, sitting across the table from Joelle and glowering suspiciously at her. "Suddenly here you are in Holmdell."

If Joelle hadn't intended to tell her mother why she'd traveled to Holmdell, she wouldn't have rung her mother's doorbell. Yet she wasn't sure what exactly to say. Wanda had never been the sort of warm and cuddly mother a woman would want to confide in.

"Bobby and I needed a break," Joelle said. "And I—" she shrugged "—I had this urge to visit my old haunts."

"What kind of break?" Wanda leaned forward. "You tell me that boy is cheating on you, Joelle, and I swear I'll fly to Connecticut and tear his eyes out."

"He's not cheating on me," Joelle hastened to assure her mother. Her mother's loyalty would have been more welcome if Joelle had actually believed Bobby had done something wrong. He hadn't, though. He'd just been himself—closed in, shut down, sucked into a black hole.

"Then what kind of break? You hungry? I've got some Danish, left over from the diner. It's a little stale, but still good.

Cheese and apple," she said, rising and moving to the refrigerator. She removed a platter covered in aluminum foil and deposited it on the table. Then she sat back down and peeled the foil back. "Here, take one. This one's apple," she said, pointing. "You always liked apple Danish."

"No, thanks." Joelle's stomach felt leaden from the eggs she'd eaten at the West Side Motor Lodge.

"You look thin. You're not on one of those crazy diets, are you? South Beach or whatever. Why do they always name diets after fancy towns? Why isn't there a Holmdell Diet?"

"Or a Tubtown Diet," Joelle joked.

"That would be a liquid diet," Wanda muttered with a grin. "Lots of beer and whiskey." She grew abruptly solemn. "He's not drinking, is he?"

"Bobby? No," Joelle said, praying that it was the truth.

Wanda lifted a cheese Danish from the platter, pulled a napkin from the plastic holder on the table and used it as a plate, tearing the pastry in half and arranging the halves on the napkin. "It took me twenty-five years to decide that marrying Bobby DiFranco wasn't the dumbest thing you ever did in your life. I'll admit it, Joelle—he turned out a hell of a lot better than I would have predicted. A businessman, a college education—who would have guessed that long-haired boy in torn jeans and boots would wind up like that? I always thought he was wild, with that good-for-nothing father of his and no mother to take him in hand, and that god-awful truck he rattled around in. He had no prospects, no money, nothing but an induction notice when you ran off with him."

"He was a good man. I always knew that."

Wanda nodded. "He's a good man. He's proved it a whole bunch of times. So why are you here and he's in Connecticut?"

Joelle sighed. Crumbs fell from her mother's hands as she broke her Danish into bite-sized pieces and popped them, one at a time, into her mouth. Even as she ate, her eyes remained on Joelle, sharp and assessing. "He won't talk to me," Joelle finally said, the power of her mother's stare forcing the words out. "It's always been a struggle to get him to open up, but now he won't talk to me at all. How can you have a marriage when your husband won't open up?" As if her mother were in any position to offer marital advice.

Wanda devoured another chunk of pastry, then dusted the crumbs from her hands onto her napkin. "It's Claudia, right?"

Joelle flinched. "What?"

"How many years now, Joelle? Thirty-seven? Tell me the truth."

"What truth?"

"Bobby isn't Claudia's father."

Joelle fell back in her chair. How had her mother guessed? What should Joelle do, now that she *had* guessed? She and Bobby had vowed to keep the truth hidden, and they'd maintained the lie successfully for all these years. No one in Holmdell knew. Maybe her mother had suspected, but why should Joelle confirm her suspicions?

"I may not be the sharpest knife in the drawer, but I'm not blind," Wanda said, her voice low and firm. "My daughter spends her whole senior year of high school dating a rich boy from the Hill. He's her ticket out of here, her gateway to a better life. They're going steady. They go to the prom together. And then all of a sudden she runs off with another guy—a guy who's her ticket to nowhere and her gateway to nothing. Why does she do that?"

"You know why I married Bobby," Joelle said, her voice scarcely about a whisper.

"Because you *loved* him." Her mother sneered. "Seven months later you have a baby. You think I can't count?"

"I've never denied that I was pregnant when Bobby and I got married."

Her mother glared at her. "You're dating Drew Foster, Mr. Wonderful—Mr. *Rich*-and-Wonderful—and on the side you let Bobby DiFranco knock you up? You weren't stupid, Joelle, and you weren't careless. You wouldn't have risked your chances with Drew Foster by getting involved that way with Bobby. Besides, you weren't the type of girl who slept around. If you were going steady with a boy, that was who you would have given yourself to."

Joelle drank some coffee while she tried to figure out what to say. No, she hadn't slept around. If she had, she'd bet Bobby would have known how to use a condom better than Drew had. Bobby would have protected her. He was that kind of boy, that kind of man.

"How I got pregnant is irrelevant," she said.

"I'm aware of *how* you got pregnant, honey. There's really only one way for that to happen." Her mother shook her head. "Claudia is Drew Foster's daughter, right?"

Once the truth was out, it was out, Joelle supposed. Sustaining the lie about Claudia's parentage was pointless. Claudia might as easily have told her grandmother who her father was, now that she'd been informed of the fact. It was no longer Joelle's secret to keep. "Claudia is Bobby's daughter," she said quietly. "Drew Foster provided the sperm."

Her mother made a face. "God, I wish I still smoked," she muttered. "I could use a cigarette." She reached for another

Danish, instead. "I guess you *were* stupid. You're pregnant with Drew's baby—why didn't you make him do the right thing?"

"I didn't want to *make* him do anything," Joelle retorted. "I sure as hell didn't want to marry him, not after he told me to get an abortion. He even sent me money and the name of a doctor."

Wanda, not the most religious woman, clicked her tongue and crossed herself. "That would have been a sin. And it wasn't even legal then."

"Legal or not, it wasn't what I chose to do. I wanted my baby."

Her mother's piety departed as quickly as it had arrived. "So you had the baby. That baby was Drew's. You could have milked him for child support, or gone after his snooty parents. You could have made Drew pay through the nose. If he wouldn't marry you, the least he could have done was give his daughter a good life."

"Bobby provided her with the best life in the world," Joelle countered, irritated by her mother's crass calculations. "I didn't want money, Mom. I wanted my daughter to have a father. I wanted her to have a real family. I didn't want her to grow up the way I did, never really knowing the man who provided the sperm for me."

Her mother bristled. "Dale Webber—"

"Dale Webber was a trucker passing through. You invented that nice story about how you and he got married, but I knew better. I had no father."

"He visited you," her mother argued. "He gave you a doll."

"And then he conveniently died in a highway accident." Sarcasm stretched Joelle's voice thin. "The way I figure it, that insurance check you got from his sister was insurance against your going after him. And his sister was probably his wife. Or maybe him. 'Here's some money, Wanda. Now, stay out of my life.'"

Wanda's eyes narrowed and her mouth tightened. The lines grooving her brow dipped into a frown.

"That's not what I wanted for my child," Joelle said. "I wanted a husband. I wanted my daughter to grow up knowing who her daddy was." And she did, Joelle tried to reassure herself. Bobby was Claudia's daddy. Always. Still.

"Fine. So you had yourself a little Father-Knows-Best family," her mother snorted. "And now your husband isn't talking to you. I guess things didn't work out so well for you after all."

The vindictiveness in her mother's tone stung. Joelle had come here for comfort, for support, maybe even for advice. She'd come because she had desperately needed someone to talk to, and Bobby was no longer listening. She hadn't come so her mother could break her into pieces like a day-old piece of breakfast pastry.

"You're right," she said, pushing away from the table. "Things didn't work out well. Thanks for pointing that out."

Before she could stand, her mother had clamped a hand over hers. Wanda's hand was hard, her joints knobbed with arthritis, her skin freckled with age spots. But her palm was warm and she held Joelle tightly. "Don't go running off, honey," she murmured. "You're hurting. I'm hurting for you. Seems to me there are worse things in this life than having a man who lives with you, gives you a nice home and good children, pays the bills, doesn't drink and doesn't like to open up. Men can be that way. I've known a whole lot more of them than you have, Joelle. They're like clams. They could have a pearl inside—a whole damn pearl necklace—but God help 'em, they won't open up and let you see the good stuff."

Just the touch of Wanda's hand was enough to thaw the knot of anger inside Joelle. Her words turned that thawed knot into a warm rush of tears and gratitude. "He doesn't love me, Mom," she said in a wavering voice. "That's the bottom line."

"He doesn't love you? What are you, nuts? He's crazy about you."

She shook her head. A few tears slithered down her cheeks, and she pulled a napkin from the plastic dispenser and wiped her face dry. She didn't want to weep. She didn't want to believe her situation was bad enough for tears. Yet here she was at her mother's house, hundreds of miles from home, hundreds of miles from Bobby.

"I've seen him with you," Wanda said. "He looks at you like a teenager checking out a centerfold. It's all he can do not to drool."

"That's lust, Mom. Not love."

"Don't knock it." She loosened her grip on Joelle's hand, then patted it gently. "Lust'll get you a lot closer to love than you realize."

Not close enough, Joelle thought. The last time she and Bobby had made love was the night after they'd told Claudia the truth about her conception. Bobby hadn't reached for Joelle that night. She'd initiated their lovemaking. And afterward, Bobby had warned her that the wall they were perched on was about to collapse and hurl them down.

Lust couldn't get her to love. If anything, it demonstrated just how far from love she and Bobby were.

Chapter 12

June 1998

Bobby gazed around the interior of Our Lady of Lourdes and decided he could survive an hour in church. He'd gotten through both his sons' christenings without melting down—he'd missed Claudia's christening, thanks to 'Nam—and he could get through today. The church was just a place, after all. Just a building.

Before Mike's christening, the last time Bobby had been in a church he'd been twelve. St. Mary's in Holmdell had been a dreary church in the best of times, with dark stone walls and stained-glass windows depicting the most gruesome scenes in the life of Jesus. That day when Bobby was twelve, all those fractured images of Christ with is head wrapped in thorns, and Christ dead on the cross and Christ bleeding in his mother's arms, had served only to magnify Bobby's misery.

A coffin had stood in front of the altar, smooth and polished, shining like a freshly waxed car. His father had said, "That's your mother in there," and Bobby had wanted to kick things. Instead he'd held Eddie's hand and let their father lead them down a hall to the priest's office.

"Let me talk to the boys alone for a minute," Father Paul had said, ushering them inside.

The room had smelled of cedar and cigar smoke. Eddie had been too small for the chair next to Bobby's; he'd had to shift forward so his legs wouldn't stick straight out in front of him. His face had been blotchy red and damp. By Bobby's calculation, Eddie had been crying pretty much nonstop for four days.

Father Paul had sat behind a huge desk, facing them. He'd been old and balding, his face as round as a volleyball. He'd seemed to have no neck, just his clerical collar. It kept his head from rolling away, Bobby had thought.

"Do you boys know why your mother died?" he'd asked. Eddie had given his head a vigorous shake, but Bobby had remained still, staring at Father Paul, daring him to come up with any possible justification for such a tragedy. "She died because God loved her so much. He wanted her in heaven with him. He knew that was where she belonged."

Eddie had sniffled. Bobby had pulled a Kleenex from the box on Father Paul's desk and handed it to him. Doing that had kept him from saying what he was thinking: that God must not have loved Bobby and Eddie very much if he would take their mother away from them.

"Your mother is an angel," Father Paul had told them.

"She's an angel among angels, in God's kingdom, where God wants her to be because He loves her so much."

Bullshit, Bobby had thought.

"Now your father is all alone, and he's suffering," Father Paul had gone on. "It's very important that you boys mind him. You don't want to increase his suffering. So whatever he tells you to do, you do it. Don't disobey him. Don't talk back. Don't give him a hard time. He's lost his wife, and your job from here on in is to be obedient, well-behaved boys and do as your father says. Whatever he asks of you, you do it. Do you understand?"

Eddie had been blubbering openly by then. Bobby had nodded, because he'd figured agreeing with Father Paul was the fastest route to escaping from the stuffy office.

"Very well." Father Paul had stood, which had given Bobby and Eddie the freedom to stand, as well. "Be good boys, now. Don't make your father's life harder than it is. Do as he says. I don't want to hear about you giving him a hard time."

"Okay," Eddie had mumbled, and Bobby had echoed him.

Out in the hall, Eddie had collapsed against Bobby. "Do we have to do whatever Daddy says?" he'd asked plaintively.

"Nah. That was a crock. You steer clear of Dad as much as you can. I'll take care of things."

He wasn't sure he'd done a particularly good job taking care of things, but somehow, thirty-plus years later, he was standing at the back of a church, sunlight streaming in colored shafts through the much cheerier stained-glass windows of the Catholic church in Gray Hill. The pale oak pews were filled with people, among them Eddie and his partner, Stuart, and Louie, the man Father Paul had ordered Eddie and Bobby to obey. Joelle had arranged the seating so that Louie was positioned at the end of a pew, Joelle's mother next to him and

Eddie and Stuart on Wanda's other side. After all these years, Louie DiFranco hadn't yet come to terms with the fact that his younger son was gay.

Coming to terms with things wasn't one of Louie DiFranco's strengths. He was much more adept at mouthing off like a fool and drinking like a fish.

He was sober this morning, at least. Eddie had assured Bobby of it. Eddie and Stuart and Louie were all staying at a hotel in Arlington, and Eddie, who had rented a car, had volunteered to chauffeur Louie wherever he had to be. "You're the father of the bride," Eddie explained. "You've got enough on your plate. I'll babysit Dad."

Father of the bride. God, how had that happened? Bobby shook his head and grinned.

Mike and Danny looked spiffy in navy blue blazers, khaki trousers, white shirts and burgundy ties, each with a red rose boutonniere pinned to his lapel. Claudia had decided they didn't need to wear tuxedos just to be ushers. Lucky boys, Bobby thought. Wearing a tux made him feel as if he ought to be trick-or-treating. He, Gary, Gary's father and the best man had all gone to a tuxedo-rental place in Arlington, where they'd agreed on the least frilly, fancy style available—plain black with black satin lapels, straight black trousers, pleated white shirts and black bow ties. Bobby had struggled a bit with the shirt's studs, but Joelle had gotten them all fastened and tied his bow tie so it lay smooth under the weird stand-up collar and didn't resemble a fat butterfly too much.

She was beautiful, almost as beautiful as the bride. She'd sewn her own dress, a simple thing of flowing blue silk that fell to midcalf, with a blousy jacket over it. It was the same color as her eyes, the same color as the prom dress she'd sewn for herself so many years ago. Bobby still remembered that day. He remembered the pang he'd felt when Drew Foster had shown up—looking ridiculous in a matching blue tux, as Bobby recalled—and Joelle had looped her hand through the bend in his elbow and gazed at him with adoration.

Bad memory. Bobby shook his head again, then stepped aside as Claudia's bridesmaids began their procession down the church's center aisle, leaving clouds of perfume in their wake. Claudia inched closer to him, her dress rustling. Joelle had sewn Claudia's dress, too. It had taken her two months, and it was a work of art, panels of ivory silk with a gently curving neckline and a sweeping skirt that trailed behind Claudia. Rather than a traditional veil, she'd pinned a scarf of lace into her hair. In her hands was a bouquet of red, pink and white roses.

"Are you sure you want to go through with this?" he teased as they watched her bridesmaids march down the aisle. "It's not too late to change your mind."

"Gee, I don't know," Claudia whispered back. "If I marry him, will you still be my dad?"

"Forever and ever." He wasn't joking anymore.

Her smile was so real he knew she wasn't joking, either. "Good," she said, then tucked her hand around his arm and led him through the doors, into the church.

The reception was held at a country club in northern Fairfield County. Gary's parents were members, and they'd made the arrangements, even though Bobby had insisted on paying. The venue was damn expensive, although Gary's father had informed Bobby that because he was a member of long standing, the place had offered them a generous discount.

Discount? Bobby would hate to think what the undis-counted price was.

But he could afford it. If this was what Claudia wanted, she would have it.

The club was pretty, at least. The room they were in was bright, afternoon sunlight flooding through the French doors that lined one wall and opened out onto a fieldstone patio. The tables were draped in linen, the bartender was filling orders nonstop in one corner of the room and a three-piece combo played mellow music. Claudia and Gary had considered hiring a deejay, but they'd gone with a band instead, for which Bobby was thankful. Not that they showed any flair for playing Doors and Jimi Hendrix songs, but at least they weren't playing hip-hop, or that deafening heavy-metal junk the boys were listening to these days.

Claudia was in her element, circulating among the guests, dancing with Gary, laughing, hugging, kissing and showing off her ring set. The wedding band had diamonds in it, and the engagement ring contained a rock so big Bobby needed sunglasses to stare directly at it.

Joelle glided over to him, holding a glass of white wine for herself and a club soda for him. The sense of dislocation he felt in this ritzy room, hosting this ritzy reception, was replaced by an even greater amazement that a woman so elegant and confident could be his wife.

"How are you holding up?" she asked as she handed him his drink.

"Fine. You?"

"I don't know." Her smile was bittersweet. "I'm not old enough to be someone's mother-in-law."

He chuckled and glanced toward his own mother-in-law.

Wanda was seated at a table with some of Gary's relatives, blathering about something. As mothers-in-law went, he supposed there were worse. Over the past few years, she'd started acting as if she liked him, or at least respected him. He supposed she had to be nice to him, as long as he and Joelle were helping her out financially. And since she lived in Ohio, he didn't have to see her too often.

"You'll be a great mother-in-law," Bobby assured Joelle.

"And you're a wonderful liar." She reached up to adjust his collar. He'd untied the bow and unfastened the shirt's top stud a while ago, which had undoubtedly destroyed the odd shape of the collar.

He eased her hand away from his neck and gave it a gentle squeeze. Then he studied her ring. So plain, so thin. It had been all he could afford twenty-seven years ago. At least it was fourteen-carat gold.

"I should buy you a diamond," he said.

She was in the middle of a sip of wine, and she coughed a couple of times. "A diamond? Why?"

"Your daughter's walking around with the Rock of Gibraltar on her hand. That stone could cover the boys' tuition costs when they go to college."

She stretched out her arm and inspected her wedding band. "I like this ring just fine."

"It's cheap."

"It's priceless," she said, then rose on tiptoe and kissed his lips.

He closed his eyes and sank into the kiss, astonished that he—Bobby D—could be lucky enough to have this woman as his wife. When someone seated at a table near them whistled softly, he chuckled and pulled back. And immediately frowned when he spotted his father at the bar again.

How many drinks had the guy consumed? At least four, and the formal dinner hadn't begun yet. There weren't enough appetizers in the entire country club to absorb all the booze he'd been swilling.

If his father got drunk… Hell, he was already drunk. At this point, the only question was whether he'd get drunk enough to start breaking things.

Bobby cursed softly and handed his club soda to Joelle. "I've got to head Dad off at the pass," he said, squaring his shoulders and working his way across the room. It wasn't easy. Too many people had to stop and congratulate him. Who were all these folks, anyway? He and Joelle had very small families, but they'd invited neighbors, friends, a few of Joelle's fellow teachers, a few of Bobby's colleagues and associates from work. Bobby's first boss in Connecticut, the cousin of his physical therapist. Suzanne, the woman Joelle had lived with while Bobby was in 'Nam. A goodly portion of Claudia's classmates from high school and college. It seemed as if every single one of them had to stop him and offer congratulations, or share some anecdote about Claudia, or reminisce about some silly thing Gary had done years ago.

By the time he reached the bar, his father had already been served a highball glass full of scotch. Glenlivet, expensive stuff—wasted on Louie. At this point he'd probably think motor oil tasted great, as long as it had a high enough alcohol content.

Louie turned from the bar and wove toward a table. Bobby swooped down on him, slung his arm around the old man's shoulders and said, "Let's take a walk." Before Louie could muster any resistance, Bobby had him through the room's door and out into a chilly, air-conditioned hallway.

"What's going on?" Louie asked.

"You and I could use some fresh air," Bobby said, steering him down the hall, past the pro shop and the restrooms, through the airy lobby and out the front door. The patio that bordered their reception room ran the length of the building, but in front of the main entry it extended outward into a broad stone stairway that descended to a plush lawn and a circular driveway. Meticulously pruned arborvitae lined the driveway. Blossoming rhododendron flanked the patio. Not bad, Bobby thought. DiFranco Landscaping could do better, but the view was attractive and the lawn was extremely green.

"I don't need fresh air," Louie groused, wrinkling his nose as the summery evening wrapped around him. Like Bobby, he'd loosened his tie. His shirt and the jacket of his suit were wrinkled. Bobby wondered when he'd bought the suit, and where. It looked old, but his father never gained weight. He might have bought it when Bobby was a kid. Lapel widths came and went, and Bobby had no idea which width was considered fashionable when.

"I think you do need fresh air," Bobby said quietly. A blue-bird alighted on the stone ledge bordering the patio and then flew off. A couple of pink-faced men in casual apparel, with golf bags slung over their shoulders, emerged from the building, nodded a greeting at Bobby and Louie and then headed down the steps to the driveway.

"A flipping golf club," Louie muttered. "Since when did you get so fancy?"

Bobby chose to laugh off his father's implicit criticism. "It was what Claudia wanted," he said, his gaze settling on the glass in his father's hand. Was there a tactful way to get it out of Louie's grip? A way that wouldn't cause Louie to snap?

"You spoil that girl rotten, Bobby."

Anger bubbled up inside Bobby, but he swallowed it back down. He wasn't going to let his father goad him, not today. "It's her wedding. The only wedding she's ever going to have."

"People get divorced all the time," Louie pointed out.

"There's a happy thought." Keeping his voice mild required greater and greater effort. "If she gets a divorce, she's still doing this—" he gestured toward the building "—only once. One big wedding, and after that she's on her own. But I don't see a divorce happening here. Gary's a good guy, and Claudia's crazy about him."

"Lucky to marry a woman who's crazy about you, huh," Louie said, his tone tinged with sarcasm.

What the hell was that supposed to mean? Was he implying that Joelle wasn't crazy about Bobby? She'd said her simple little wedding band was priceless. That sounded pretty crazy to Bobby.

His father slugged down some scotch. His eyes had a milky appearance, but he wasn't staggering or reeling. "So, how much did this shindig set you back? You got that much money to spare?"

"We budgeted for it," Bobby said cryptically. He wasn't sure what direction the conversation was taking, but he didn't like it. "How about a cup of coffee, Dad?"

"I don't want coffee. I've got a drink." He took another sip from his glass. Damn the bartender for having filled it so full. "I hear you send money to Wanda."

"We don't send her money." They only helped her out when she needed it. They'd paid her airfare to visit Connecticut—and they'd paid Louie's airfare for this wedding, too, and his hotel room. But he'd been union at the rivet factory, and he received a decent pension in retirement. That he spent most of it on booze wasn't a justification for Bobby to give him financial support. "Dad, you're getting in a mood. I think you should have some coffee."

"What mood? I'm not in a mood." Louie shot him a defiant glare. "I'm here, okay? I came to the flipping wedding. Put on a suit, got on a plane, saw the girl get married. This part's called the reception, right? This is when we get our reward for sitting through the boring parts."

"Reward yourself with a cup of coffee. There's going to be a nice dinner soon, and—"

"Oh, a *nice* dinner. Everything's very nice here. Who are you trying to kid, Bobby?"

Bobby sighed. His gaze was still on his father's glass. He felt his eyes swiveling in their sockets, following the movement of Louie's hand as he moved it, the glass shifting right and then left.

"You're a piece of crap like me, Bobby. You can dress up in a fancy tuxedo, but it doesn't change what you are. A kid from Tubtown. Cannon fodder, all shot up in Vietnam. Now you lug stones and plant shrubs. You wear boots to work and breathe dirt. You married that snotty blond girl—I don't know why. Why didn't you marry the dark-haired one? She was like us. This one—" he gestured toward the doors "—this Joelle, she always put on airs. Thought she was better than us. I never liked her."

"I'll be sure to tell her," Bobby said dryly. "Give me the glass, Dad."

"Like hell." He took another sip. "I never liked her. She had a superior way about her. I don't know why the hell you married her—"

"Dad."

"But I can guess. I can guess, Bobby. You think I'm an idiot? She was pregnant. You got her in trouble. You were stupid, sleeping around with too many girls. Thought you were the stud of Holmdell, but Mr. Stud got caught."

"Give me the glass," Bobby said, extending his hand.

His father stepped back, out of reach. "At least you had the balls to get a girl pregnant, which is more than I can say for your pansy brother. But I'll tell you this, Bobby, since you're too stupid to figure it out yourself. Joelle tricked you. She conned you. That pretty little girl you walked down the aisle today? You claim she's my granddaughter, but she sure as hell doesn't look like a DiFranco."

Rage exploded, flaring red in Bobby's brain. He made a dive for the glass and wound up catching his father's wrist. The glass tipped, splashing scotch onto the fieldstone beneath their feet. With his free hand, he wrenched the glass from his father's grip and hurled it over the ledge, onto the grass below.

"You little punk," his father snarled.

"You've had too much to drink, Dad. You're saying things you don't mean to say—"

"I mean every word of it." He yanked his arm away from Bobby and started toward the door. "I'm getting another drink."

"No. You're done drinking for today."

"You think I'm a drunk?"

"I know you're a drunk."

The punch came so quickly, so unexpectedly, Bobby didn't have a chance to duck. He felt the sting in the corner of his mouth, the grinding ache in his cheek as his feet danced under him, struggling to hold him upright. Behind him he heard someone shout, and then a pair of hands pressed against his shoulders, steadying him. "Christ," Eddie muttered. He pressed a frosty glass and a cocktail napkin into Bobby's hands. "Put some ice on your lip. I'll take care of Dad."

Bobby's vision slowly cleared. He watched his brother storm across the patio to Louie, who was trying to climb over the ledge to retrieve his glass from the lawn below. Sucking air into his lungs, he lowered his gaze to the glass in his hand. Some sort of liquid in there, a stirrer and ice. He pulled out a cube and pressed it to the corner of his mouth. The cold felt good, but the alcohol made his lip sting even more.

The ice melted fast, dripping between his fingers. He used the cocktail napkin to dry his hand and then his mouth. When he drew the napkin away, he saw blood on it.

Eddie seemed to have calmed his father down. He held him tightly and led him back toward Bobby. "How 'bout that?" Louie said, studying Bobby's face and smiling with dazed pride. "Didn't know your old man had it in him, huh."

"I always knew you had it in you," Bobby retorted, wondering if the hatred burning in his gut was visible in his eyes.

"It's not that bad, Bobby," Eddie assured him. "Use more ice."

"You can just tell folks you walked into a door," Louie said, then laughed. Maybe he wasn't so drunk after all. Or maybe being drunk didn't dull his memory. This punch, Bobby understood, was payback. It was settling a very old score. It was letting Bobby know that the hatred was mutual.

"I'm going to drive him back to the hotel," Eddie said.

"I can call a cab for him."

"Here? In the middle of golf country?" Eddie snorted.

"I don't want you to leave. They'll be serving dinner soon."

"That's all right. I'll get him into his room and come back. You can tell Stuart where I've gone. Anyone else, just tell them Dad wasn't feeling well."

"I'm feeling fine," Louie protested. "I'd feel even better if I had a drink."

"I'll talk to the bartender at the hotel lounge," Eddie added.

Bobby shook his head. "If the bar cuts him off, he'll just go through whatever's in the minibar in his room."

"At least he won't be drinking in public. Let me leave so I can come back."

Bobby glanced at his father, who appeared to be deflating, adrenaline no longer pumping through his veins. Just blood and booze. "Eddie, I—"

"Hey." Eddie silenced him. "How many times did you shield me from him over the years? This is the least I can do for you. Now, your princess just got married. Go back inside and be a proud papa."

Bobby felt his energy drain away. "Thanks."

He watched as Eddie led their father toward the stairs and down. Louie's legs seemed rubbery beneath him, even though Bobby was the one who'd gotten walloped. If he and Eddie were lucky, the son of a bitch would collapse as soon as he got to his room and sleep until morning. If they weren't lucky, he'd work his way through the minibar, make himself sick and stick Bobby with a whopping bill at checkout time.

Screw it. Eddie was right. He had to go inside and be a proud papa. With a split lip and a bruised cheek.

He made his way back to the building, shivering as the air-conditioning blasted him. Refusing to show his face in the reception room until he'd cleaned up, he ducked into the men's room.

The bathroom was brightly lit and as he studied his reflection in the mirror that stretched the length of a wall above a row of sinks, the striped green wallpaper made him look even paler than he was. His hair was mussed, the skin above his jaw slightly puffy. Blood leaked from the corner of his mouth. At least it hadn't dripped onto his tux. How would he have explained the bloodstains when he returned the suit to the rental place?

I walked into a door, and the door won.

Frickin' bastard, he thought as he tossed the cocktail napkin into the trash can and twisted the faucet.

The door swung open. He hoped it wasn't one of the wedding guests. His peripheral vision caught a flutter of pale blue and he spun around. "Jo? What the hell are you doing here?"

"Someone in the lobby said you were in here."

"It's a men's room."

"Big deal." She swept across the room, pinched his chin between her thumb and index finger and inspected his face. "Did you hit your father?"

"No." He eased out of her grasp and turned back to the sink. "I wish I had," he added before bowing and splashing water onto his face.

"Where is he now?"

"Eddie's driving him back to the hotel." He lifted a paper towel from the stack beside the sink. It was as soft as cloth. He dabbed his lip, then stretched it to see where the blood was flowing from. Just inside, where his teeth had jammed into the flesh.

"Let me," Joelle said, taking a fresh towel, soaking it and pressing it lightly to his mouth and cheek. "I think you'll live." She smiled, obviously trying to cool his anger as much as his face.

"I look like shit."

"You look like the most handsome man at the wedding," she argued. "With a slightly puffy lip. If you smile, no one will notice."

He attempted a smile. It hurt not just his face but his soul.

Behind Joelle, the door cracked open and a man started to enter. "Oh—excuse me," he said, hastily retreating.

"Come on in," Joelle called to him. "Don't pay any attention to me."

"No, that's all right—I'll find another restroom." The man vanished, letting the door whisper shut behind him.

Joelle grinned up at Bobby. "I scared him away, huh."

She was the scariest woman he'd ever known. So calm, so sure of herself, so determined to whip him back into shape. He could force a smile so the wedding guests wouldn't notice his swollen lip, but he was a long way from back into shape. The anger inside him had mutated into something else, something that felt like panic, or helplessness. Something weak and frightening, something Bobby didn't want to be.

Joelle must have sensed it. "Talk to me, Bobby."

"I'm fine," he insisted.

"You're upset, but your father's gone. Eddie's taking care of it. Put it out of your mind, okay?"

"It's not—" He swallowed. When she gazed at him that way, her eyes so blue, so beseeching, he wished he could tell her everything. He wished he could sob on her shoulder. But he couldn't. He was a man, her husband, the person who had promised to make everything right for her. "I'm not upset," he said.

"You are, Bobby. Why do I always have to fight with you to get you to open up? For God's sake, talk to me."

What could he say? How could he admit what he was feeling? "I hate my father," he admitted at last.

"I don't blame you."

"Not because of him, or this." He brushed his hand against his throbbing mouth. "Because…because what kind of father can I possibly be if he's who I learned from? He's all I know about how to be a father." Eddie was wise not to have kids—even gay couples became parents these days, but Eddie and Stuart had no interest in that. Bobby should have been that wise, too. He carried his father's genes in him, his father's imprint. He'd spent every day of his life struggling to be a better man, but what if he'd failed? What if he was his father's son?

He should never have married Joelle. He'd done it only because she'd been desperate and he would have done anything for her—even if it meant turning into his father.

She cupped her hands on either side of his face and forced him to meet her gaze. Her fingers were cool, firm but unbearably gentle. "You are the finest father I've ever seen," she told him. "You're nothing like him."

"I'm his son."

"He's not a father." Her voice dipped to a near whisper. "Contributing sperm isn't what makes a man a father, Bobby. You know that. I know that."

Bobby's father probably knew that, too. The words he'd said outside, the insinuations—had he guessed the truth? Did it matter?

"*You,* Bobby DiFranco—*you* are what it means to be a father." She guided his face down to her and kissed him, a sweet, warm touch of her mouth to his, light enough not to hurt his injured lip. Then she released him. "Come," she said, slipping her hand into his and leading him out of the bathroom. "You have to make a toast to the bride and groom. Try to smile, okay?"

Smiling would hurt. But for Joelle he would do it.

Chapter 13

Danny showed up at five-thirty, lugging a shopping bag full of take-out Chinese food. The aroma of soy and ginger emanating from the bag tore through whatever had been wrapped around Bobby's appetite all day. One whiff and he realized he was starving.

He wasn't sure what to make of his kids' fussing over him, though. That morning Claudia had barged in and ordered him to eat something. Now Danny was standing on the front porch, armed with food.

At least he hadn't taken inspiration from his brother and shown up with booze. Of all the mistakes Bobby had made in the past week—and he still wasn't sure what all those mistakes were; he just knew he'd made plenty—downing drink after drink with Mike at the Hay Street Pub had been the biggest.

Or maybe not. Joelle hadn't left him after that debacle. Maybe meeting with Helen Crawford behind Joelle's back had been a worse mistake.

Or maybe his biggest mistake was that he was who he was—a man who couldn't give Joelle what she wanted. A man who could provide her with a home and a car, all the security in the world, but couldn't go all touchy-feely about his emotions.

She wanted him to open up and let everything out? Well, damn it, he'd been as open as he could be. She wanted to know what was inside him? Rage. He'd sure as hell let that out.

"How about it, Dad?" Danny said with forced cheer. "Can I tempt you with some General Gao's chicken?"

"Come on in." Bobby waved Danny inside, then shut the door. The house didn't have its usual Saturday fresh-scrubbed smell. He supposed he could have cleaned the place in Joelle's absence, but instead he'd spent much of the day working on her garden. She labored over it, and she liked to believe it was hers, but gardening wasn't her forte. She didn't understand that you had to thin out the carrots and radishes if you hoped to harvest edible vegetables and not scrawny little roots. You had to check the undersides of the tomato leaves for aphids, and you had to weed ruthlessly. Joelle insisted that her garden be organic and she'd forbidden Bobby from spraying weed killer and insecticide on the plants. But you couldn't get a crop of organic produce if insects ate whatever the weeds hadn't choked to death.

He'd finished gardening a couple of hours ago, taken a long shower and thought about how, if he were a drinker, a cold beer would have hit the spot. Instead, he'd poured himself a glass of iced tea, left another message, less pleading and more demanding, on Joelle's cell phone and then called Wanda. "Have you seen Joelle?" he'd asked.

"I don't want to get in the middle of this," she'd replied, which indicated that she *had* seen Joelle and knew something about what was going on.

"She won't return my calls," he'd said.

"I suppose she will when she's good and ready."

"Will you ask her to get ready soon?" He'd been unable to sift the impatience from his voice. "We can't work anything out if she won't talk to me."

"Or if you won't talk to her," Wanda had said.

He'd almost retorted that he'd been attempting since yesterday to talk to Joelle, but she kept refusing to accept his calls. But why argue with Wanda? She didn't want to get in the middle of this, and he didn't blame her. "Tell her I called," Bobby had said. "Tell her I'll keep trying."

"You better try *something*," Wanda had said cryptically before hanging up.

Discouraged, he'd turned the CD player back on. The carousel was still full of Doors disks, and the first song to play was "The End." He'd sat listening to the dirgelike number, absorbing Jim Morrison's howls of pain. "The end of laughter and soft lies," Morrison sang, leaving Bobby so depressed he almost hadn't heard Danny ringing the doorbell.

All right. Food had arrived, food and his youngest son. He was still depressed, but not quite as much as he'd been a few minutes ago.

"Lauren says Asian cuisine tastes better with chopsticks," Danny said as he removed plastic tubs and waxed cardboard containers from the bag and spread them out on the kitchen table.

Bobby reminded himself that Lauren was Danny's girl-friend, the woman who'd dragged Danny off to Tanglewood to listen to symphonies. Bobby had met her a couple of times, most recently at a barbecue at Claudia and Gary's house to celebrate Memorial Day and Claudia's birthday. Lauren seemed nice enough—but she also seemed like the sort of person who'd use words like *cuisine* and insist on using chopsticks.

"This is America," Bobby said. "I'm using a fork."

Danny grinned and accepted a fork, too. He helped himself to one of the microbrewery beers in the refrigerator door while Bobby poured himself a fresh glass of iced tea. Then they settled at the table and dug in. While Bobby inhaled a third of the General Gao's chicken and a small mountain of steamed rice, Danny described the client he and Mike had visited earlier that day. "He asked for terracing, but his property doesn't slope. If we did terracing, we'd have to recontour the land first. It seems like an awful lot of effort just so the guy can have terraces."

"It's a profitable job," Bobby explained. "If that's what he wants, we'll rent some earth movers and recontour his property. And we'll make a lot of money doing it."

"Yeah, well, Mike and I wrote down the guy's specs and figured you'd have to calculate the cost. We weren't sure whether the company can do that kind of job."

"We can."

Danny nodded. He was eating even faster than Bobby. Twenty-four years old and he still went through food like a ravenous teenager. He piled some spring rolls onto his plate, then picked one up with his fingers and chomped on it, managing to consume half of it in one bite.

"So, what's the deal?" Bobby asked once Danny had made it through all his spring rolls. "You kids are on some kind of rotation?"

Danny gave him an innocent look. "Rotation?"

"Yeah—taking turns feeding me. Is Mike scheduled for tomorrow morning?"

"Mike." Danny snorted. "He's pissed. I told him to stay away from you."

That brought Bobby up short. He lowered his fork. "Why?"

"Because of the whole Claudia thing. He doesn't want to forgive you for not telling us the truth."

"You *do* want to forgive me?"

Danny shrugged. Along with his adolescent appetite, he still had a lanky adolescent build. Working for DiFranco had added some heft to his torso, however. His chest and shoulders filled his T-shirt well. The front of the shirt featured a picture of a rock band Bobby had never heard of. "I figure, what the heck," he said. "Claudia's my sister. End of story."

"You don't mind that your mother and I lied to you?"

"People lie. They have their reasons." He rummaged through the food containers, apparently contemplating what to eat next.

Danny had apparently made his peace with Bobby and Joelle's decision not to tell anyone about Claudia's origins. Why couldn't Mike? Was it simply that Danny was a mellower guy, or happier because he was in love? And where did Claudia fit on the scale? She'd agreed to have her blood tested, but she seemed agitated about the whole thing.

Beyond the kids, what about him? What about Joelle? What would they do if Claudia wound up being a genetic match for Foster's son?

Would they even still be married by then?

"So, when do you think Mom'll be coming home?" Danny asked after washing a dim-sum dumpling down with a swig of beer.

"I don't know. She won't talk to me."

"Man, what did you do to her?"

"Nothing," Bobby said, then pressed his lips together and stared at the thick brown sauce spread like an oil slick across the surface of his plate. He'd done *something*. Saying he'd done nothing was just another lie.

He and Joelle had survived worse, hadn't they? They'd survived his return home from Vietnam, his nightmares, his long, arduous months of rehab. They'd survived years of scrimping, years when the only vacation they could afford was a day at an amusement park with the kids, when their idea of a new car was anything less than ten years old.

"Maybe you ought to go out to Ohio," Danny said as he scooped a pile of beef and broccoli onto his plate. "Sit down with her and talk things out."

"I just told you—she won't talk to me," Bobby said.

"Maybe you ought to get in her face. Then she'd have no choice but to talk to you."

Bobby regarded Danny. Danny tended to be more impulsive than Mike or Claudia. He thought a thing and then he did it. *Get in her face,* he'd said. *Go out to Ohio.*

Bobby wasn't one for dramatic gestures, and he'd never chased after a woman who didn't want him. But this wasn't just a woman. This was JoJo. His wife.

The woman who'd betrayed him. The woman who'd taken his daughter away from him.

The woman he'd adored since he was ten years old.

He couldn't fix this mess alone. He wasn't sure he and Joelle could fix it together. But apart, they would never make things right.

"I wonder how soon I could get to Ohio," he said.

Joelle's childhood bed was a lot less comfortable than her bed at home in Gray Hill. It was even less comfortable than the hard king-sized bed in the room at the West Side Motor Lodge, where she'd stayed her first night in Holmdell. Yet after checking out of the motel and moving into her old bedroom at the rear of the first-floor flat on Third Street, Joelle slept as if someone had clubbed her over the head, a thick, black sleep without dreams.

The small room overlooking the backyard was warm and stuffy. Her mother had never installed an air conditioner in that room, and she left the door shut most of the time so the air-conditioning gusting through the rest of the apartment wouldn't be wasted in a room she rarely used. She'd set up her sewing machine on Joelle's desk, and an ironing board along the far wall. A pile of fabric squares in a basket next to the sewing machine indicated that she was working on a quilt. Joelle could sew it while she was in town, but it was her mother's project, so she left the fabric and the machine alone.

She used to sew a lot when the kids were younger. They were always outgrowing things, always in need of a new shirt or dress. Ratty old furniture had to be spruced up with new slipcovers and pillows. But lately she'd been neglecting her sewing. When she went home, she'd start a new project.

When she went home. Once she decided it was time to return to the house in Gray Hill. Once she knew whether the mistakes she'd made were reparable, whether her children would forgive her, whether her husband would ever, ever open his heart fully to her.

Until she was ready to face everything that awaited her in Connecticut, the cramped back bedroom on Third Street would do, even without air-conditioning. The scuffed chest of drawers that used to hold all her clothing now contained stationery supplies, old magazines and odds and ends, but the bottom drawer was empty, enabling her to unpack her suitcase. The closet was empty, too—except for her high-school prom dress, still hanging from the rod, draped in clear, protective plastic. As if she'd ever wear the thing again. Just touching the synthetic fabric made her skin itch.

The pillow on her bed smelled musty, but the sheets were cool. She'd opened the window to let in the night air and asked her mother to let her sleep late. She hadn't slept well for so many nights. Maybe a night alone, without Bobby lying right beside her yet light-years away from her, would allow her to get some rest.

It did. In her thin T-shirt, with the blanket kicked to the foot of the bed, she lay unmoving in the heat. She might have slept straight through Sunday if she hadn't heard a tapping at the window.

She opened one eye and found the room hazy with a gray light seeping through the voile curtains. Then she heard the tapping again, and a whisper: "JoJo?"

She bolted upright, blinking furiously. Once her eyes were in focus, she saw the familiar silhouette against the floating curtains. Inhaling deeply to steady her nerves, she swung out of bed, crossed to the window and spread the curtains apart.

There stood Bobby, just as he had when they'd been children, when he'd sneaked over to visit her late at night and hadn't dared to ring the front doorbell. She stared at him through the screen, his face shadowed, his shoulders broad and strong. "What are you doing here?" she asked.

"Danny said I should get in your face," he told her.

Her brain moved sluggishly, still woozy with drowsiness. She blinked again, took more deep breaths, shook her head to clear it. "I mean *here,* at the window."

"No one answered the front door."

"What time is it?"

He lifted his wrist. "Almost eleven."

Her mother must have gone out. Maybe she'd met Stan Sherko at the Bank Street Diner for brunch. Just friends, indeed.

Unsure what to do, Joelle decided to concentrate on facts and chronologies. "How did you get here? You were still in Connecticut last night. You phoned."

"And you had your mother run interference." He sounded annoyed when he said that, but his tone grew more conversational when he explained, "I hitched a ride to Cincinnati on a FedEx plane."

"What?"

"Danny's girlfriend, Lauren—her father is an attorney for some big shot at FedEx. Danny talked to Lauren, and she made a few calls and got me a seat on one of their overnight flights. Me and a bunch of fruit crates and sandals from L.L. Bean. I like that girl." She saw the outline of his cheeks move and realized he must have smiled. "I rented a car at the airport."

"You must be exhausted."

Although she couldn't see his eyes, she felt his gaze. "You look a lot more tired than I feel."

"Bobby…" She sighed. "I'm not sure I'm ready to talk to you yet."

"Too bad. I'm in your face."

She smiled, imagining Danny giving him in-your-face coaching.

"So, are you coming out or am I coming in?"

"I'm not climbing over the windowsill," she said. "I'm too old. Go around to the front door. I'll let you in."

She turned from the window, wondering whether she should get dressed before she let Bobby inside the apartment. Why bother? He hadn't touched her in days. The last time he had, it had felt more like fear than love. No way would he interpret her sleep apparel as seductive.

She ran her fingers through her tangled hair and yanked the knob on the bedroom door. The heat had made the wood swell, and the door stuck for a moment before opening. Willing herself to full alertness, she strode barefoot down the hall to the front door.

Bobby stepped inside, closed the door behind him and stared at her. He had on a pair of old jeans worn to flannel softness and a plain navy blue T-shirt that hinted at the lean strength of his body. She ached to bury her face against his chest, to feel his arms tight around her. But he didn't reach for her, and she kept her distance.

"Are you okay?" he asked.

"Yes."

"It was a long drive for you, all alone."

She shrugged. "Would you like some coffee? Something to eat?"

"Why is everyone trying to feed me? You all think I don't know how to feed myself?"

Irked by his response—by his presence—she pivoted on her heel and stalked into the kitchen. Bobby might not want coffee, but she did.

He followed her into the kitchen and opened the blinds while she prepared a pot of coffee. "What have you been doing here?" he asked.

By here, she knew he meant Holmdell. She wasn't sure she should say anything when she was still not completely awake, but having Bobby talk to her, pepper her with questions, attempt a conversation, was a treat after the past week. She ought to encourage him. "I've been retracing my steps," she told him.

"What do you mean?"

"Figuring out how I wound up where I did."

"Have you figured it out?"

"I don't know." The coffeemaker churned. She pulled two cups and saucers from the drying rack and set them on the table. Typical Bobby: he wanted her to give him a simple answer. He wanted her to say yes, she'd figured it out, so he wouldn't have to offer anything of himself. In fact, she *had* figured it out, at least some of it. She'd figured out that for the past thirty-seven years she'd been married to a loyal, reliable, generous man who couldn't face the demons inside himself, who couldn't face the even greater goodness there, who couldn't love her the way she'd always dreamed of being loved. But how could she tell him that?

The coffee finished brewing, and she lifted the decanter from the machine. "I'll go to a marriage counselor with you," he said, startling her so much she nearly dropped the pot.

She steadied herself before carrying the pot to the table and filling the cups. "You will?"

"I can't stand the idea, Jo, but if it'll make you happy, I'll do it."

"I don't know how successful counseling would be if you went into it saying, 'I can't stand the idea.'"

He snorted. "Sitting in an office and baring my soul to a stranger? I don't do that kind of thing."

You don't bare your soul to anyone, she thought, returning the pot to the counter.

"I don't even know what we'd talk about," he added.

"We'd talk about why…" Her voice started to crack, and she took a sip of coffee to cover the sound. "We'd talk about why you can't talk about anything. About why when you're angry or afraid, you won't talk to me. You lock everything up inside yourself and pretend it doesn't exist."

He ignored his coffee, his attention fully on her, his eyes as intense as lasers. "Sometimes that's a pretty smart strategy."

"But the truth doesn't always stay locked up. It escapes."

"Yeah." He looked past her and drank some coffee. "Why don't you get dressed and go downtown with me. I can drop off the rental car at the bus station. No sense having two cars here."

He was shutting down again. Despair whispered in her heart, but she refused to listen to it. He was here. He'd traveled all the way to Cincinnati on a FedEx cargo plane. Maybe that was as close as he'd ever get to telling her he loved her.

Abandoning him to the steaming coffeepot and whatever edibles he might scrounge—there were probably some more stale Danish stashed somewhere—she detoured to her bedroom to grab a robe, then headed for the bathroom to shower. She didn't need to wear a robe around him. He was her husband; he'd seen her naked plenty of times. But she still felt a barrier between them, like the spring-pressured gates he'd bought to block off the stairways when the boys were toddlers. The gates wedged between the walls at the top or bottom of a flight of stairs, or in a doorway and tension held them in place.

Tension was holding a barricade in place between her and Bobby, too.

She showered, brushed her teeth and returned to the bedroom to dress. Her mouth tingled with mint. She wondered whether Bobby would kiss her. He'd traveled all this way— in a cargo plane—but he hadn't even touched her.

Dressed in shorts and a polo shirt, her hair brushed and sandals buckled onto her feet, she emerged from the bedroom. She found Bobby where she'd left him—in the kitchen, staring out the window above the sink. All he could see from there was the duplex next door. The buildings along Third Street were separated from one another only by alleys no wider than a car. When Joelle was about ten, a fat woman with poodle-curly hair lived in the neighboring building, and she liked to stack Andy Williams and Dean Martin albums on her hi-fi and waltz around her flat. Joelle used to spy on her, half amused and half transfixed by the way the woman danced, as graceful as a ballerina despite her size. She'd moved away a couple of years later and a family with a bunch of bratty children who were always screeching moved in. In the summer, when people kept their windows open because no one in those days had air-conditioning, the children's constant whining and bickering became an excruciating sound track to Joelle's dinners.

Now everyone had air-conditioning units and all the windows were closed.

Bobby gave her a tenuous smile and led her out of the building into the overcast morning. His car was a nondescript dark green sedan. Before folding himself behind the wheel, he reminded her that the car-rental drop-off was at the bus station. She nodded, climbed into her Prius and followed him down the street.

Once he dropped off his car, she'd have to drive him places, or else he'd appropriate her car to drive himself around. Maybe it would have been better for him to keep the rental.

Except that he'd journeyed to Holmdell to get in her face, and she had to admit she wanted him there. Maybe he was ready to start talking, *really* talking. In any case, that he'd go to such an effort to be with her had to mean he wasn't ready to give up on their marriage.

The bus station's parking lot was full, every space occupied and a huge Greyhound bus occupying most of the curb. Bobby double-parked and approached her car. She pushed the button to open her window. "I'll park in the lot behind the bank," she said. It was less than a block away.

Nodding, Bobby slapped the roof of her car and then strode into the terminal.

Since it was Sunday, the bank was closed, but several cars were parked in the lot. Parking on the downtown streets was metered, so people often left their cars in the lots behind the stores and office buildings. Joelle eased into a space between a Dodge Ram and a glossy Mercedes sedan. Swanky car, she thought as she climbed out of the Prius, careful not to let her door bump the Mercedes. No doubt it belonged to someone from the Hill.

By the time she'd walked back to the bus station, Bobby had completed his task. She observed him as he swung out of the terminal. Although their marriage was in shambles, he walked with a confidence that dazzled her. He'd had that long-legged, sure-footed stride for as long as she'd known him. Even during the year he'd been on crutches, undergoing rehab on his left leg, he'd hobbled with a certainty and determination that announced to the world that he knew where he was going.

"Hi," he said, meeting up with her at the parking lot's entrance. The gray sky washed his face with wan light.

"Is there anything you need to do downtown?" she asked.

"No." He gazed down at her, his expression inscrutable.

"Well, what should we do? We're not going to find a marriage counselor on a Sunday morning."

He laughed, a welcome sound above the rumble of the bus's idling engine and the whisk of cars cruising down the street. "Downtown didn't use to be so busy on a Sunday," he said, observing the traffic. "Everyone used to be in church."

"Or sleeping late. And all the stores used to be closed. I guess they did away with the blue laws. Lots of stores are open today."

"Holmdell meets the twenty-first century." He shrugged and started toward the bank. "Let's get some lunch. It's too late for breakfast."

She wasn't particularly hungry, but she supposed he was, after his overnight flight on the cargo plane. They couldn't go to the Bank Street Diner, though. Her mother might be there, and if she was, she'd meddle.

As Joelle and Bobby entered the parking lot behind the bank, she spotted a woman ahead of them, approaching the Mercedes. The woman had silver hair as smooth and shiny as a mirror, and she wore white slacks and a sleeveless cotton blouse. Her hair placed her well past middle age, but her tan and freckled arms were firm and muscular, as if she swam or played a lot of tennis.

She reached her car just before Joelle and Bobby reached the Prius, and when she pressed the button on her key to unlock the sedan, she turned to offer a friendly smile. It froze on her face, and her eyes widened in astonishment. "Joelle Webber?"

The woman's shock arced like lightning, striking Joelle and causing her to flinch. She recognized that nut-brown face, the elegant cheekbones, the prim lips glossed with pink lipstick. Drew Foster's mother was the sort of woman who never left the house without first donning a full layer of makeup.

"Mrs. Foster," she said politely, trying to hide her surprise. Hadn't she seen a strange young woman picking up the mail at the Foster house yesterday? Hadn't she concluded that the Fosters no longer lived there? Stupid assumption. The young woman could have been a guest, or hired help.

Joelle scrambled for something innocuous to say to Drew's mother. But before she could come up with a friendly observation, Mrs. Foster had stepped out from between their cars, marched over to Joelle and slapped her cheek.

The slap didn't hurt—for all the muscle tone in her arms, Mrs. Foster was a petite, elderly woman. But it hurt Joelle's composure. She sprang back and Bobby sprang forward. Joelle gripped his arm, afraid he'd take a swing at Drew's mother and send her clear across the lot.

"How dare you!" Mrs. Foster railed. "How dare you keep my granddaughter from me!"

"Don't touch my wife," Bobby growled.

"Bobby, no." Joelle tried to calm him.

"You're her husband?" Mrs. Foster glowered at Bobby, her expression as lethal as his. "You're the man who stole my granddaughter?"

Before Bobby could retort, Joelle yanked on his arm, moving him back a step. "No one stole your granddaughter, Mrs. Foster," she said.

"Then tell me why my son had to hire a detective to find out he even *had* a daughter."

Joelle could feel Bobby bristling next to her; energy pulsing through him. He wanted to defend her, he wanted to lash out. Yet he restrained himself. She knew how much that restraint cost him.

"Drew ran away from his daughter," Joelle said, her voice muted. Something cold and wet struck her cheek and she glanced up to see a dark cloud passing over the parking lot. "When I told him I was pregnant, he asked me to get an abortion."

"He didn't know any better," Mrs. Foster said, defending him. "He was just a child. He was scared."

"I was young and scared, too."

"You should have come to Marshall and me. We would have supported you, paid your medical expenses."

And then stolen my baby from me, Joelle completed the thought. She wasn't sure why she believed this, but she did. The Fosters had never cared for her. She'd been a poor girl from the wrong side of town, and while they'd tolerated her and maintained a pleasant civility around her, they'd never embraced her.

If she'd shown up on their doorstep with the news that their son had gotten her pregnant, they would have hated her.

They would have done the right thing—they were the kind of people who recognized their obligations—but they wouldn't have done it for her. Only for her child.

"I made the choice I believed was best," Joelle said firmly, ignoring another raindrop that struck the tip of her nose. "And I'd make the same choice today."

"Keeping our granddaughter from us? Does she even know she has grandparents?"

Joelle felt another wave of energy surge through Bobby. She slid her hand down past his wrist to twine her fingers through his. The tension in his grip could have broken her bones if he'd let it. "She knows her grandparents," Joelle said, not bothering to add that Claudia's allotment of grandparents was pretty skimpy.

"Marshall and I need to meet her. She's our grandchild, too."

"She's an adult. If she wants to meet you, I'm sure she'll arrange it."

Mrs. Foster closed in on her. "You have no idea," she said, her teeth clenched and the tendons in her neck standing out beneath her skin. "You can't begin to comprehend what it's like to have only one grandchild and he's dying. In your worst nightmares, you can't begin to imagine it."

Joelle suffered a pang of sympathy for the woman, but it was fleeting. If Mrs. Foster had raised her own son to be more responsible, she might have spent the past thirty-seven years doting on a granddaughter. But things happened. One decision led to another, and to another, until people wound up so far down one path that they could never retrace their steps and try another route.

"I've had my own nightmares, Mrs. Foster," Joelle said quietly.

Bobby broke in, apparently unable to hold back any longer. "We're done here." He dug into the pocket of Joelle's purse where she stashed her keys and pressed the button on her car key to unlock the doors. Swinging the passenger door open, he nudged Joelle onto the seat, then loped around the car and crammed himself behind the wheel, not bothering to adjust the seat for his larger frame before he ignited the engine and backed out of the parking space. In the side mirror, Joelle saw Mrs. Foster calling to them, her face stretched into a grimace, her hand hacking the air.

Bobby didn't speak as he drove out into the street, his knees banging against the steering wheel. Stopped at a red light, he slid the seat back and tilted the rearview mirror to accommodate his height.

She considered asking him where they were going, then thought better of it. He was seething with anger, most of it aimed at Drew Foster's mother but some of it reserved for Joelle, too. She knew Bobby well enough to understand he was furious with her for having spoken gently to a woman who had slapped her. Joelle should have been furious, too. But…God help her, maybe she deserved that slap. And maybe she deserved Bobby's wrath. She'd made a choice so long ago, the only sensible choice she could grasp at the time, the only one that would enable her to keep her baby and her dignity. It might have been the wrong choice, but she wouldn't have done anything differently if she'd had it to do all over again.

Next to her, Bobby said nothing. Random raindrops had accelerated into a drizzle and he flicked on the wipers. She could tell he was gnashing his teeth by the twitching muscle in his jaw.

He drove through downtown Holmdell, past Harley's and

the new Starbucks. He drove past where the A&W stand used to be. It was gone, replaced by a carwash. Farther down the road, a Home Depot had sprung up, a large concrete structure surrounded by an even larger parking lot. Bobby kept driving.

She realized where he was driving her when he veered off the main road and onto a two-lane strip of asphalt that snaked into the woods outside of town. Over one hill, a jag in the road, up another hill and the trees thinned out, opening onto a stretch of dirt and gravel and beyond it the lake.

No other cars were there. Sunday at noon wasn't exactly a popular time for teenagers to make out in cars—if they still did that sort of thing these days—and the damp day kept swimmers from gathering along the edge of the lake on the narrow strip of sand that Holmdell residents extravagantly called a beach. Bobby had his choice of places to park, and he angled the car to provide a clear view of the lake and the pine forest surrounding it. The water was slate-colored, pockmarked by the rain striking its surface. When he turned off the engine, Joelle heard the tap of raindrops against the roof.

"You never brought me here before," she said.

"Yeah, I did." He pushed his seat back as far as it could go and attempted to stretch his legs. "We'd bike up here to swim."

"When we were kids. I meant..." She remembered the summer nights Drew drove her to the lake in his Corvette and she'd struggled to figure out how far she ought to let him go.

"I know what you meant."

More silence. More raindrops pattering on the car's roof.

Joelle stared at the lake and ran her fingers lightly over her cheek where Mrs. Foster had slapped her. "You wanted to kill Mrs. Foster back there, didn't you," she finally said.

"And you wanted to shoot the breeze with her."

"I did not!"

"You treat the Fosters like they're decent people. They're not. They're spoiled, demanding, manipulative users. And that woman hit you. I can't believe she did that."

"I can."

"It's her son's fault she never knew about Claudia. She shouldn't be blaming you."

"Maybe she should." Joelle felt as bleak as the grim, gray clouds lying low above them. A sob filled her throat and she gulped it down. "I did everything wrong, Bobby. I shouldn't have had sex with Drew. And when I got pregnant…"

"Don't say you should have gotten rid of the baby." His voice was taut with indignation.

No, she shouldn't have gotten rid of Claudia, either through abortion or adoption. She couldn't imagine her life without Claudia in it, her precious daughter, her blessed first-born. She couldn't imagine her life without Claudia—or without Bobby. If it hadn't been for Claudia, he would never have married her.

He reached across the gearstick and captured her hand in his. It was the first time he'd touched her voluntarily, with affection, since Drew Foster had entered their house a week ago. He pulled her hand toward him, sandwiched it in both of his, traced his thumb aimlessly over her palm. "You weren't acting alone, Jo. If you did everything wrong, so did I."

The caress of his thumb felt so good she wanted to moan. She wanted to vault herself over the gearstick and into his lap, and hold him and kiss him and believe he loved her the way she loved him. But there was no room, and her seat belt was still fastened and she was afraid to risk having him push her away. So much remained wrong between them, so much unsaid. "Maybe marrying you was just another thing I did wrong. But I can't help feeling it was the right thing to do."

He twisted in his seat to face her. She kept her eyes on the lake, but she sensed his movement. She felt his scrutiny, his gaze solid and warm. "We were nuts to think we could keep the truth about Claudia a secret forever," he conceded.

"We kept it a secret for a long time." At last she looked at him, but now he'd turned away and was staring at the lake, at the rain streaking the windshield. "Unfortunately we never figured out what we'd do if the secret got out."

"What should we do?" he asked.

"If I knew, we wouldn't be here now."

His lips moved, as if he wanted to taste his words before he actually spoke them. "You walked out on me, Jo."

"We walked out on each other," she corrected him. "I just traveled more miles."

His thumb moved back and forth against her palm, exploring the lines, the skin worn dry by so many years of cleaning, digging weeds, sewing, demonstrating craft projects to her students, writing, hugging, clinging to her children and then prodding them out into the world. "All my life, I've tried to give you what you want," he said, his voice low but steady. "I did the best I could. But I don't think it's enough."

No, she acknowledged. It wasn't enough. He'd given her so much, but not the one thing she truly wanted. "I need to know what's in your heart," she said. "That would be enough."

He exhaled. "I—I don't do that stuff. Baring my soul and all that. Talking to shrinks, punching pillows to get out the rage, meditating, chanting, whatever. That's not the way I am."

She agreed with a nod.

"But I've tried."

She eyed him skeptically. "Have you?"

"I told you what happened in 'Nam. I didn't want to, but you pushed me, so I told you. And when I was starting the business, I talked to you about the finances, the loans, everything I was worried about. Everything I dreamed the business would be." He hesitated, and his voice emerged hoarse when he said, "I told you I hated my father. And I told you how I felt when Foster walked into our house last week. What more do you want?"

"I want…" God, she hated to beg. She hated to ask him for what he couldn't give. But they were actually talking, and he was holding her hand and she couldn't back out now. If the truth hurt… Well, it often did. She would simply have to endure the pain. "I want you to love me, Bobby."

"What?" He half shouted the word, half laughed it.

"You've never said it. Not once in all the years I've known you, all the years we've been married. You've never told me you love me."

"I tell you all the time. Maybe not in words, but—come on, Jo. You ask for a Prius—I buy you a Prius. You decide to try gardening—I give you a garden. Anything you want, anything I can give you—"

"Those are things, Bobby." He might be laughing, but she heard anger in his words, as well. She herself was far from laughter. It was all she could do to keep from erupting in tears. "When you were in Vietnam, every time I got a letter from you, I'd say a little prayer that you'd signed it 'Love, Bobby.' Then I opened it, and it never said *love*. I was sure you were planning to divorce me as soon as you got home. That was the deal, after all—we'd get married and then we could get a divorce. You never said you loved me, so I figured you didn't.

But then you came back broken and wounded, and you couldn't divorce me while you were in rehab, and then you kind of got in the habit of being married to me and—"

"Are you insane?" He tugged her hand, urging her to meet his gaze. "I've been in love with you since the first day of Mrs. Schmidt's fourth-grade class."

"You were ten years old. How could you have been in love with me?"

"Damned if I know. But I was."

"You never told me, Bobby. You never even hinted—"

"Because you were Joelle Webber." He sighed, his gaze pinned to the horizon. "You were going places. I realized even then that you were going to wind up someplace better. You were going to escape Tubtown. You weren't going to tie yourself to a boy whose father drank a lot and knocked him around, who went off to Vietnam because even that hellhole was better than his own home. I loved you enough to stay out of your way."

"I did wind up someplace better," she said, wishing he didn't look so distraught. "You were right about that."

"Everything I did, Jo—buying a house, building a business, getting the damn college degree—I did it so you would never have to think you'd gotten ripped off. You had dreams, you had expectations, and I did everything I could not to disappoint you. You married me only because you were in a bad situation, but—"

"The day you asked me to marry you was the best day of my life," she said. "I'd walked up that hill in the cemetery certain it was the absolute worst day of my life, and you turned it into the best day."

"You didn't know that at the time," he argued.

"No. It took me a while to figure out, but I know it now."

She unclasped her seat belt and leaned across the console to kiss Bobby. "Tell me. I need to hear the words."

"I love you, Jo," he said. "I always have."

They kissed, a deep, lush, loving kiss. His hand remained around hers and his mouth took hers, possessive, hungry... loving. She believed that. He'd said the words, and this time the truth didn't hurt at all.

By the time they stopped kissing, she was half in his lap, one knee propped on her seat, the steering wheel digging into her shoulder and the car's windows steamed. Bobby cupped her face with his free hand, brushed her hair back from her cheek and peered into her eyes. "So here we are at the lake, and this car is too small."

"It's not too small."

"It's too small and I'm too old." He smiled and caressed her mouth with his fingertips. "I'm sorry I never took you here to do anything besides swimming."

"You were busy with half the girls in Tubtown. I don't think you're all that sorry."

"I am," he insisted. He grazed her lips with his, and then her cheek and then the sensitive spot just below her ear. Desire throbbed deep inside her. "I would have made it good for you if I'd brought you here," he murmured, and she knew he would have. He'd made it good for her on their wedding night, when all she understood about sex was that it was unpleasant and painful and embarrassing. He always made it good for her, even when they were tired or angry or distracted. If only Bobby had told her he loved her back then, when she'd been young and hadn't made any terrible mistakes yet, who knew where they'd be today?

As if he could read her mind, he let his hand fall still and his eyes grew darker. "I could say I love you nonstop for the rest of our lives, Jo. But that wouldn't make things any better."

"Why?"

He closed his eyes for a moment, then opened them. "I'm still going to lose Claudia."

If Bobby had loved Joelle as a teenager, Claudia would never have existed. They would never have had their wonderful daughter. "You won't lose her, Bobby. She adores you."

"She went for a blood test."

Once again silence filled the car. The rain was falling harder now, drumming against the car's surfaces, blurring the world beyond the windows.

"If she isn't a match, it's all over," Joelle said, wishing she could convince them both of that.

"It's not over." His gaze slid past her and fixed on the silver shimmer of the rain. "She said he was her brother. Foster's son—her brother." He stared into her eyes, the sorrow and accusation in his gaze piercing her. "You told her about Foster, and now I'm losing her. You want me to bare my soul? Here's what's in my soul, then. I love you, Jo. I always have and I always will. But when you told Claudia that Foster was her father, you took her away from me." He turned from her, once again staring out at the rain spilling down into the lake.

"She loves you."

"She calls him her father." He swallowed, his eyes distant, seeing not the scenery outside the car but something invisible, something inside himself. "I love you, Jo, but I wish to hell you'd never let Foster into our lives."

"He was in our lives all along," she pointed out sadly.

She felt Bobby's withdrawal, a subtle motion, a slackening of his hold on her. He seemed to slip away from her like the rain slipping into the lake, water vanishing into water. "Yeah," he muttered, nudging her back into her seat and reaching for the car keys. "He was, wasn't he."

Joelle watched him, struggling to read his expression. For one fleeting moment he'd opened to her and spoken his heart. Now he was locking himself up again, sealing himself away. What she'd said was only the truth, but like the truth that he feared had cost him his daughter, this truth might cost Joelle her husband.

Don't close down, she wanted to plead. *Don't leave me.* But he was easing away, drawing back, in full retreat. She'd had him for that one precious moment, and now he was gone.

Chapter 14

Two weeks later

"Here you go," Mona said, entering Bobby's office with a stack of application forms. "I put the three best prospects on top. One's a college kid just back from a school program in London. He plans to make some money before he has to go back to college in September. The other two are cousins of Hector Cabral's wife. Here legally. I checked their papers. They don't speak English too well, but Hector vouches for them. They said he told them you're a good boss." She grinned. "You want to fire him for lying?"

Hector had been working for DiFranco Landscaping for several years. Bit by bit, he was transporting his entire extended family from Brazil to New England, and Bobby had already hired several Cabral relatives. Over the years, he'd learned a lot about immigration law.

"You ought to move on these soon," Mona continued, placing the stack on his blotter. "You really need some more employees. The price of success, Bob. You've got more contracts than you can staff."

"I'm not complaining." DiFranco Landscaping had landed a lot of jobs this summer. His staff size waxed and waned with the seasons, but this year the firm was in serious demand. He was desperate to add some more personnel, and he would.

He eyed the top application, from the college student. The words made no sense to him; the letters were just squiggly ink shapes. "Something on your mind?" Mona asked.

He shoved back the pile. "I can't concentrate. My daughter's undergoing a medical procedure tomorrow morning."

Mona's eyes widened. "Nothing serious, I hope."

"She'll be fine." Bobby was reasonably convinced of that, even though marrow extraction was a lot more complicated than getting a tooth filled or suturing a cut. Claudia would be given general anesthesia, and then a doctor would insert a needle into her pelvic bone and suck the marrow out. Bobby consoled himself with the understanding that Drew Foster would hire only the best doctors in New York City to treat his son. The doctors would know what they were doing with Claudia.

"If her procedure is tomorrow morning, those applications can wait until tomorrow afternoon," Mona said, tapping the pile with her fingernail and giving Bobby a sympathetic smile before she turned and left his office.

He dug his thumbs into his temples and rubbed, trying to stave off the headache that had been circling his skull all morning. Claudia would be fine, he assured himself. She wanted to do this. It was her choice.

And he ought to review the applications and find some new hires.

He slid open the top drawer of his desk to get a pencil so he could jot down notes. His gaze snagged on the photo of Joelle he kept there, and he paused.

Despite the washed-out colors of the photo, Joelle glowed in her pretty prom dress, with her loose, loopy curls and her bright smile. She'd been so happy that evening, so excited about attending the prom.

With Drew Foster.

It wasn't just the medical procedure that was eating at Bobby. It was the knowledge that Claudia was about to meet her real father.

Foster had arranged for a car to pick up Claudia that morning and drive her to the city so the extraction could be done in the same hospital where his son was a patient. They were all going to meet with the doctor later that afternoon, ostensibly to discuss the procedure. She would spend the night as the guest of Foster and his wife and then get to the hospital by seven the following morning.

Bobby couldn't obliterate the pictures in his mind of Claudia meeting Foster, acknowledging their kinship and believing that she'd finally found her real father. No matter that Bobby had been the only dad she'd ever known. There was a bond between her and Foster, and once they were in the same room, it would blossom.

Thinking about their meeting opened the doors to his headache, which rushed into his brain with booms and flashes of red. Damn. Claudia and Foster. Claudia and her father.

Claudia and the guy who'd escorted Joelle to the prom the night that photo was taken, the night she'd worn that beautiful blue gown and worried about whether she had enough class to hang off the arm of a boy from the Hill.

Bobby shoved the drawer shut, locked his desk and stormed out of his office. "I can't work," he told Mona, who peered up at him from her desk in the outer office. "I'll review the applications tomorrow. I just can't do it today." Before she could question him, he swept out of the building.

He was halfway home before he paused to figure out what the hell he was doing. His mind swam with images of Claudia and Joelle's old boyfriend, Claudia searching the man's face and seeing in it a reflection of herself. Bobby had tried so hard, since the day she'd phoned to tell him and Joelle that she was a match for Foster's son, to be calm and reasonable about the whole thing. He'd tried to focus on his work, to make conversation with Joelle over dinner, to slip into the comfortable routines that had marked his days before Foster had barged in and screwed everything up.

He'd tried to be the husband Joelle wanted him to be.

But just as Foster dreaded the possibility of losing his son, Bobby dreaded the possibility of losing his daughter. And in his case it was his own fault. His and Joelle's. They'd lied, and now they were paying the price. He hated himself—and he hated Joelle, too.

He sped up the driveway to their house, slowing only for the automatic garage door to open. Slamming out of the truck, he took a deep breath to calm himself. It didn't help.

By the time he reached the door to the mudroom, Joelle had opened it and was staring into the garage, frowning. "Bobby? What's wrong?"

He strode past her, his boots thumping against the floor, and halted in the kitchen. Several shopping bags stood on the counter. Apparently she'd just arrived home from the supermarket.

"What happened, Bobby?" she asked, concern planting a flutter in her voice as she joined him in the kitchen.

He must have looked half-mad, because she shrank back when he turned to her. "She's going down there today," he said.

"Of course. I know."

"She's going to meet him."

Joelle watched him. "Yes."

"I can't stand it." He roamed around the kitchen, too edgy to stand still. "I've been trying to be a good sport about this, but I…" Emotions tore at him like thorns. "We shouldn't have told her."

"Who? Claudia?"

"We shouldn't have told her about Foster. We should have kept the secret."

"We couldn't, Bobby."

He bore down on her and she shrank back again, pressing against the counter, her eyes wide with alarm. Did she think he would hurt her?

His anger frightened him, too, and he wrestled with it, forcing it down into his gut. He would not become his father. He would not throw things, break things, hit the people in his life.

He spun away from her and moved to the window, hoping the sight of their perfectly landscaped backyard would soothe him. Joelle's garden lay lush and fresh in the late-morning sunlight. He'd done a fine job of weeding and pruning it after she'd run off to Ohio, and she'd done a decent job of keeping it tidy since they'd returned home.

If only raising children were as simple as raising tomatoes and zucchini. If only maintaining a marriage was as simple as digging out a few weeds and adding a little fertilizer.

"We should have kicked Foster out of our house that day."

"If we had sent him away…" Her voice sounded tight, breathy with anxiety. "He would have gone behind our backs to find her. He'd hired a detective, Bobby. He knew about Claudia. He would have found her, with or without our help."

He refused to look at her. "You're sure he'd do that? You know him that well?"

"I'm a mother," she answered, her voice drifting across the room to him. "I know what a parent will do for a child."

"You're a mother. He's a father." What was Bobby? When it came to Claudia, what the hell was he?

He closed his eyes, unable to bear the sight of Joelle's thriving garden anymore. But closing his eyes left his mind free to see what he didn't want to see: Claudia and Foster together, shaking hands. Hugging. Claudia calling that son of a bitch Dad.

"I've tried," he said slowly, his voice breaking. "Ever since we got back from Ohio, I've tried to accept this. I've tried to forgive you and me both." He sighed. "I just can't do it."

For a minute neither of them spoke. The hum of the refrigerator's motor spread around them, and the hiss of one of the upstairs air conditioners cooling down the bedrooms. Then Joelle said, "All right. Let's go."

"Go?"

He heard the bell-like rattle of her keys and the clapping of her sandals hitting the soles of her bare feet as she headed for the mudroom. "Let's go," she repeated.

He had no idea where they were going. Away from the garden, away from the patio he'd built, away from the house in which he'd raised his sons—and his daughter. Away from this house Claudia had once called home.

Going couldn't possibly be worse than staying. He followed Joelle out.

Even with the passenger seat shoved all the way back, Bobby seemed cramped in the Prius. He also looked forbidding, his eyes dark and brooding, his brow low as he stared at the road in front of them. Waves of tension, hot and pulsing, rolled off him.

She should have changed her clothes. She had on a pair of khaki shorts and a cotton shirt with a pastel striped pattern. Her hair was arranged in a ponytail, but as she drove she tugged off the elastic and ran her fingers through the locks to loosen them.

Ponytail or no, she looked like a dowdy middle-aged suburban lady, someone who'd abandoned a pile of groceries on the counter and bolted on an insane mission. To save her husband, to save her daughter, to save her marriage—for all she knew, everything she cared about was beyond saving by now. At least she'd gotten most of the perishables into the refrigerator. She'd saved their groceries.

"Where are we going?" Bobby asked.

"I'm not sure. Do you have your cell phone with you?" At his nod, she said, "Call Gary."

He eyed her dubiously but punched in his son-in-law's number. After listening for a couple of seconds, he said, "Gary? It's Bob. I…uh…" He flashed a quizzical glance at Joelle.

"Ask him Drew Foster's address."

Bobby's frown intensified. He said nothing.

"Go ahead. Ask him. Somewhere in Manhattan. I need the address."

Bobby continued to glare at her. Into the phone, he said, "No, I'm still here. I just…"

"Ask him," Joelle ordered.

Twisting away, he spoke into the phone. "Do you know Drew Foster's address?" He listened for a moment, then said, "Thanks. No, nothing's wrong. I'll talk to you later." He folded the phone shut and grunted, "Nothing's wrong? Add that to the mile-high heap of lies."

"What's the address?" she asked. "Write it down so we don't forget it."

"We're not going to New York."

"Yes, we are."

Skepticism mingling with the tension that radiated from him, he opened the glove compartment, pulled out a pen and a wrinkled napkin with a fast-food logo on it and jotted the address. "I wrote it down. Now, turn the car around and take me home."

"You don't want Claudia to do this. You won't admit it, Bobby, but it's obvious you don't want her to do it. So we're going to New York to get her."

From the corner of her eye she could see his disbelief. "We are *not* going to New York to get her," he retorted. "This was her decision. She wants to do it. She's a grown-up. If this is what she wants to do—"

"But *you* don't want her to do it. You don't want her to save that boy's life."

"That boy's life has nothing to do with it," Bobby snapped. "Of course I want the boy to live. Damn it, Jo…"

He seemed as furious as he'd been in the kitchen. But at

least he was strapped in by a seat belt, trapped in a moving car. He couldn't act on his anger as long as she kept her foot on the gas pedal.

She had tried to reach him through talk. She'd tried to reach him through food, preparing his favorite meals. She'd tried to reach him physically. Since their return from Ohio, their bed had seen its share of activity—but something had been wrong. There was no hostility when they made love, but there was no rapture, either. There was no life at all. The bed was like a garden without water. Nothing could bloom there.

She'd tried leaving him, and he'd chased after her and brought her home. He'd told her he loved her. But still the demons danced inside him. He was in agony, and in the pauses of their lives, in the quiet moments when conversation died, when sex was over and they retreated to their own sides of the bed, she felt blame flowing from Bobby and spilling all over her.

If the only way she could save her marriage was by snatching Claudia away from Drew Foster, she would do it. She'd tried everything else.

Perhaps she should have thought through this mission a little better. She wasn't sure she was ready to meet Drew's wife—the woman who'd insisted she and Bobby were two corners of a trapezoid when they'd gone out for drinks. Drew's wife would be sleek and chic, and Joelle would be frazzled and ragged. She'd be forced to tell the woman her son would have to find another donor, because until Bobby got his daughter back, he would never forgive Joelle for allowing Drew to cross their threshold. How could Joelle do that? How could she deny a woman the chance to keep her son alive?

"This is nuts," Bobby muttered.

"I don't care if it's nuts. You want Claudia? We'll get her."

"This isn't about Claudia," he said.

Joelle was so startled she almost veered off the road. She straightened the wheel, glanced at him and refocused on her driving. "Of course it's about Claudia."

"It's about you," he argued, spite edging his voice. "It's about you and Foster."

Joelle took a minute to collect herself. All along, Bobby had been anguished about Claudia, about losing her, about losing his place in her heart. He'd never acknowledged that anything else was troubling him. Of course, that was Bobby. He never said anything at all, anything that mattered.

"There is no 'me and Foster,'" she said quietly.

"There was."

"Years ago."

"All right." He sank back in his seat, his hands curled into fists on his knees, and shut his eyes. "Never mind."

He was finally opening up. *Never mind* wouldn't do. "Talk to me, Bobby. For once in your goddamn life, talk to me."

She heard him inhale, then let his breath out on a broken sigh. "I always loved you, Jo. Maybe I didn't say it in words, maybe I didn't express it the way you wanted, but I always loved you. And you loved Drew."

"In high school," she emphasized. "I was young, I didn't even know what love was. It was a schoolgirl crush."

"You wanted to marry him. You planned your future around him." Now that he was talking, *really* talking, the words sprayed from him like water from a garden hose, soaking and chilling her. "I asked you to marry me because I loved you. You were the only good thing in my life back then, and I saw a way to keep you in my life, and I grabbed it and held on tight. That's why I married you. And you married me because you couldn't have Drew."

"That's not—" she stumbled over the next word "—true." But it *was* true. If, when she'd phoned Drew to tell him she was pregnant, he had sent her bus fare to travel not to an abortion doctor in Cincinnati but to New Hampshire, to his college campus, so he could marry her, she would have gone. She would have been his wife and had his baby.

And she would never have had the life she'd lived with Bobby. She would never have struggled with him and celebrated each triumph with him, whether that triumph was his tossing away his cane or starting his own business or earning a college degree. She would never have had her two glorious sons. She would never have built her own world with Bobby. She would never have had all those loving nights in their bed, trusting, touching, connecting in the most elemental way.

"Back in Holmdell, you accused me of never saying I love you," he reminded her, sounding oddly drained. "And I've spent this whole damn marriage knowing I wasn't your choice, I wasn't the one you loved. You settled for me in desperation. The son of the town drunk. The kid who mowed the grass at the cemetery. You didn't marry me for love." He sighed again, almost a moan. "You want me to open up, Jo? There. I've done it."

She didn't realize she was crying until the double yellow line striping the road turned into a blur. Somehow she managed to steer onto the shoulder and stop the car. How could he have thought she'd *settled* for him? Hadn't she loved him enough? Hadn't she given him everything she had—her joy, her sorrow, her patience, her passion?

He had lived the past thirty-seven years doubting her love, just as she'd lived the past thirty-seven years doubting his. If only he'd opened up, if only he'd shared his feelings with her. If only she'd known he felt that way.

The last time she and Bobby had kissed in this car, he'd been in the driver's seat and she'd had the wheel jammed into her back. This time, she climbed over the console to the passenger seat and settled onto his lap. She clung to his shoulders and wept into his shirt until he closed his arms around her. Only then did her sobs subside. "I love you so much, Bobby," she murmured, brushing her mouth against the hollow of his throat with each word she spoke. "The only thing I love about Drew was that his stupid selfishness sent me to you."

"You came to me because you were panicked," Bobby insisted.

"No." She lifted her head and gazed at him. "When I found out I was pregnant, the first person I thought of was you."

His eyebrows arched in surprise. "We'd never done the deed," he reminded her. "You couldn't have pinned it on me."

She managed a feeble smile. "I wouldn't have pinned anything on you. It was just...you were the one I wanted to share my pregnancy with. My first thought was, 'I've got to tell Bobby.'"

"Why?"

She struggled to remember that day, when the nurse at the community college clinic had given her the news and she'd immediately thought of Bobby. "Because you were my friend?" she said, testing the idea as she spoke it. "Because you were my soul mate? Because—" she let out a damp, bleary sigh "—because I trusted you in a way I never trusted anyone else. If that's not love, Bobby, I don't know what love is."

He twined his fingers into her hair, pushing it back from her tear-soaked cheeks. Then he kissed her forehead, tucked his thumbs under her chin and angled her face so he could kiss her lips. A soft kiss, not steamy, not erotic, yet it was the most loving kiss he'd ever given her. "For all these years," he said, barely above a whisper, "you kept me going. You rescued me from that graveyard, from Holmdell, from 'Nam, from a million kinds of hell. And I always told myself that was enough. I loved you, you saved my life, and that was enough. If Foster hadn't come through our door that day, I probably could have kept on going, believing it was enough. But he came through our door…and I realized it wasn't."

"Is it enough now?" she asked. "Knowing I love you with all my heart—is that enough?"

He kissed her again. "It'll have to be, because I can't go through this opening-up shit every day. It hurts, Jo."

"Not every day. Just now and then," she assured him. "When it's absolutely necessary." They kissed again, and she felt the dampness on his cheeks, too. Her tears or his? She didn't know and didn't care.

"We don't have to go to New York," he said. "Claudia'll be fine. Let her save some poor boy's life. Just like her mother." He kissed her again, one last, deep, lingering kiss. "Can we go home?"

She wanted to go home, too—home with Bobby, her husband, the man she loved. But she didn't want to leave the warmth and safety of his arms. She wanted to remain this way with him forever. Their lips touching, grazing. Their bodies pressed together. "Will you take me to bed?"

"Yeah," he said, then smiled gently. "I'll do that."

She returned his smile and blinked back a few fresh tears.

Reluctantly she eased off his lap and back into the driver's seat. She turned on the engine, merged back onto the road and risked an illegal U-turn. Then she cruised north, away from New York City, away from the Fosters and her daughter and the boy whose life she would save.

Joelle and Bobby drove away from their past, away from the lies, away from the doubts, heading home. The sooner they got there, the sooner they would be in each other's arms, in their bed, expressing their love in the most honest way they knew.

★ ★ ★ ★ ★

Mediterranean Nights

Join the guests and crew of Alexandra's Dream,
*the newest luxury ship to set sail on the romantic Mediterranean,
as they experience the glamorous world of cruising.*

*A new Harlequin continuity series
begins in June 2007 with*
FROM RUSSIA, WITH LOVE
by Ingrid Weaver

Marina Artamova books a cabin on the luxurious cruise ship
Alexandra's Dream, *when she finds out that her orphaned
nephew and his adoptive father are aboard. She's determined to be
reunited with the boy…but the romantic ambience of the ship
and her undeniable attraction to a man she considers her enemy
are about to interfere with her quest!*

Turn the page for a sneak preview!

Piraeus, Greece

"THERE SHE IS, Stefan. *Alexandra's Dream*." David Anderson squatted beside his new son and pointed at the dark blue hull that towered above the pier. The cruise ship was a majestic sight, twelve decks high and as long as a city block. A circle of silver and gold stars, the logo of the Liberty Cruise Line, gleamed from the swept-back smokestack. Like some legendary sea creature born for the water, the ship emanated power from every sleek curve—even at rest it held the promise of motion. "That's going to be our home for the next ten days."

The child beside him remained silent, his cheeks working in and out as he sucked furiously on his thumb. Hair so blond it appeared white ruffled against his forehead in the harbor breeze. The baby-sweet scent unique to the very young mingled with the tang of the sea.

"Ship," David said. "Uh, *parakhod*."

From beneath his bangs, Stefan looked at the *Alexandra's Dream*. Although he didn't release his thumb, the corners of his mouth tightened with the beginning of a smile.

David grinned. That was Stefan's first smile this afternoon, one of only two since they had left the orphanage yesterday. It was probably because of the boat—according to the orphanage staff, the boy loved boats, which was the main reason David had decided to book this cruise. Then again, there was a strong possibility the smile could have been a reaction to David's attempt at pocket-dictionary Russian. Whatever the cause, it was a good start.

The liaison from the adoption agency had claimed that Stefan had been taught some English, but David had yet to see evidence of it. David continued to speak, positive his son would understand his tone even if he couldn't grasp the words. "This is her maiden voyage. Her first trip, just like this is our first trip, and that makes it special." He motioned toward the stage that had been set up on the pier beneath the ship's bow. "That's why everyone's celebrating."

The ship's official christening ceremony had been held the day before and had been a closed affair, with only the cruise-line executives and VIP guests invited, but the stage hadn't yet been disassembled. Banners bearing the blue and white of the Greek flag of the ship's owner, as well as the Liberty circle of stars logo, draped the edges of the platform. In the center, a group of musicians and a dance troupe dressed in traditional white folk costumes performed for the benefit of the *Alexandra's Dream's* first passengers. Their audience was in a festive mood, snapping their fingers in time to the music while the dancers twirled and wove through their steps.

David bobbed his head to the rhythm of the mandolins. They were playing a folk tune that seemed vaguely familiar, possibly from a movie he'd seen. He hummed a few notes. "Catchy melody, isn't it?"

Stefan turned his gaze on David. His eyes were a striking shade of blue, as cool and pale as a winter horizon and far too solemn for a child not yet five. Still, the smile that hovered at the corners of his mouth persisted. He moved his head with the music, mirroring David's motion.

David gave a silent cheer at the interaction. Hopefully, this cruise would provide countless opportunities for more. "Hey, good for you," he said. "Do you like the music?"

The child's eyes sparked. He withdrew his thumb with a pop. *"Moozika!"*

"Music. Right!" David held out his hand. "Come on, let's go closer so we can watch the dancers."

Stefan grasped David's hand quickly, as if he feared it would be withdrawn. In an instant his budding smile was replaced by a look close to panic.

Did he remember the car accident that had killed his parents? It would be a mercy if he didn't. As far as David knew, Stefan had never spoken of it to anyone. Whatever he had seen had made him run so far from the crash that the police hadn't found him until the next day. The event had traumatized him to the extent that he hadn't uttered a word until his fifth week at the orphanage. Even now he seldom talked.

David sat back on his heels and brushed the hair from Stefan's forehead. That solemn, too-old gaze locked with his, and for an instant, David felt as if he looked back in time at an image of himself thirty years ago.

He didn't need to speak the same language to understand exactly how this boy felt. He knew what it meant to be alone and powerless among strangers, trying to be brave and tough but wishing with every fiber of his being for a place to belong, to be safe, and most of all, for someone to love him….

He knew in his heart he would be a good parent to Stefan. It was why he had never considered halting the adoption process after Ellie had left him. He hadn't balked when he'd learned of the recent claim by Stefan's spinster aunt, either; the absentee relative had shown up too late for her case to be considered. The adoption was meant to be. He and this child already shared a bond that went deeper than paperwork or legalities.

A seagull screeched overhead, making Stefan start and press closer to David.

"That's my boy," David murmured. He swallowed hard, struck by the simple truth of what he had just said.

That's my boy.

"I CAN'T BE PATIENT, RUDOLPH. I'm not going to stand by and watch my nephew get ripped from his country and his roots to live on the other side of the world."

Rudolph hissed out a slow breath. "Marina, I don't like the sound of that. What are you planning?"

"I'm going to talk some sense into this American kidnapper."

"No. Absolutely not. No offense, but diplomacy is not your strong suit."

"Diplomacy be damned. Their ship's due to sail at five o'clock."

"Then you wouldn't have an opportunity to speak with him even if his lawyer agreed to a meeting."

"I'll have ten days of opportunities, Rudolph, since I plan to be on board that ship."

★ ★ ★ ★ ★

*Follow Marina and David as they join forces to uncover
the reason behind little Stefan's unusual silence,
and the secret behind the death of his parents....*

*Look for FROM RUSSIA, WITH LOVE
by Ingrid Weaver
in stores June 2007.*

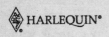

Every great love has a story to tell™

Every picture tells a story…

Anyone looking at Celia Butler's scrapbook
would see a portrait of a wonderful marriage,
but her life is not so easily summed up in these
photographs. The value of these moments frozen
in time is the stories behind them—the lifetime
of love, heartache, sacrifice and commitment
that brought her to this point.

From the love that began, almost by chance,
all those years ago…

Pick up a copy of

The Scrapbook

by

Lynnette Kent

Available in June.

n o c t u r n e™

IT'S TIME TO DISCOVER
THE RAINTREE TRILOGY...

There have always been those among us
who are more than human...

Don't miss the dramatic first book by
New York Times bestselling author

LINDA
HOWARD

Raintree:
Inferno

On sale May.

Raintree: Haunted by Linda Winstead Jones
Available June.

Raintree: Sanctuary by Beverly Barton
Available July.

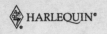

REQUEST YOUR FREE BOOKS!

2 FREE NOVELS PLUS 2 FREE GIFTS!

EVERLASTING LOVE™

Every great love has a story to tell™

YES! Please send me 2 FREE Harlequin® Everlasting Love™ novels and my 2 FREE gifts. After receiving them, if I don't wish to receive any more books, I can return the shipping statement marked "cancel." If I don't cancel, I will receive 4 brand-new novels every other month and be billed just $4.47 per book in the U.S. or $4.99 per book in Canada, plus 25¢ shipping and handling per book and applicable taxes, if any*. That's a savings of about 15% off the cover price! I understand that accepting the 2 free books and gifts places me under no obligation to buy anything. I can always return a shipment and cancel at any time. Even if I never buy another book from Harlequin, the two free books and gifts are mine to keep forever.

153 HDN ELX4 353 HDN ELYG

Name	(PLEASE PRINT)
Address	Apt.
City	State/Prov.	Zip/Postal Code

Signature (if under 18, a parent or guardian must sign)

Mail to the **Harlequin Reader Service®:**
IN U.S.A.: P.O. Box 1867, Buffalo, NY 14240-1867
IN CANADA: P.O. Box 609, Fort Erie, Ontario L2A 5X3

Not valid to current Harlequin Everlasting Love subscribers.

Want to try two free books from another line?
Call 1-800-873-8635 or visit www.morefreebooks.com.

* Terms and prices subject to change without notice. NY residents add applicable sales tax. Canadian residents will be charged applicable provincial taxes and GST. This offer is limited to one order per household. All orders subject to approval. Credit or debit balances in a customer's account(s) may be offset by any other outstanding balance owed by or to the customer. Please allow 4 to 6 weeks for delivery.

Your Privacy: Harlequin is committed to protecting your privacy. Our Privacy Policy is available online at www.eHarlequin.com or upon request from the Reader Service. From time to time we make our lists of customers available to reputable firms who may have a product or service of interest to you. If you would prefer we not share your name and address, please check here. ☐

HEL07

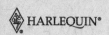

EVERLASTING LOVE™

Every great love has a story to tell™

COMING NEXT MONTH

#9. *The Scrapbook* by Lynnette Kent
Anyone looking at Celia's scrapbook would see a portrait
of a wonderful marriage, from Celia and Mack Butler's
beautiful white wedding—the beginning of her life as a
navy wife—to her growing, smiling family. But Celia's life is
not so easily summed up in photographs. The true value of
these moments frozen in time is found in the stories behind
them....

#10. *When Love is True* by Joan Kilby
What do you do when you realize that your one true
love has been with you all along? For twenty years
Daniel Bennett has been Chloe's rock. But something
has always held her back from fully giving him her heart.
Suddenly she sees Daniel with new eyes, but does her
realization come too late?

www.eHarlequin.com

HECNM0507